"Landmines and Grizzlies? H [...]
                    —Dav [...]

Praise for *Bad Citizen Corporation*

"Bad Citizen Corporation pumps fresh blood into the corpse of American mystery. Lauden debuts with the storytelling ease of a veteran author. It's fun, sun-scorched, and salty as the beaches it hails from." **—Tom Pitts**, author of *Hustle* and *Knuckleball*

"Like a punk rock Lew Archer novel, *Bad Citizen Corporation* challenges you to keep up with the twists and turns. A murder mystery that goes from sun-kissed LA beaches to dirty rock clubs in a story filled with damaged souls and the lasting bonds of friendship." **—Eric Beetner**, author of *Rumrunners* and *The Devil Doesn't Want Me*

"Beach noir with some serious punk rock bonafides. *Bad Citizen Corporation* is a rush of a debut novel that poses timely, thoughtful questions set to a breakneck tempo." **—Rob Hart**, author of *New Yorked*

"Carrying on in the tradition of musicians turned mystery writers like Jo Nesbo and Bill Moody, S. W. Lauden's *Bad Citizen Corporation* pounds out an impressive rock-and-roll thriller. The story comes on strong and never lags behind its neck-breaking beat. Greg Salem, part-time punk rocker, now disgraced cop, plays like the bastard love child of Poly Styrene and James M. Cain. Add to the mix murder and mayhem—the girl who got away, seedy bars, real estate scams, vengeful heiresses, and an oddball assortment of thugs from the old neighborhood—drop it all under the warm California sun, and you've got the hit song—and must-read—of the season." **—Joe Clifford**, author of *Junkie Love* and *Lamentation*

GRIZZLY

S W LAUDEN

SEASON

IZZY

AUDEN

SON

A Genuine Rare Bird Book
Los Angeles, Calif.

A Rare Bird Book | Rare Bird Books
453 South Spring Street, Suite 302
Los Angeles, CA 90013
rarebirdbooks.com

Set in Minion Pro
Printed in the United States

Book Design by Robert Schlofferman

10 9 8 7 6 5 4 3 2 1

Publisher's Cataloging-in-Publication data

Names: Lauden, S. W., author.
Title: Grizzly season / S. W. Lauden.
Series: Greg Salem Mystery.
Description: First Trade Paperback Original Edition | A Barnacle Book | New
York, NY; Los Angeles, CA: Rare Bird Books, 2016.
Identifiers: ISBN 978-1-945572-02-9
Subjects: LCSH Drug traffic—Fiction. | Kidnapping—Fiction. | Organized
crime—Fiction. | Marijuana—Fiction. | Angeles National Forest (Calif.)—
Fiction. | Mystery and detective stories. | BISAC FICTION / Mystery &
Detective / General.
Classification: LCC PS3612.A9323 G75 2016 | DDC 813.6—dc23

September 2011—*The white van crawled down Hollywood Boulevard. Streetlights and gated storefronts reflected off the tinted windows, like a never-ending silent film. The countless dents and scratches read like battle scars around the vehicle's battered body. All four hubcaps were missing, but somebody had spray painted the rims a splotchy silver. Faded stickers covered both back doors where the brake lights blinked like the eyes of Satan himself. It looked like any other indie rock tour van at three in the morning, but the only gear inside was some rope and a couple of cameras.*

The driver scanned the street for cops. The passenger was looking for junkies and runaways. It wasn't easy to pick them out scattered among the homeless and streetwalking whores. Desperation trumped good decisions at this time of night, blurring lines that seemed so clear in the light of day. The two men in the van were counting on it.

They had almost reached the western end of the strip when they saw her: tall and thin with greasy brown hair that shifted and swung as she scratched at her arm. She was walking fast like there was somewhere to be, but they all knew she was just killing time, burning away the hours while she waited for dealers to come out of their apartments in the morning, keeping herself awake until she could find somewhere safe to sleep when the sun came up. She didn't seem surprised when the van pulled alongside her and the passenger window came down.

"You cold?"

The girl kept walking. The van kept pace.

"Can we give you a ride? We have party favors."

A hand emerged through the window, shaking a small baggie.

"I'm not working. Try the parking lot behind the library."

"Slow down, honey. We aren't looking for a date. Just want to help a few of you street kids out."

She eased her pace a little, considering their offer. Adults always told her to avoid getting into cars with strangers. They also warned her never to get strung out on drugs. But here she was, twenty-one years old and weighing the options between getting well and getting killed. The same decision she was forced to make daily.

"You two aren't cops, are you?"

The passenger laughed. The driver didn't. The girl was somewhere in between.

"Axe murderers?"

"Stop being silly and get in. It's cold out tonight."

She opened the side door, leaning in to take a look. The warm blast of heated air felt good against her face. It almost made her forget about her aching muscles and itchy skin. Never mind the desperate hunger that coursed through her veins.

There was nobody else in the van that she could see—just a couple of bags of chips on the back seat, and a six-pack of beer.

"Got anything stronger than that?"

"Start by smoking this."

She climbed in and slammed the door shut, taking the small pipe and lighter in her hand as she sat.

"What is it?"

"A little relief."

She brought the pipe up to her lips and let the flame dance across the top. The driver turned the blinker on and merged across two lanes. It would be a shame to get pulled over now that they'd found the girl they'd been searching for.

The passenger turned around to watch her take a deep pull from the pipe. She wouldn't be awake much longer.

"What's your name?"

She knew to lie, but couldn't. Her vision began to narrow and pulse.

"Mary."

"Goodnight, Mary."

CHAPTER ONE

The kid in the blue hat was standing in the alley in Virgil Heights. His older brother, Manny, was right there beside him. They were both bringing their guns up in slow motion. Greg Salem reached for his weapon, but came up empty handed. The shots rang out, reverberating off the brick walls all around them. Greg tried to duck for cover, but there was nowhere to hide. Two bullets struck his chest. The impact sent him backwards onto the pavement. He could hear the brothers laughing as they fired again…and again…

"Wake up, bro!"

Marco shook Greg by both shoulders. His stringy blonde hair brushed across Greg's terror-stricken face. Greg's fingers dug into the twisted sheets, his teeth gnashing. The murky depths of his rattled mind kept pulling him back under. He clung to the terror and inched himself upward, afraid he might drown if he screamed.

His eyes shot open. Marco was staring down at him.

"You're kinda freaking me out, bro."

Greg's pounding heart brought the real world into sharp focus. He heard birds chirping in the trees outside of the cabin now. He smelled bacon cooking in the kitchen. It was starting to seem like everything might be all right.

Marco stood up and went for the door.

"Happy birthday, old man. Breakfast will be ready pronto."

Greg sat up and rubbed the wetness from around his eyes. It could have been sweat, or it could have been tears. It was always hard to tell on mornings like these.

He jumped out of bed like somebody fleeing the scene of a crime. He and Marco weren't anywhere near the ocean, but Greg always felt better when he wore board shorts. He slipped them on and went into the bathroom.

Greg checked himself in the mirror, running a hand over his fresh buzz cut. His hair was still more blonde than grey, but not by much. He massaged his sunburned scalp and studied the bags under his eyes. The tattoos on his arms peeked out from under the sleeves of his T-shirt as he stretched and twisted. He splashed a handful of cold water onto his face and headed for the living room. It had only been a few minutes, but so far his fortieth birthday wasn't agreeing with him.

Flames were dancing in the fireplace as Greg took a seat at the table. Marco set a plate of pancakes, eggs, and bacon down in front of him. He left a syrupy thumbprint behind on the edge of the plate. Marco didn't seem to notice, but Greg definitely did. It might have killed his appetite if he'd had one to start with.

"Thanks. Did you make coffee?"

"Cool your jets, bro. I'm on it."

Marco went back to the stove to deal with the boiling water. He'd become a pretty good cook since they started living off the grid in the Angeles National Forest. It gave him something to do with all the manic energy he had after getting sober. His wiry, shirtless body darting around the kitchen was a permanent fixture in the small cabin they'd shared for the last six months.

Greg was amazed at how tired two people could grow of each other in such a short amount of time. It reminded him of when their punk band, Bad Citizen Corporation, used to tour. Back when Greg still went by the stage name Fred Despair, and Marco played drums. They were just four young beach kids who took off in a van to conquer the world. Fighting over who had to drive and who got to sleep as they hurtled down the highway in the dead of night, bouncing between backwater clubs and living off of less than twenty bucks a day. It surprised him sometimes that his brother Tim was the only one who didn't make it out alive.

Greg took a bite of his bacon, letting the grease coat the inside of his mouth. He knew that all this heavy food should be taking a toll on his body, but the constant hiking kept him lean and mean for his age.

Marco set a steaming mug down on the table in front of him.

"What the hell were you screaming about in there? You scared the crap out of me."

"It was just a nightmare."

Just a nightmare. The same one he'd been having a couple times a week, since he'd lost his Virgil Heights Police Department badge last year. Even after months at this remote cabin in the mountains, away from the news coverage and constant reminders of the kid that he shot: the kid in the blue hat.

Greg was nervous that the nightmares might never go away, but he wasn't about to admit that to his roommate.

"Doesn't take much to scare you these days, Marco."

"Sounded like there was a raccoon in there with you."

"You afraid of raccoons now too?"

"Hell yeah. Little bastards are mean."

Marco wandered off to do the dishes. Greg pushed his plate away and headed into the living room. Every piece of furniture in the cabin had come up the mountain from Greg's childhood home in North Bay. There was more hunting and fishing gear in the closets than most sporting good stores kept in stock.

He glanced at the family photos that lined the paneled walls. His brother and his dad had both been gone for many years now, but Greg still felt their presence whenever he was up here. Breathing the clean air and wandering around the wide-open spaces reminded him of who he really was, and what really mattered. It took his mind off of the murder and mayhem that followed him around these days like an angry black cloud.

Marco came over to refill his mug. The smell of the fresh coffee brought him back to reality. Greg motioned to the packs leaning against the wall by the front door.

"You ready to get going soon?"

"I don't know, bro. Seems kind of gnarly."

"It's just a week."

"And a hundred miles."

"It'll be good to get out of this little cabin for a while. Before I strangle you."

Greg punched Marco on the shoulder. Marco returned the favor.

"Whatever. It's your birthday."

Marco went back to clean up the mess in the kitchen before they left. Greg stepped outside to wait on the porch. The sun was poking up behind the mountains to the east, shafts of light dancing across the hood of his baby blue El Camino in the distance. He studied the dents and dings that covered the body, and the long crack that still split the windshield. They'd brought some gear with them to fix her up, but never got around to it. He was beginning to wonder if they ever would, or if it even mattered any more.

A woodpecker started hammering out a rhythm nearby. It echoed off the surrounding hills and briefly interrupted the almost constant silence. Greg scanned the pine trees that ringed the cabin on all sides, trying to spot the bird. He was still looking when Marco dragged both packs outside.

"What was that noise?"

"A big scary monster coming to eat you."

"Hilarious. But seriously—you're bringing a gun, right?"

"No guns on the trail, Marco. That's the rule."

"That's *your* rule."

"And it's *my* gun."

They shimmied into their straps and headed off side by side. Marco had his pet iguana, Godzilla, tucked under one arm like a football. Greg reached up and adjusted his ear buds. The thin black cords flowed from the sides of his head and came together at the back of his tattooed neck. The cable snaked along the outside of his pack and into a smartphone connected to a solar charger. His eyes were on the dirt road ahead of them, as Black Flag kicked into "Rise Above."

꙰

"DUDE!"

A few hours later, Greg was twenty yards ahead of Marco on the Pacific Crest Trail. It wound through a desolate stretch of the San Bernardino Mountains seventy miles north of LA's foothill communities. He was sure that his partner was just freaking out about his own shadow again.

There was a steep incline to their right covered in sagebrush and sunbaked rocks. To their left, the trail dropped down to a flat valley floor. A thick stand of pines stood between them and the green fields below. A pungent smell swirled in the air all around them, along with a swarm of annoying little bugs. Greg wiped the sweat from his eyes and was transported back to the cliffs above the tidal pools in The Bay Cities. To the night he saved his best friend Junior and her son Chris from a serial killer.

He was relieved when Marco pulled him back from this flood of unwanted memories.

"Dude! BEARS!"

Greg smelled them before he saw them. A full-grown black bear with two furry cubs tumbling around at her enormous paws. Marco was standing behind the imposing ursine trio, slowly backing up the trail. His eyes were bugging out of his head. Greg tried in vain to get his attention.

"Marco. Listen to me. They won't hurt you. Just don't run—"

"Run" was the only thing Marco heard. He immediately ditched his pack and took off at a sprint in the opposite direction. The sudden commotion spooked the two cubs, and it looked like momma bear was about to give chase. Greg knew that Marco had plenty of experience outrunning middle-aged cops, but bears were a different story. He screamed at the top of his lungs to save his friend's life, "Hey, bear! Over here!"

The bear rose up on its hind legs, casting a twisted shadow several yards long. It was more than seven feet tall, gnashing its teeth and swiping at the air. Greg tried not to panic. He'd spent whole summers in these mountains as a boy, and had heard every piece of advice about how to deal with bear attacks. His father always told him to make a bunch of noise and jump around, so that's what he did. It didn't work.

The bear dropped down to all fours and charged at him. A rippling mass of muscle and fur was on him in a heartbeat. Greg's only option was to take off toward the valley. The heavy pack helped him keep his balance as he gained momentum, but he couldn't sustain it. Gravity took his feet out from under him, so he finished the trip down to the tree line by sliding on his back. He bumped and skidded along while brambles and jagged stones tore at his exposed skin. The trees were coming up fast when a gunshot split the air.

It surprised both Greg and the bears. He sprang to his feet and spun around in time to see the momma and two cubs in full retreat up the slope. Greg appreciated that Marco came back to save him, but thought they had agreed on no guns. A second bullet ricocheted off the boulder right beside him before he could think it through. This definitely wasn't friendly fire. Greg could still hear the piercing ring as he scrambled into the trees.

The ground was covered in pine needles, and dappled in sunlight. Thick branches up above brought the temperature down a few crucial degrees. Greg crept from trunk to trunk, keeping his head low and bracing himself for the next shot. The green field on the other side of the trees quickly came into focus.

Greg backed up against an outcropping of boulders, catching his breath before wriggling out of his straps. He unhooked the canteen from the side of his pack. His gaze wandered out across a sea of marijuana plants as he chugged the water.

The third shot split the bark in the tree right behind his head. He tripped over the pack as he turned to flee, heading straight out into the field. He'd taken only a few steps when his foot caught hold of a trip wire. His palms were inches from the ground as a flash of light consumed him. He flew through the air for a few feet and hit the ground hard. The Minutemen were half way through "Corona" in his headphones, when everything went black.

∽

SOMEBODY WAS GRUNTING LOUDLY nearby. Greg tried to open his eyes, but the blinding sun was right overhead. His lips were fried, and his tongue felt thick and swollen in his mouth. He might have simply passed out again if it weren't for the putrid smell suffocating him.

Greg tried to roll onto his side, but the rope caught his left wrist. The result was the same for his other arm and both legs. His shirt rode up as he squirmed, trying to wriggle free. Plastic trash bags seared the skin on his lower back, causing his eyes to shoot open. It took a few minutes to figure out that he was staked down on a pile of garbage in the middle of a campground. But that still didn't explain the grunting.

He lifted his head to make sense of the situation. An enormous black bear was tearing into a pile of garbage only yards away. A slightly smaller bear was further down the mound, sitting on its haunches and ripping a bag apart. Every muscle in Greg's body tensed as he craned his neck to look for Marco. What he saw instead was a crowd of silent spectators watching his every move. He almost didn't recognize his own voice as he screamed for help

Everything went still before the audience gave a collective gasp. They must be seeing what Greg only heard—both bears were making their way toward him to inspect the sudden commotion. The musky smell of filthy fur filled his nostrils as the bears approached. He closed his eyes and clenched his teeth, trying to go somewhere safe in his mind. It wasn't long before he was bobbing on the ocean in South Bay, waiting to catch a wave.

The crowd laughed as he thrashed and bucked. That's when the sirens started shrieking. The bear that was gnawing on his shoe froze before darting from the mountain of trash. The second bear followed right behind it. Greg gulped for air and tried not to move. He imagined the Virgil Heights Police Chief coming to rescue him once again. But the voice that came crackling through the bullhorn wasn't familiar at all.

"We really don't appreciate trespassers up here."

A murmur started to swell in the crowd. Greg was overwhelmed with exhaustion. He let his head drop and waited for whatever came next.

"Don't pass out on us, now. I want to pick your brain about a few things."

Greg brought his head up again. That's when he spotted the man, perched on a branch high up in a tree. He wore stiff blue jeans held up by black suspenders. His plaid shirt was tight across his barrel chest, sleeves straining against bulging arms. The thick stubble on his round face was on the verge of becoming a beard. He was every bit the mountain man, except he spoke like a drunken manager on a corporate team-building retreat.

"I hate to sound like a broken record here, but those bears look pretty hungry."

"I was out for a hike." Greg's voice was gravelly, but thin. The altitude and dehydration were taking their toll. "Where's my friend?"

"You were by yourself when we found you out in our field. What's this friend of yours look like?"

It was relief to know that Marco had gotten away, even if it meant that Greg was on his own. His only hope was that Marco might make it back to a phone where he could call for help. That meant he had to buy some time. The man with the bullhorn started speaking again before Greg could formulate his next lie.

"I suggest you answer before the bears come back."

"Okay, okay. He's about six feet tall, heavy-set, with spiky black hair. You couldn't miss him out here."

"Liar!"

The word blared through the bullhorn and the crowd started chanting it. They stomped, clapped and shouted. It went on for several minutes before the siren on the bullhorn began wailing again. Greg heard footsteps thundering toward him across the hard-packed ground. The mob was clawing their way up the mound of trash.

They were a filthy group, like farmhands fresh from the fields. The women wore no make up and kept their hair pulled into long braids that hung down their backs. The men had choppy haircuts and wispy beards, like college-aged camp counselors. Greg guessed that most of them were younger than him by several years, if not decades—all except for the men who hacked the ropes from his hands and feet. They looked more like career criminals enjoying a brief vacation between prison sentences.

The crowd tore his sweat-soaked clothes off and pulled him to the ground. They lifted his naked body overhead, parading him around the garbage heap and out of the makeshift stadium. The man with the bullhorn was waiting when they finally put him down. He was shorter than Greg originally thought, but in better shape than any grandpa pot farmer should be. He swiped the flies away from his face, squinting at Greg as he spoke.

"Care to change your story?"

Greg tried to force a smile. His lips split and bled.

"I'll tell you whatever you want to hear, as long as I get my clothes back."

"Funny. Let's see who's laughing when we toss you down into the pit."

The man stepped aside to reveal a large hole in the ground. Huge paw prints covered the dirt ramp leading down into the darkness. Greg could just make out a tall stake erected in the center of the subterranean space. He decided to be a little more polite now that he understood what they had in mind. Anything would be better than getting mauled to death, or freezing in the chilly desert night.

He decided to play his last card.

"This is all a misunderstanding. I'm actually a police officer, out on a weekend hike."

Now it was the other man's turn to smile.

"We know exactly who you are. We've had our eye on you and your sidekick for a while now. Isn't that right?"

Greg heard a chain rattle. He looked down into the pit where Marco stepped out into a sliver of sunlight. His naked skin glistened as he looked up with an annoyed scowl on his face.

"What the hell's going on, Marco?"

"Ask that psycho standing next to you."

Greg spun to face their captor.

"What's all over him?"

"Honey. It's like crack for these bears."

"What the hell is this place?"

"We call it Grizzly Flats. I'm Magnus Ursus."

Greg never studied Latin, but he thought he knew what that meant.

"Big Bear? Seriously?"

"I prefer Magnus."

"Mind telling me what my friend is doing down there?"

Greg motioned to the pit. Marco spoke up before Magnus could.

"Dude's got a screw loose, bro."

Greg spun to face Magnus, waiting for his answer. Magnus stood up on his toes and waved to a girl in the crowd.

"Ursula. Please come over and join us. *Now.*"

She emerged with a shopping bag, setting it at Greg's feet. Her blue eyes sparkled as she pulled out several honey bottles. Every one of them was shaped like a smiling little bear.

Greg took a step back and almost tumbled into the pit. Magnus grabbed his shoulder to stop him from falling, but Greg spun around behind him. He had his forearm wrapped around the old man's neck before anybody in the crowd could react.

"Nobody move or he's a dead man."

Several of the men inched closer. Magnus brought his hands up to wave them off. Greg thought he could kill the crazy bastard if he had to, but then he and Marco would never get out alive. He dug his heels into the ground at the edge of the pit, tightening his grip around the old man's windpipe.

"Have one of your men untie my friend."

"Why don't you do it yourself?"

The words were barely out of Magnus's mouth before he pushed back with all of his might. The instant momentum sent them both plunging into the pit. Marco was screaming as Greg slammed back-first into the ground. Magnus came crashing into him a second later, knocking the rest of the air from his lungs.

The old man grunted as he rolled onto his side and stood up. Marco took a swing and missed. The old man countered with a straight arm that sent him to the ground. Greg could see the bloodthirsty crowd lining the edges of the pit. He willed himself to breath as he looked up. Magnus took a step forward and brought his boot hard into the side of Greg's head. Cheers erupted from up above as Greg 's vision blurred, flickered and faded.

CHAPTER TWO

reg twitched and stirred. He felt the ropes rubbing against the skin on his wrists and ankles, but knew he wasn't on the trash pile. The smell was different this time, like campfire mixed with perfume. He lifted his head to look around, when somebody giggled.

The girl with the bag of honey was down at the end of his cot. She was wringing a washcloth into a bucket of water. He took one look at her face and knew that she was stoned out of her mind. But her eyes were the iciest shade of blue that he had ever seen. He felt drawn in by her peaceful gaze, trapped inside of the shy smile that was slowly parting her lips.

She was in her early twenties, maybe a little younger. The rough tips of her work-worn fingertips were gently massaging the bottom of his foot.

"Rise and shine. That tickle?"

Greg let his head drop back to the pillow as she gently washed him with warm water. He was almost asleep again when he heard a familiar voice.

"That's enough for now, Ursula."

Greg turned back to look at honey girl. She gave his toes a little peck and stood up. There was a bear paw tattoo on her left shoulder blade. He was tracing her spine with his eyes as she sauntered out into the cool night air.

Magnus strolled around the cot like he was lost.

"Sorry to break up your little party."

"I'm just glad you didn't get here until *after* she licked all the honey off."

"Keep cracking jokes, if you want. Just remember that your friend isn't exactly enjoying the same amenities that you are."

Greg strained against the ropes, but knew it was no use.

"Is he okay?"

"For now. The bears don't usually come until after dusk. Unless it's trash day, of course."

Magnus chuckled and picked at his fingernails. Greg jumped right back in: "You can't leave him down there all night."

"I can, and I most definitely will. It all depends on you, Greg."

"How do you know my name?"

"We know exactly who you are. I've had my eye on your cabin ever since you arrived in our neck of the woods. It's not every day we get a celebrity up here."

Bad Citizen Corporation was the last thing that Greg wanted to talk about at the moment. But, he was willing to try anything to save Marco from being eaten alive.

"How do you know about my band?"

"What band? I was talking about those people you saved down by the beach. It was all over the local news for a few weeks."

Magnus held a folded newspaper up for Greg to see. It was a regional rag called *The SoCal Sentinel.*

"I'm just screwing with you. Everybody's probably heard of your band by now. See for yourself."

Magnus held the newspaper up for Greg to read. The page was open to a trashy gossip column. Greg checked the date. It was weeks old.

LA Buzz: What Happened To The 'Punk Rock Cop'?

by Leslie Thompson, Staff Reporter

According to acquaintances, Greg Salem, a Virgil Heights police officer who burst into the spotlight last year, hasn't been heard from in months.

Salem was involved in an on-duty shooting during which he claimed the underage suspect pulled a gun. He was put on leave. The weapon in question was never recovered, but the search for it led to one of the biggest gang busts in recent years.

He was back in the spotlight two weeks later when he rescued a couple of hostages during a tense beach standoff, which left one suspect dead. But Salem, who is also a former singer for LA-based punk band Bad Citizen Corporation, hasn't been heard from since. Is he dead, or simply hiding out? Working undercover, or writing another album?

There were another dozen paragraphs, but Greg stopped reading. He already knew how that story ended. Magnus brought the paper down with a slap.

"Like I said, you're famous."

"She's got a pretty good imagination."

"Perception is reality."

Magnus folded his arms across his chest. He was looking up at the ceiling of the tent, deep in thought when he went on.

"I actually used to work in the music industry myself. Did marketing for a few hair metal bands in the eighties."

Greg was having a hard time picturing this ragged pot farmer in a corporate boardroom.

"So, why'd a marketing guy leave entertainment for agriculture?"

"Who says I left entertainment? It's all about diversification these days."

Greg motioned to the inside of the tent with his head.

"This isn't exactly The Ritz, but I'm guessing you come and go when you feel like it."

"Life's about choices. I did my time in fancy hotels, ate at all the hip restaurants on both coasts, but I was suffocating. Fat and happy, like a caged animal waiting to be slaughtered. Don't get me wrong, the money was great and there were plenty of perks. But the people? All sharks."

"And you prefer bears."

Magnus finally brought his gaze down to lock eyes with Greg.

"I'm always looking for the next opportunity. A man can learn a lot about himself by living out here. Speaking of which, I've got something to show you."

Magnus walked over to a backpack on the ground and pulled out a piece of cloth. Greg watched as he slowly unfolded it, careful not to let it touch the ground. He was soon holding the corners of a California state flag in his outstretched hands.

"See that? It's a grizzly bear. They used to live all over these mountains a hundred years ago. Fierce hunters. True individuals."

"So what?"

"They were hunted to extinction. Completely wiped out. But there they are, right on the state flag. A constant lie that we perpetuate."

"There are still plenty of black bears up here."

"Imported from Yosemite a century ago. There's less and less that's native about Southern California."

Greg was happy that Magnus was getting to the point, whatever it turned out to be.

"You and I are special, Greg. Born and raised here. Natives. Just like the grizzlies."

"Meaning we're almost extinct?"

"Might be unavoidable, if we don't stop the hemorrhaging. All the transplants coming here only care about money and the weather, but they're destroying our soul. Sure, they like their symbols. They want you to think that they're all about individualism and freedom, but it's not true. The minute you become a threat—BOOM—they take everything away from you."

"So all of this is about illegal immigration?"

"To the contrary. I'll take Mexicans, Guatemalans, Nicaraguans—anybody from South of the border—over these East Coast assholes that just keep coming like locust."

"What's that have to do with me and Marco? Let us go and we'll forget this place even exists."

"You hard of hearing from all that punk rock crap? I'm giving you the opportunity to get in on the ground floor of something huge."

It took Greg a moment to figure out what this whack job was driving at. A job offer was the last thing he expected. Greg tried to look like he was considering it, but his mind was only focused on getting out of there.

"Seems like you have plenty of people here who can help you out."

"These kids? They're strays and runaways, mostly here for the weed and sex. All they're good for is working the fields and keeping the product moving. I need a business partner. Somebody who can handle the day-to-day while I work on taking this thing to the next level."

"Let my friend go and I'm all ears."

Magnus stood up and lumbered over to the door. He wore a pinched expression when he turned to face Greg again. Like something was boring into the back of his skull.

"I'll consider taking him out of there tonight. What happens tomorrow depends on you."

"Can you at least untie me?"

"Not sure that's in my best interest, but I can send one of the girls back in. That should keep your mind off of those ropes."

Greg wasn't up for any soulless cult sex, but thought he might get some useful information out of Magnus's harem; or at least one of them.

"Maybe just Ursula."

"You'll have to be more specific. They're all called Ursula."

〰

THE KID IN THE blue hat was standing in the alley with a gun to Marco's head. Giant grizzlies burst through the brick walls around them, choking the air with red dust. Greg stumbled forward, but the dirt ramp under his feet kept stretching out before him. His foot caught hold of a trip wire and he went flying through the air...

Ursula woke Greg from his bad dream with a kiss. He smelled her sweet skin, and felt her lips brushing his. He opened his eyes. She laid her head on his shoulder and caressed his cheek.

"That sounded scary. What were you dreaming about?"

"It was nothing. Just my imagination getting the best of me."

"You were screaming about some kid in a blue hat. Who is he?"

"Nobody important."

They spent the entire night talking, but Greg had gotten very little information out of her. What she did share made it seem like Magnus was extremely violent and unpredictable. *Or maybe that's just what Magnus told her to say.*

She claimed her real name was Kristen Raines, but swore him to secrecy about that. She told him that Magnus would put her down in the pit if she responded to anything other than Ursula.

"I moved to Hollywood after high school, but things got a little out of control. Then Magnus showed up one day, about a year ago, and promised me money and weed."

Kristen said that he'd been true to his word, but it came at a serious price. She didn't give any specifics when he pressed her on it, except to say that a few recruits had been "sacrificed" since she arrived.

"He can be a little unpredictable. And violent."

"Why don't you just leave?"

"Believe me, I've tried. Somehow he always convinces me to stay."

The main question she avoided all night was the one that mattered most to Greg—"Who is Magnus Ursus really?" He knew that she might not know the answer; it was entirely possible that nobody at Grizzly Flats did.

Kristen gave his nipple a little pinch. It brought him hurtling back to the moment.

"Was the kid in the blue hat the one you shot when you were still a cop?"

There was no point in hiding it. His life had become an open book, thanks to the media. That's the main reason he and Marco stayed living in the Angeles National Forest for so long. Greg needed everybody else to forget what had happened before he could forget it himself.

It wasn't working so far.

"Yeah."

"But he's in jail, right?"

"Him and his older brother, Manny, pretty much their whole gang. For now."

They probably could have gone on like that for the rest of the day, but Magnus came in. He had two cups of steaming hot coffee in his hands. Kristen immediately stood up to put her frumpy frontier dress on. Greg still wasn't sure how or why he'd resisted her body the night before.

She smiled at him and slid out of the tent. Both men watched her go before Magnus got down to business.

"Coffee?"

Greg looked between his tied hands and raised an eyebrow. Magnus set the two cups down on the ground and loosened the ropes around his wrists. Greg immediately sat up. Two men were standing outside of the tent with rifles in their hands.

"What about my feet?"

"You're fine. Drink up. Long day ahead if I'm going to get you up to speed."

Greg reached for the cup, but his hands were still tingling. He tried to shake the numbness away instead.

"Where's Marco?"

"He's safe, for now. How'd you and Ursula get along?"

Greg didn't want him to find out that all they'd done was talk. He could only imagine what Magnus would do to her if he knew what she'd said.

"Sweet girl. Great body."

"Lots more like her here. You can have your pick, if you play ball."

"I'll keep that in mind."

"First thing we need to do is get you dressed. Then we'll take a little tour of the operation. But I'll warn you, my men won't hesitate to shoot you if you try to run." nodded to the door and "And if they don't get you, the booby traps will."

Greg drank half of his down in a single gulp.

"Almost sounds like you're daring me."

"Take it however you want. But even if you do get away, it'll be much more painful for your friend." He stood up and headed outside. "Get your feet untied and grab a uniform. I'll give you a few minutes."

There was a cardboard box filled with stiff blue jeans. A second box was filled with colorful plaid shirts. Greg put on a dusty old pair of work boots from a pile in the corner and went outside to face the day.

Magnus was waiting with a group of armed guards when Greg walked up. It was only eight, but the mountain air felt like a blast furnace on his face. Flies were buzzing around Greg's neck, where thin streams of sweat were already starting to form. Magnus greeted him like an old friend.

"Hot enough for you?"

"I want to see Marco."

The familiar charm was gone, as quick as it had arrived.

"We all want something. Right now I want you to shut up and come with me."

They started off across the camp, two guards in front, and two behind. The tent that Greg was staying in stood at one end of a long row. He peeked into the other tents as they passed, noting that they all looked about the same inside. As they walked, they saw a few men and women, but the camp was mostly empty.

"Where is everybody?"

"Out in the fields. Let's cut through here. Look familiar?"

They were back in the stadium. It seemed smaller now that Greg wasn't so disoriented. They came out on the other side and walked by the pit. A couple sheets of plywood, held in place with broken cinderblocks, covered the hole. He wondered if some other poor bastard had replaced Marco down there, but didn't dare ask. There were a lot of other questions he had about Grizzly Flats. It seemed smart to start with an easy one.

"What do you do with the bears when you don't need them?"

Magnus stopped in his tracks. The same pained expression was back. He was either deeply annoyed or in terrible pain.

"Those bears aren't trained. They're wild."

Greg's stomach dropped. Magnus chuckled and pressed on. A large outcropping of cactus and rocks was just beyond the pit. It created a natural corral that was filled with a couple of dune buggies and a dozen or so motocross bikes. A few of Magnus's men were working on the vehicles as Greg and Magnus walked by, but none of them looked up. Greg could see workers in the distance as he followed Magnus right up to the edge of an area the size of a football field filled with marijuana plants. It had taken less than ten minutes to tour the entire camp.

Magnus swept his arm out in front of himself.

"This is what it's all about."

Greg wasn't that impressed, but decided it was best to hide it.

"Did you guys plant all of this?"

"We've got other fields around here, but this one's the biggest. I bought it from some local bikers."

"Don't you ever worry about getting discovered?"

"Not many people come this deep into the Angeles National Forest. The few hikers that happen by don't want any trouble, and the government doesn't pay the Forest Service employees very well, if you know what I mean."

"What about the Sheriff's Department?"

"Everybody has a price—even people with badges—but we've definitely done our share of relocating."

Greg no longer thought of himself as a police officer, but dirty cops still made his skin crawl. Maybe that's what Magnus wanted from him, to broker deals with local law enforcement. Greg decided it might be worth considering if it meant that he and Marco could get out alive.

Magnus brought Greg back from his dark thoughts.

"What do you think?"

"It's impressive, but I have to wonder—what will all of this matter once the Feds finally legalize marijuana and give those fat contracts to the cigarette companies?"

"I knew I liked you. That's the same question I've been asking myself. Come with me."

They walked along the edge of the field for a couple hundred yards, finally reaching a stand of pine trees.

"If you want to stay ahead of the changes, you have to evolve. Think outside of the box. My former colleagues in the music industry couldn't do it, and now look at them running around with their heads cut off."

Magnus kept speaking as they wound their way through the trunks to a small camouflaged tent. It was the same size and shape as the ones that they slept in, but much harder to spot from a distance, or overhead by plane or helicopter.

"Tell me, Greg, what do *you* think will happen once marijuana is totally legal and taxed?"

"It'll become normal, I guess. Like booze."

"Right. Just like booze, and for most people that'll be enough. But what about the people who want a little bit more?

"More what?"

"Something more thrilling than just buying a pack of joints and some pork rinds from the liquor store."

"Street drugs?"

Magnus was getting excited. He was talking faster, emphasizing key points with quick hand motions.

"Yes, but nothing too serious. That won't fly in the suburbs. Half the fun of getting high is knowing that it's illegal, but your average consumer isn't quite ready for serious narcotics. I'm talking about something in between. Something you can smoke like a cigarette, but with a kick. No needles or snorting. You have any idea what somatic fusion is?"

Greg was starting to wonder how soon this information was going to get him killed.

"Is that something you studied in school?"

"Among many other subjects. I must have changed my major fifty times. But this is way over my head, so I hired some pros to figure it out."

"Figure what out, exactly?"

Magnus lifted his chin and flashed a confident smile.

"We've almost cracked the code on creating a marijuana and coca leaf hybrid. We're calling it 'Grizzly Bear'. Like the noble beast itself—totally mellow, but able to rip your head off. Catchy, right?"

Greg did a piss-poor job of feigning excitement. Magnus didn't seem to notice or care.

"Most of the real science takes place at our state-of-the-art facility in Van Nuys. It'll blow your mind when you get a chance to see it."

"So why are you out here rolling around in the dirt then?"

"You have to get your hands dirty if you want to build an empire."

The answer rolled off of Magnus's tongue with the ease of an actor reciting a line. He didn't miss a beat getting right back to his presentation.

"The plants I'm about to show you are strictly for field test purposes. Hope to have the first crop by next spring, if everything goes according to plan."

Greg shook his head in disbelief.

"Cocaine is cartel territory."

Magnus flinched, but so quickly that Greg almost missed it. Something about the word "cartel" struck a nerve with him. It might explain why he was hiding out in the mountains. Magnus recovered fast.

"That's the whole point. Grizzly Bear isn't some long-term business plan; it's my golden parachute. I just need to find a place I can test it without drawing too much attention. Once it's perfected, I'll sell the plants to the highest bidder and check out."

"Sounds like a solid plan."

"I'm just an opportunist, like everybody else in this great state. Come on, I'll show you."

The guards lowered their weapons and stepped out of the way. Greg and Magnus were almost inside when there was a loud explosion nearby. The original four escorts took off at a sprint toward the commotion. The remaining two trained their guns on Greg while Magnus carried on.

"What'd I tell you about the booby traps? The one that brought you here is nothing compared to some of the surprises we've got hidden out there. Bear stepped on a landmine last week. An ear was the biggest piece of the body we could find, and that was way up in a tree."

Two guards returned a few minutes later, dragging a third man between them. They looked like triplets, except that the man in the middle was bloodied and battered. He could barely stand up when they pulled him to his feet and explained the situation.

"He was trying to escape. Had this with him."

One of them handed a shredded backpack to Magnus. He opened it up and took a look inside. The disappointment that swept across his face quickly turned into pure rage. He snatched a rifle from one of the guards and broke the prisoner's jaw with the butt. The man fell to the ground face-first and lay there groaning. Magnus stood over him, shoving the tip of the barrel into the back of his neck.

"I get your sorry ass off the streets and this is how you repay me?"

The prisoner didn't have a chance to respond before Magnus pulled the trigger and blew his head off. Greg jumped back, but the other two guards grabbed him. His jeans were splattered in blood and his hands were shaking.

Magnus dropped the rifle on the corpse and turned toward camp, muttering to himself as he stomped off through the pine needles. Greg watched him go. *The tour might be over for the day, but the nightmare's just beginning.*

⁊

GREG HADN'T SEEN MAGNUS since the shooting. The guards eventually took him back to his tent and told him to stay put, but didn't tie him up. They probably assumed he wouldn't run, after what he'd just seen. Besides, he still wasn't exactly sure where Marco was.

They brought him lunch a few hours later, and dinner around sunset—a baloney sandwich and a cup of beans both times. In between, he rifled through every box and backpack in the tent, but found nothing. It was dark outside when the guards came in again to tie him down for the night. He was so bored out of his mind by then that he went straight to sleep when they left. Greg rolled over in the middle of the night to find that he was free. He sat up and rubbed the rope burns on his wrists. Kristen was sitting on his cot beside him in the dark, tears streaming down her face. She lunged for him and dug her nails into his back. Greg was still groggy and thought he might be dreaming, but managed to sit up.

"What happened?"

"They killed him."

"Who? The guy who tried to escape today?"

She nodded and started sobbing. He brought her face up from his shoulder and tried to wipe her cheeks.

"Did you know him before you came here?"

"No. His name was Nicholas. He was just a kid...I'm the one who brought him to Grizzly Flats."

She sat up and sniffled. Her wet eyes sparkled in the light of the lamp. Greg thought he caught a glimpse of the woman that she was supposed to become. *Maybe in another lifetime.*

"What do you mean 'you brought him here'?"

"Magnus has a few of us go down to Hollywood sometimes, to pick up new recruits. I found him up on Sunset Blvd. last month."

"That doesn't make this your fault."

"Everybody at Grizzly Flats has blood on their hands, Greg."

"So why don't you just leave?"

"I had my reasons, until you came along."

She collapsed in his arms again. There were still so many questions he wanted to ask her, but he doubted she could answer right then. He sat holding her for several minutes, until she lifted her head and wiped the remaining tears from her eyes.

"I have something to show you."

Kristen went over to a bag at the foot of the cot. A map was in her hands when she sat down beside him again. He rose up onto his elbows to watch her unfold it.

"What is that?"

"A map of Grizzly Flats."

He wanted to grab it from her hands and commit the contents to memory, but resisted the urge. This could still be some kind of twisted test orchestrated by Magnus.

"Where'd you get it?"

"I have my ways."

She flashed an evil smile and spread the map out across his legs. The intricate lines and complicated symbols were hand drawn in pencil. The paper was worn thin in spots where it had been erased and altered several times before. There was only one person who knew the operation that well.

"Jesus, Kristen. Magnus will kill us both if he notices this is missing."

"I'll put it back tonight, after he's asleep. Trust me."

"Why should I?"

"Because I've got the map that's going to get us out of here. All three of us."

His hand was still on her shoulder as she leaned in for a kiss. Kristen took his face in her hands and bit the tip of his tongue. Whatever reservations he'd had about sleeping with her were quickly evaporating in the warmth of her body. She pushed him back, running a finger down his chest. A shy smile danced across her lips as her dress fell to the floor.

She lowered herself on top of him. Their eyes were only inches apart, searching each other in the dark. He inhaled her sweet breath as she opened her mouth to speak.

"You're the only one I can trust here anymore."

"You don't have to do this, for Magnus I mean—"

She shut him up with another kiss—harder this time, with greater intent. He brought his hands up onto her back to let them explore, but slowed down when he reached the bear paw tattoo. She pulled back when his hands stopped moving.

"What's the matter?"

"You all have the same tattoo."

"You cops don't miss a thing, do you?"

Greg didn't know what to make of her comment. She rolled off of him and giggled.

"It's no big deal. Just like branding a cow, I guess."

"Is that what you think of yourself?"

She traced the outline of his tattoos with her fingers.

"Can we maybe discuss this a little later? Seems silly to have a lover's spat before we're actually lovers."

She started kissing his bicep before working her way up to his neck. It was hard for Greg to know if she was telling the truth about her feelings for him. Either way, there was no going back—at least not for tonight.

CHAPTER THREE

I t was pitch black and freezing cold. Again.

Marco wrapped his arms around his bent knees and rocked in place to keep warm. Bears were no longer an issue since Magnus and his men started sealing him into the pit at night. Now the only monsters he fought were the ones he conjured himself. Most of them, these days, looked like some version of Magnus.

He spent many sleepless nights throwing pointless punches into the surrounding darkness. Rattling the chain clamped to his ankle, and shouting into the void. Sometimes he made promises to get his revenge on Magnus. Other times he prayed out loud that Greg would come to rescue him.

And in the morning they would rip the plywood back, letting the sunlight blind him. Magnus was there to greet him for the first few days, coffee in hand and a smile on his face. He always seemed excited for Marco about the backbreaking work that lay ahead. Lately, it was just his soulless soldiers with their guns and grunted orders.

Marco wondered how many more nights like this he could survive, when somebody pulled the plywood back. Stars filled the night sky behind the woman who peeked down at him over the edge of the pit.

"I have something for you. From your friend Greg."

She tossed down a folded blanket that hit the ground with a dull thud. He reached over and immediately wrapped it around his body. The unexpected warmth was better than any drugs he had ever taken.

Marco looked up to thank her, but his guardian angel was already gone. The last sliver of light disappeared as she slid the plywood back into place.

⁓

"Wake up, love birds."

Greg saw a strange look on Magnus's face when he opened his eyes. It was a cross between fury and joy. Then he saw the rifle in the old man's hands, and felt the tip of the barrel pressed against his chest. Kristen was already up and getting dressed, but Magnus told her to stay put.

"I've got something to say to the two of you."

She had practically moved in with Greg over the last two weeks. They'd spend their days apart, but come together every night when the long workdays were done. Greg was spending most of his time with Magnus, following in his shadow, learning everything he could about Grizzly Flats. He had no idea what Kristen did with her time, or what her role was in the organization. Only that Magnus seemed to trust her more than the other girls. That made Greg want to trust her less, when he wasn't clinging to her to get him through the long nights.

Kristen dropped her dress and climbed back on top of the bearskin. Greg could feel her trembling next to him. He took her hand in his and squeezed it tight. If Magnus noticed, he didn't let it show.

"We need to talk, Greg. It's time for you and I to come to some kind of agreement."

Greg's eyes flicked to the gun barrel. There had to be a right way to respond, but he couldn't decide what it was.

"I'm listening."

"I've shared my master plan with you. You know everything about my business plan, but time's running out. It's becoming a distraction. That stops right here, right now. I've already told you that I want you to come work for me—with me. We would be partners, splitting some of the profits. I also told you what I would do if you refused my offer."

Greg could picture Marco with a gun to his head somewhere in the camp. The image made his stomach turn. He nodded, trying hard not to show any emotion.

"I need to know your answer right now."

"What exactly would this partnership entail?"

"I need somebody I can trust to keep the cash coming in while I work with the other team on perfecting Grizzly Bear."

"Why me?"

"I don't have a lot of other options at the moment. From what I've seen you know how to handle yourself."

"And you'll kill Marco if I say no."

Magnus swung the rifle from Greg's chest to Kristen's forehead.

"Not just him."

Kristen was digging her nails into the palm of Greg's hand now. She shut her eyes and gritted her teeth. Greg thought about wrestling the gun away from Magnus, but knew who would pay the price if he failed. There really wasn't much of a choice.

"I need to see Marco first."

Magnus lifted the rifle, turning to face the exit.

"Boys! Bring him in."

There was a scuffling sound outside of the tent. Greg watched the flaps of the door split open. Marco came flying through in a pool of sunlight and dust. His hands were tied tight in front of him, but he still managed to break his fall. He stood up and shook the hair from his face.

"What the hell's going on, dude?!"

"Your friend and I are in the middle of a negotiation. He requested your presence."

Marco went to look at Greg, but overshot the mark and landed on Kristen's naked body instead.

"Hey, you're the chick that—"

"That put the honey all over you?"

Greg looked over at Kristen. The way she interrupted Marco made it seem like she was hiding something. Whatever it was, he didn't want to discuss it in front of Magnus. Greg figured he could ask her about it later, when they were alone.

"Marco, you doing okay?"

"Not as good as you, from the looks of things."

"Are they feeding you?"

"Getting a little burned-out on baloney and beans, but I've had worse. One thing's for sure, bro. It'd be nice not to sleep in that pit for change."

Greg swung his head to look at Magnus, trying to contain his anger.

"He sleeps with me from now on."

Magnus grinned.

"I'll agree to move him into his own tent if it'll make you feel better."

"Hell yeah you will."

Both Greg and Magnus turned at the sound of Marco's voice. He had his chest puffed out like a strutting rooster.

"And I want my iguana back."

Magnus threw a punch, knocking Marco to the ground. Greg lunged, but Kristen held him back. All he could do was scream.

"Leave him alone! I'll do whatever you want."

"I assume we have a deal then?"

Magnus took a step forward with his hand out. Greg brought his up and they shook on it.

⁊

GREG'S FIRST DAY ON the job started immediately. Kristen tried to pull him back to the cot once Magnus left, but he managed to get his clothes on anyway. There were some things he needed to figure out if they were going to get out of Grizzly Flats in one piece. He had more than just Marco to worry about now.

She held up one of the ropes and flashed a wicked smile.

"Next time I might have to tie you up myself so you can't get away."

Greg turned to leave, but stopped.

"What was Marco talking about earlier, when you cut him off?"

She tried to act surprised, but her eyes betrayed her.

"It was cold last night, so I snuck a blanket out to him. No big deal."

But it was a big deal to Greg. He bent down and gave her a kiss before he said goodbye.

Magnus was waiting for him in the stadium with three of his men; none of them could have been older than twenty-one. They were wearing thick leather gloves and fully-loaded backpacks. One of them handed Greg some identical gear, and Magnus started barking out orders.

"I need you to get a better sense of the property, so I'm sending you out with these three. Booby trap blew a big hole in one of the fences on the far side of the main field. Don't do anything stupid, *partner.*"

Magnus winked as he gave Greg a fatherly slap on the back. His three escorts took off at a fast clip, jogging out of the camp and all the way across the field. Greg was in pretty good shape from all the hiking he'd been doing, but still a little stiff from the blast. He did his best to seem like he was keeping up, while also keeping his distance.

Greg tried to remember the details of their route, memorizing every turn they took. It all seemed at least a little familiar thanks to the map that Kristen had shown him. He still wasn't sure if that was a brave or stupid move on her part, but he had to admit that it made him trust her more.

Small clusters of women popped up between the plants to watch as they passed. Greg guessed they were doing some harvesting, but he didn't have the first clue about marijuana cultivation. He was several yards behind the rest of his crew when he saw them stop. One of them pulled out a map and studied it while the other two scanned the nearby trees and rabbit trails. They were having some kind of hushed debate when Greg caught up.

"This the spot?"

The guy closest to him motioned to a shattered fence post. There was another one in better shape a few yards in the other direction. Greg figured that this was close to where he had entered Grizzly Flats.

"Should we get to work?" Greg said to the guy next to him; but the guy with the map answered.

"Hang on. We're trying to figure out if there's another trip wire right here."

The kid spun the map ninety degrees, as if reading it sideways would help.

"Is that a master map?"

"Supposed to be, but it doesn't make much sense."

"Let me take a look."

"That's okay, we've got it."

They huddled and exchanged a few whispers. The map got folded up and put away before Greg could see anything. Wire and tools were starting to come out of the backpacks when there was a rumbling sound in the distance. They all turned in the direction of the rapidly approaching noise. The first shouts came from somewhere in the middle of the field.

"Helicopters!"

Greg watched as heads dropped from view across the leafy green horizon. The rest of his team did the same, ducking behind boulders and backing-up against trees. Greg stayed right where he was, trying to play dumb for as long as he could. The Sheriff's Department helicopters were in full view when somebody yanked him to the ground.

"Are you crazy?"

Greg looked up at the sky as the whirlybirds buzzed by. It seemed like they might be moving too fast to even notice what was going on beneath them. Or maybe these officers were already on Magnus's payroll.

The helicopters echoed away into the distance just as quickly as they had arrived. Greg cursed under his breath as he stood up to dust himself off. One of the trio slapped some wire cutters into his hand and they all went straight to work on mending the fence. They were done in a couple of hours and back in camp just in time for lunch. Greg didn't see Kristen around, so he grabbed a tray of food and took a seat next to Magnus.

"We had some unexpected visitors out there in the fields today."

Magnus snorted and took a drink from his mug. He wiped his lips with the back of a dirty hand.

"So I heard. Friends of yours?"

"I was about to ask you the same thing."

"Hard to keep track. Seems like they send new recruits up here for training."

Greg gave a dismissive snort.

"Yeah. They save the cushy desk jobs for us veterans."

"Well, at least the rookies are cheaper to bribe. By the way, don't be surprised if there's a different Ursula in your cot tonight."

Greg stopped mid-bite, a spoonful of beans hovering in front of his face.

"Excuse me?"

"Don't forget, she's my girl. You two had your fun, but it's time to mix things up. Keep it fresh. Cheers."

Magnus stood up and left. Greg finished his bite and took a look around. Whatever plan was brewing in the back of his mind had just been destroyed.

He was tearing into his sandwich when he heard several explosions in the distance. First, one—followed by two more in quick succession. Each time it got a little closer. Soon they were going off every few seconds. Somebody was systematically detonating the booby traps as they made their way toward the camp.

CHAPTER FOUR

eople all around Greg jumped up from their tables and started running. The women made a beeline for the tents, while the men scattered. A few of them headed for the corral to pull out the motorcycles. Two dune buggies tore across camp in the direction of the tent where they were growing the Grizzly Bear. Greg assumed that Magnus must be in one of those vehicles, but couldn't spot him.

Two men yanked tarps back from where the motorcycles had been stashed and started handing out guns. Greg grabbed a rifle and headed straight for his tent. He had no idea if Kristen would be there in the middle of the day, but he didn't know where else to look. She had their backpacks ready to go when he arrived.

"We have to hurry."

"We can't leave without Marco."

She took both of his hands in hers and looked him straight in the eye.

"I know. I'll take you to him."

The tents on either side of theirs were already collapsing when they emerged. He could hear gunfire on the other side of the camp, and motorcycles revving. The unmistakable scent of burning marijuana choked the air as the field went up in flames. Smoke was closing in all around them as they fumbled along to the few structures that still remained standing. Marco was nowhere to be found, but Kristen wasn't ready to give up.

She grabbed Greg's wrist, pulling him along behind her. It was hard to see even a few feet in front of them now, but they managed to find the bear pit. She pulled off the cinderblocks while Greg ripped the plywood back. They raced down the ramp together, but found only dirt and bones at the bottom.

The first shots buzzed by their heads as they reemerged. Greg pushed Kristen to the ground and chanced a look over the edge. He could see the silhouettes of Magnus and a gaggle of goons closing in fast. It looked like they were dragging Marco behind them.

Overloaded motorcycles were whizzing out of the camp all around them, heading for the hiking trails. Greg lifted his rifle and fired, narrowly missing one of the young guards. He fell hard and the others dropped on their bellies beside him. Magnus screamed to Greg over the automatic gunfire that echoed through the camp.

"Now or never! Give me the girl or your friend is bear food!"

Greg looked down at Kristen. She looked back with pleading eyes, begging him not to hand her over. He knew that he needed to save both Kristen and Marco, but he didn't know how.

Visibility was almost down to zero, and an army of Forest Service, Sheriff's Department, and Drug Enforcement Agency officers would be on them soon. Greg knew that saving Kristen entailed more than just getting her away from Magnus. He had to find a way to keep her from getting arrested and thrown in prison too.

He lifted her up and pointed toward the field.

"Straight across the middle, where the smoke's the thickest. Just like on the map you showed me. Don't stop until you reach the other side. Keep climbing up the slope until you find the trail."

"Aren't you coming with me?"

"I'll be right behind you, as soon as I get Marco. Ready?"

She bit her lip and nodded, stroking his face with the back of her hand. Greg took aim in the direction of Magnus and started squeezing the trigger in a slow rhythm. He wasn't trying to hit anybody, just buying her some time.

"Go!"

Magnus and his men returned fire, but none of the bullets came close. The fields were engulfed in flames now. Smoke billowed over Greg like whitewash from a massive wave. He thought he could hear Marco whimpering, but tried to block it out. Then he heard him scream.

"Greg! He's got a gun to my head!"

"Last chance or your friend dies."

Two stun grenades went off in the stadium, knocking several people to the ground. Dark figures in combat gear were swarming the camp. Greg heard a single shot ring out, followed by a heavy thud and the sound of Magnus and his men running away. He sprang from the pit and sprinted to where he thought Marco might be. He was halfway there when two helmeted figures emerged from the smoke. He put his hands behind his head and dropped to his knees. Tears sparkled in the little red dots that danced across his face.

"Take it easy. I'm a cop."

It wasn't true, but it kept him from getting shot. Especially since he was dressed like all the others. They zip-tied his wrists behind his back, leading him out of the camp. There was a command center set up several hundred yards beyond the burning field. A dozen other men in jeans and flannel shirts were seated with their backs against huge boulders. Greg sat down beside them and kept his mouth shut tight.

The gunfire didn't die down for another hour, getting farther and farther away. Fire planes arrived a little while later and dumped lake water on the flames. The steam it generated brought the temperature up for a few minutes, just as everything got silent again. Agents led the prisoners away one by one for questioning.

Greg was practically alone when the sky turned a deep blue, a spray of stars slowly emerging. He looked up, trying to think about Kristen more than Marco—praying his friend had survived.

"You the cop?"

A Sheriff's Deputy was standing above him. His helmet was tucked under his arm and his face was smeared with greasy sweat. He held his hand out to Greg and helped him up.

"Depends on who you ask."

"What the hell were you doing all the way out here? You undercover or something?"

"It's a long story."

They entered the tent and Greg plopped down into a folding chair. He answered an avalanche of questions, careful to keep his responses short and consistent. His interrogators seemed annoyed at first, but the light eventually went on behind their intense eyes.

"Tell us about your friend."

"His name is Marco Johnson. Stringy, blonde hair. About five-foot-nine, maybe a buck forty, soaking wet."

"We'll let you know if we find anybody that meets that description. In the meantime, you mind telling us what precinct you supposedly work in?"

"Virgil Heights. At least that's where I used to work."

The commander took a step forward, shoving the deputy aside.

"I thought you said you were a cop."

"Call the Police Chief there. He'll give you all the details."

"What'd you say your name was?"

"Greg Salem."

They traded looks. The commander nodded and the deputy went to make the call. He was back with the radio five minutes later.

"He wants to talk to you."

Greg brought the device to his ear and waited. The Chief's voice sounded like a ghost from another lifetime.

"Greg, you there?"

"That you, Chief?"

"Jesus Christ. Why the hell can't you stay out of trouble?"

❧

IT COULDN'T HAVE BEEN easy to get those bulky news vans up the mountain, but there they were. A line of them stretched along the curving road for as far as Greg could see in both directions. He kept his head down and followed the two officers who were supposed give him a lift. ATVs had gotten them from the smoldering field and out to the road, but now they had to walk a hundred yards to where the cruisers were parked. He hoped the windbreaker they'd loaned him would be enough of a disguise. It wasn't.

They'd only made it a few feet when he heard somebody shout his name. He didn't respond or even turn around, but his shoulders tensed and he broke his stride. That was confirmation enough for the media vultures. An army of reporters and their camera-wielding crews descended on him, forming a circle that was impossible to break.

Greg found himself bathed in a blinding glow of light. Microphones shoved into his face. Questions yelled at him from every direction.

"Are you the cop that solved those murders in The Bay Cities?"

"Where have you been hiding out?"

"Why did the Sheriff's Department call you in to help with this raid?"

"Are you working undercover for the DEA?"

"Is it true that they were growing a mutant strain of marijuana up here?"

Greg kept his mouth shut tight and waited for the cavalry to arrive. Ten officers broke up the news crew blockade, whisking him away to a waiting car. Reporters were still shouting after him as they chased the car on foot. Greg kept his eyes forward, trying hard to catch his breath.

It was only a few minutes before the cruiser pulled up to the end of the road that led to Greg's cabin. Greg pulled on the handle and swung the passenger door open as the officer spoke.

"You're the hero cop, right? The one that brought that gang down in Virgil Heights."

"All I did was shoot some kid."

He slammed the door shut, turned and walked off. The cruiser pulled away, taking all the light with it. Greg shuffled along the winding gravel road, letting his memory guide him through the dark. His El Camino came into view just before the darkened cabin did.

The back door was unlocked, just like it used to be when he was a kid. He stepped inside and started peeling his pants and shirt off as he walked. The strong odor of wood smoke from the fireplace in the living room was no match for the stench of his clothes. Greg tried to make sense of everything that happened as he made his way to the bathroom.

He pulled the chain on the overhead light and turned the faucet on in the sink. His body was suddenly sore all over, now that he wasn't worried about escaping from Grizzly Flats. Images of Marco flashed in his mind as he splashed cold water on his face.

"What took you so long?"

Greg almost sprang backwards through the bathroom door. He was still gasping for air when she sat up in the bathtub. The bear paw tattoo flexed and danced on her shoulder as she rubbed a washcloth across her neck.

"You mind getting my back?"

He took a step forward and knelt down. Kristen pulled his head against her naked chest and ran her fingers across his cropped hair. A whisper was the most he could manage.

"I couldn't find him."

"Magnus?"

"No, Marco. It looks like Magnus got away with a few of his men."

"I'm sorry, sweetie."

She stood up and grabbed a towel from the rack. Greg let his cheek rest on the edge of the bathtub, too exhausted to move.

"We need to get out of here right away."

"Kristen, you have to turn yourself in."

"No way! He kept me there against my will. He kept me high and he…he used me. You saw it with your own eyes. Besides, none of these cops even know that I exist."

"For now, but what about down the road? They're questioning everybody they caught. Any one of them could give up your name to make a deal."

"Hardly any of them even *know* my real name."

"You've got blood on your hands, Kristen. You said so yourself."

She was trembling now. He wanted to comfort her, but couldn't bring himself to stand. Everybody he got close to seemed to get killed.

"Listen to me, Greg. If Magnus is still alive, then he's gonna come looking for me. For both of us. Probably tonight."

"Are you insane? The Sheriff's Department has officers searching for him all over these mountains."

"That won't matter to him. Turn me in if you want to, but not until we're far away from here."

There was a cup of instant coffee waiting for him when he emerged from the bedroom in clean clothes. She had a pair of his loose-fitting board shorts on and a tattered tour shirt. He thought she looked just like every surfer girl he'd ever known. They threw her pack beside his in the back of the El Camino and started down the winding mountain roads.

They got waved through several checkpoints on their way out of the Angeles National Forest. The first signs of civilization came into view less than two hours after they'd left. Greg was merging onto the freeway ramp when two motorcycles came speeding up behind them. Kristen dug her fingers into his thigh as he stepped on the accelerator.

"What's the matter?"

"Magnus does business with some of the local bikers."

The two motorcycles were gaining on them fast. Greg knew he couldn't lose them. He reached across her legs and yanked the Glock from the glove compartment. His finger was on the trigger just below the window as the bikes whipped around them. Greg tapped the brakes and tried to steady his aim. That's when he saw them—just a couple of cocky teenagers taking their girlfriends out for a ride on their crotch rockets.

Greg set the gun down in his lap and exhaled. It felt wrong to be leaving the mountains with Marco missing, but right now he needed to get Kristen out of there. He needed to take her somewhere safe, somewhere far away from Magnus and Grizzly Flats. Descendents were kicking into "Silly Girl" on the car stereo as she rested her head on his shoulder and gave a little sniffle.

CHAPTER FIVE

They'd only been home a few days, but Greg already needed to get out of the house. The Sunday night barbecue at Junior's was the perfect excuse. Greg and his friends had started it twenty years ago, back when they were still young and thought they would live forever. These days Greg felt like he was one of the last ones standing.

He threw the El Camino into park and climbed out. It felt just like old times walking across his high school girlfriend's front yard. There were almost no toys scattered around the lawn now that her son, Chris, was thirteen years old.

Greg was still worried about Kristen, but glad she decided to stay home. He hadn't spent much time with Junior and her family since he got back to town, and he was looking forward to catching up with her dad, Eddie. The old man had been like a father figure to Greg for as long as he could remember.

The door swung open before he even knocked. Eddie stepped out onto the porch and pulled him into a tight hug. It felt good, like coming home. His grey hair was a little thinner on top now, but he also looked healthier than he had in years.

"Greg! How the hell are you?"

"Doing pretty good, all things considered. How's retirement?"

"I'm bored out of my mind. Come inside."

They stepped into the living room. Greg was surprised that Chris wasn't sitting on the ground in front of the TV playing video games. He spotted Junior in the kitchen tossing a salad in a wooden bowl. She fought off an ear-to-ear grin as he walked over to give her a kiss on the cheek.

"I barely recognize you, stranger."

"I was just about to say the same to you."

Greg stepped back to take her in as she turned her attention back to the salad. Her short blonde hair had grown out a few inches and was pulled into a ponytail now. The long summer dress she wore traced her incredible curves just right.

"Grab yourself something to drink out of the fridge."

He leaned against the counter, considering the body he had gotten to know so intimately when they were teenagers. The first one he had ever seen naked, and also the last one he'd touched before Kristen. Greg noticed that Junior was carrying herself differently these days—more like a confident woman now, and less of a punk rock temptress. Although she definitely looked like she could still throw a punch.

She caught him staring, but did a bad job of pretending not to notice.

"Hungry?"

"Starving. Where's Chris?"

She slammed her tongs down and steadied herself on the counter.

"Caught that little bastard with a bag of weed yesterday. I told him to stay out of sight until dinner tonight, or I might murder him."

"Wow. Where did he even get it from? School?"

"No idea. I did find out that he's been hanging around with Jeff Barrett and his crew. Chasing after them like some desperate little puppy."

That piece of information caught Greg like a punch to the gut. Barrett was a local thug turned contractor who had made a small fortune off of the booming local real estate market. He and Greg had been at each other's throats ever since they were kids.

"Those idiots are always looking for new recruits. You don't think he gave Chris the weed, do you?"

"I honestly don't know what to think."

Greg took a moment to collect himself, controlling his anger before he went on.

"Regardless of where he got it, Chris has been through a lot in the last year. You both have."

He put his hand on her back and waited for the moment to pass. Neither of them wanted to talk about the woman who had ripped their world apart. Greg was the one who finally broke the silence.

"Does Eddie know?"

"He knows something happened, but he doesn't know exactly what. I'd prefer to keep it that way or he might have a heart attack."

Junior shook her head and went back to finishing dinner. Greg wasn't ready to let it go.

"Want me to talk to him?"

"You planning to scare him straight or something? Be my guest."

Greg was heading for Chris's room when Eddie stopped him. They took a seat on the couch in the living room. The old man's knee was pumping as he tried to form his words.

"I wanted to tell you that I'm sorry about Marco. I always thought he was trouble, but I know he was your friend."

"He still is. I just need to find him."

Greg stood up, but Eddie stopped him.

"Listen. I don't know what you're planning to do for work, but you'll always have a spot at the bar."

Eddie's L Bar was a neighborhood institution, and Eddie was the king. He ran the bar himself every day for decades, quietly building a North Bay real estate empire on the side. These days, he was worth more on paper than some of the millionaires living along the beach in South Bay. But he still wasn't willing to let the L Bar go. He'd been trying to get Greg to take the business over for almost a year now.

"I thought Junior was in charge these days?"

"She is, but she needs help. You could run the bar and let her focus on the salon. You know, keep it in the family. Just say the word."

The only word that Greg could think of at the moment was "no," but it wasn't like he had a lot of other options. His police career seemed like a distant memory and he was way too old for a full-time career in punk rock.

"Thanks, Eddie. I'll let you know."

Greg walked across the living room, grabbing the knob on Chris's bedroom door. Surfing posters were tacked up on all four walls. Greg could hear an old Bad Citizen Corporation song playing on the stereo in the corner as he stepped inside. His eyes fell on the empty bed before he saw the open window. He didn't need to investigate any further to know that Chris had snuck out. It was something Greg had done several times himself when he was about that age.

Chris wasn't even his son, but Greg suddenly understood how his own father must have felt all those years ago. That magic combination of rage, terror and disappointment that makes you want to murder the people you love the most. *Some things never change.*

Two Months Later...

September 2011—*The van wasn't moving any longer, but Mary's head was spinning. She slowly opened her eyes, looking up at the dome light and willing it stop. Wherever they'd brought her, it was much quieter than anything she was used to. There were no police helicopters whirring overhead. No addicts threatening to kill each other all night long.*

Something in the back of her mind kept telling her to get up and run. To get as far away from there as she could. But where would she go? The streets of Hollywood didn't care if she lived or died. And going back to her mom's house would be a slow death of a different kind. It was sad but true that this might be the safest place she had woken up in months. Hell, *she thought,* at least I still have my clothes on.

Mary put her hand on the back of the bench seat and pulled herself up. Her head felt thick and her mind was reeling. The view out the window didn't offer many clues, except that she was in a garage. The cluttered workbench beside the van was filled with a random assortment of greasy tools, silhouetted in the darkness. She reached for the handle and slid the door open as quietly as she could.

One foot out the door, and pause.

"Hello?"

She almost didn't recognize the fear in her own voice. It sounded so soft, so vulnerable, like the little girl she never got to be. Mary groped her way to a door that led into the kitchen. She opened it up and saw the driver standing there. He was about her stepdad's age—maybe a little older—with the same hard eyes, but otherwise more polished. The man popped a piece of popcorn into his mouth and gave her the once over.

"Want some food?"

She was hungry all the time these days, but never felt like eating.

"You got anything else?"

He smiled and nodded. "Sure. Follow me."

Scoring drugs hadn't been that easy since, well, forever. She knew they wouldn't be free.

Mary followed him through the small house. The walls were bare and there was almost no furniture. He walked fast, with a sense of purpose. She didn't hear the moaning until they reached the bedroom door. Glaring lights flooded the hallway as he pushed into the room.

Two young women were on the bed. One was blindfolded and handcuffed to the headboard. Mary recognized the second one from around Hollywood, but hadn't seen her in a few weeks. She was straddling the other woman with a riding crop in her hand.

They wound through a forest of tripods and a couple of oblivious crewmembers. There was a small sofa pushed against one wall, with a glass coffee table in front of it. Lines were already chalked up in neat little rows. He handed her a rolled up dollar bill.

"Have as much as you want. There's plenty more where that came from."

Mary hesitated for a brief moment before sitting down and getting to work.

She did two quick bumps, one right after the other. It was pure and strong. She felt the instant burn and rush as she leaned back. They sat side-by-side, watching the action on the bed. It all seemed so mechanical, like pistons and lube. A fake ecstasy compared to the narcotic euphoria that was pumping through Mary's bloodstream.

"I've never done porn before..."

"There's no rush. Just join in when the urge strikes you."

It didn't take long to make a decision. What was happening on the bed looked way better than what might happen on the sofa. He gave her a fatherly pat on the knee, but left his hand there. That made her choice even easier.

She stood up and slithered out of her tank top. The girls on the bed were waving her over as she unbuttoned her jeans. The driver looked her up and down, smiling his approval.

"There are other ways you can help me, besides all of this."

"Oh yeah? How?"

"You and I might have some friends in common, Mary. But we can talk about that later."

CHAPTER SIX

"This is bullshit, dude."

Marco was talking to himself more than the guard behind him. His bony, hairless chest heaved as he dug his shovel into the ground again. The T-shirt wrapped around his filthy hair was the same one he'd been wearing since he and Greg left to go hiking two months ago. He'd gotten it wet and wrung it out a few times since then, but it was starting to fray and fall apart. Just like him.

Marco had seen his share of hard times over the years. It was the price he paid to live the life he chose. He had survived beatings from cops, been bitten by dogs, gotten shot at by Mexican drug lords, and fought three drunks at once in a jail cell. But this was the first time he'd ever had to do hard labor. It didn't sit well with him.

"You guys want to put up fences so bad, dig the holes yourself."

"Shut up and get back to work."

The guard sounded half asleep as he spat out the order. It was hot out and none of them had taken a water break for a couple of hours. Marco's hands were raw and blistered as he kicked the blade deeper into the hard ground.

"*You* shut up."

There were a couple of other slave laborers right behind Marco. They were waiting to put the post in the ground once he finished digging the hole. He wasn't sure what they had done to get on Magnus's bad side. Marco felt like he'd been born there.

The three of them had been digging since sunrise. They'd made their new camp near a box canyon deep inside the forest where no hikers or campers ever came. There was a natural spring nearby that provided plenty of water, but they had to hunt for most of their food. Marco never thought he would miss baloney and beans so much.

Magnus and the dozen guards that escaped the raid all slept in the tents they grabbed on the way out of Grizzly Flats. Marco and the rest of his ilk camped outside on a couple of sleeping bags they shared. He didn't really mind it, except for the wildlife. A rattlesnake had bitten one of the men on his crew a few days ago; he died in his sleep. Marco discovered the body in the morning, so he got to dig the grave.

He finished the current hole and leaned on his shovel for a catnap. The guard stuck the barrel of a rifle in his back, escorting him a few yards down to dig the next hole. There were only a few more posts to sink before the fence on this part of the field was completed. Marco guessed that they would move on to clearing the brush and trees next, before they got to planting. It was anybody's guess if Magnus would let them live beyond that.

Marco had tried to escape a couple of times since the raid. He'd even gotten a few miles away once, but the overgrown animal trails all looked the same out there. Left, right or straight-ahead, there was no way to know whether you were headed for civilization or deeper into the wilderness. In the end he always made a wrong turn and practically walked right back into camp. Magnus usually gave him a slap on the back and an extra helping of venison stew.

"Welcome back," he'd say, practically laughing himself out of his chair. "We were starting to worry we'd lost you."

Marco was exhausted. He'd had enough for one lifetime.

"Just shoot me then!"

"I probably would, but then I we'd never see your friend Greg again. You're the bait in this elaborate mouse trap of mine."

Marco slammed the shovel into the ground and imagined he was digging a grave for Magnus. The hole got deep really fast, but it was wider than it should have been. Marco smiled to himself until the guard shoved him another few yards down the line.

"Take it easy, dude. Or I might have to dig a hole for you next."

GREG SET THE BOTTLE of beer down and went back to wiping glasses. He'd only started picking up shifts at Eddie's L Bar in the last couple of weeks, once the news coverage about him died down. The bar took up most of a non-descript building on Bay Cities Boulevard in North Bay. Junior's beauty parlor was the only other tenant, but now that her father had retired, she was managing both places.

The regulars were seated in their usual spots at the bar, arguing about something pointless. Eddie was right there beside them, pretending like he didn't own the place.

"Hey, Greg! Bring these idiots another round, on me."

Greg reached into the cooler and popped the cap on two bottles. He set them down and cleared the empties.

"Want a little more coffee, Eddie?"

Eddie looked down at his watch, squinting to check the time.

"You know what. I think I'll have a beer too."

"You sure? It's not even eleven."

"What the hell. It's not like I have anywhere to be."

Greg brought a third beer over. The trio tried to get him to join their conversation, but he wasn't in the mood for small talk. He went over to the jukebox instead. There was still a lot of classic rock in there, beside the punk and reggae discs that were taking over now that Junior was in charge. It was funny to hear Black Flag's "TV Party" back-to-back with "Welcome To The Jungle" by Guns N' Roses. Those songs sounded more and more similar to Greg the older he got, just an endless angry mash-up of snot, piss and angst.

A Bad Citizen Corporation song called "Heading South" came on next. Marco's drumming sounded just as frantic and unpredictable as the man himself, wherever he was—if he was still alive at all. Greg reached for the kill switch under the bar, almost ripping it from its socket. His hand was still shaking when he heard a familiar voice.

"Hello, Mr. Salem."

Greg looked straight into the neutral gaze of Bay Cities Police Chief, Robert Stanley—or as he was known locally, Officer Bob. They had been archenemies from the time Greg was a teenager, doing battle on the streets of The Bay Cities. These days it was more like a cold war, ever since Greg helped solve one of the biggest murder cases in BCPD history. It was something he was reminded of by the regulars at Eddie's during every shift he worked.

"Something to drink?"

"No, thanks. I'm actually here on police business. I thought you'd want to know that we're reopening the case on your brother."

It was the news he'd been waiting to hear for almost twenty years. The police had originally ruled his brother's death a suicide, but Greg never bought it. The Tim he knew would never do that to his friends and family, no matter how screwed up he was on drugs. They would always be brothers, no matter how bad things had gotten between them after Bad Citizen Corporation broke up.

Greg's hand instinctively went to the phone in his pocket, but he pulled it back. He could go next door to Junior's salon and tell her in person, as soon as Officer Bob left.

"I don't want to get your hopes up, but there's new information we're looking into."

"What is it?"

Officer Bob raised his eyebrows, looking around to make sure nobody else was listening. Greg made a show of doing the same and nodded along expectantly.

"You know we're still trying to track down information on Quincy McCloud."

Hearing his ex-girlfriend's name gave Greg a stabbing headache. She'd had his best friend Ricky killed, and finished-off Junior's ex-husband, Mikey, herself. She and Chris would probably be dead too if Greg hadn't rescued them before Quincy committed suicide at the tidal pools.

Officer Bob saw the blood rising in Greg's face and gave him a second before going on.

"We traced her family to a small town in Missouri. She and her brother were Army brats. Family moved around a lot before the father finally drank himself to death."

Unwanted memories of Quincy flashed in Greg's mind. He pictured the way she smiled, the way she smelled coming out of the ocean, her laugh. It was troubling how much Kristen sometimes reminded him of her.

"What's all this have to do with Tim?"

"Her brother hung himself in the attic at their aunt's house when he was a senior in high school. Sounds like Quincy found him."

Greg frowned, disgusted with himself for feeling sorry for her. They had found his brother, Tim, the same way, hanging from the rafters in the record store right next door. Officer Bob pressed on.

"She ended up going to a local college, but got thrown out freshmen year after having an affair with a professor. Does the name John Jacoby ring a bell?"

"J.J.? The bass player from Bad Citizen Corporation?"

"That's him. Local police found a diary at her aunt's house. From what we read, he apparently gave her a lot of dirt on you, Tim, and the rest of your old band."

"J.J. never could keep his mouth shut when a girl was involved."

"According to her diary, it seemed like he might have some information about the circumstances of your brother's death."

Greg slammed the bar repeatedly with his fist until all the nearby glasses and bottles were dancing. There weren't many people in the place, but they were all watching him now. Officer Bob put his hand on Greg's shoulder and motioned him outside.

"I hoped that telling you in public would have the opposite effect."

Greg snorted and kicked the side door shut.

"I need to go to St. Louis and talk to J.J."

"He's not there. University fired him as soon as they found out about the alleged affair."

"Where is he now?"

"Leave the police work to the professionals, Mr. Salem."

"I've got a little experience of my own."

"Far as I can tell, you're a bartender now. I'll be in touch."

∽

AFTERNOON TRAFFIC WAS LIGHT on Bay Cities Boulevard. The Gun Club was bashing out "Sex Beat" through the car stereo as Greg sped toward South Bay. Kristen was reclining on a lounge chair wearing only bikini bottoms when he came through the back gate. They were living in the main house now, ever since his landlady relocated up north to be near her grandchildren. She told him it would be a temporary arrangement, but there was a for sale sign in the front yard.

Kristen looked up when he came in.

"Hey, baby. You going surfing?"

"I don't know. Maybe."

"What's wrong?"

Is it that obvious? Greg muttered "nothing" under his breath and stormed inside his old garage-apartment. In the last few weeks, he'd turned it into a makeshift recording studio. A couple of guitars and amps were scattered around the room, along with a laptop computer and a small mixing board. Not that he'd managed to write or record any new songs in there. Mostly, it was just a place to keep his old gear and think about everything that had gone wrong.

Kristen came out there with him too, sometimes. At first, she would just sit and watch him play, but eventually she started singing too. She had a soft, scratchy voice that forced Greg to play gentler than he ever thought he could. Her heartbreaking lyrics were the only thing that could take his mind off of Marco, often for hours at a time. But she wasn't out there with him at the moment.

He lifted the dust cover on his turntable and watched a Peter Tosh record start spinning. Reggae was what calmed him down when he was alone. That, and surfing, but he barely had any time for either anymore. He was working the morning shift at Eddie's Monday through Friday, and up in the Angeles National Forest almost every weekend.

The official search for Magnus and his crew hadn't produced anything, and nobody who was taken into custody was talking. That didn't keep Greg from doing some searching of his own, especially since they never found Marco's body.

Greg looked up at the geological maps pinned to the walls in the garage. Large areas of the forest had been highlighted and checked off. Some of which he had done by chartering private helicopters, but it wasn't a hobby that he could afford to keep up on a bartender's salary. After that he had taken to the trails himself, riding his mountain bike to look for his friend and to clear his mind.

Some small part of Greg knew that he was just doing all of this to alleviate the guilt he felt for leaving Marco behind. The cop in him knew that his partner probably went up in flames with the rest of the camp that night. But as his friend, Greg found this image too horrible to accept. Greg's only choice was to keep searching until he had closure of one kind or another.

He looked over at his backpack, already stuffed and leaning in the corner. He half considered taking off for the mountains right then, but didn't want to leave Kristen alone for an extra night. She was still in shock from her time with Magnus and needed a lot of support from him. It was a bit draining, but there were plenty of benefits too.

He reached for a nearby guitar and strummed a few chords before somebody started banging on the door.

"I already told you that you don't have to knock, Kristen."

Junior stormed in with a scowl.

"When were you going to tell me that Officer Bob came to see you about your brother?"

Greg set the guitar down and tried to act surprised. She took a seat beside him.

"You know those drunks at the bar were listening to everything you two said."

"You were the first person I thought of when I heard the news, but things got a little out of control."

"Good to hear. I thought maybe you rushed home to tell your plaything instead. That's quite a show she's putting on out there, by the way."

"We were young once too."

He instantly felt like the dirty old creep that Junior thought he was. *Maybe it's true.*

"We both know my body never looked like that."

Greg fumbled to change the subject.

"What did the guys at the bar tell you?"

"Just that Officer Bob is reopening Tim's case. They said that he mentioned J.J."

Greg pushed himself up and went to flip the record over. Even after everything that had happened, it was still hard for him to be that close to Junior and not want to hold her. He lowered the needle onto Side Two and tried to move on.

"You think he could have anything to do with it?"

She exhaled loudly and crossed her arms. Greg could almost hear her thinking. Deep down inside they both suspected that nothing would come of this new lead.

"The only thing I remember about J.J. is that he never shut up."

"For sure. You really had to watch what you said around him, unless you wanted everybody in The Bay Cities to find out about it. But he was much quieter when we were on the road. He spent most of his time in the van reading."

"You think it could've had something to do with all the drugs he was taking? Books are a great way to isolate yourself."

"No doubt. He was probably just staring at the page and nodding out. I'm still not surprised he became a professor, though."

"Well, I always thought he was a doofus. What does he teach?"

"No idea."

Greg made a mental note to find that out. Junior stood up to leave, but had one more question to ask.

"You gonna do anything about it?"

"Officer Bob told me not to. So, yes."

❧

THERE WAS ONLY ABOUT an hour of sunlight left when Greg paddled out. The beach was mostly empty this time of day, which was just how he liked it. The waves had been pretty small all week, but he still liked getting in the water. Nothing quite compared to watching the sun set over the Pacific while sitting on a surfboard. He couldn't imagine ever wanting to live anywhere else.

He caught a couple rides before the sun dipped down behind the horizon. The last one took him most of the way to shore. He thought he saw Kristen up on the sand in the distance as he paddled the last few yards and picked up his board. She had her legs tucked under her arms and was wearing a hoody over her head. Her eyes were on him as he undid the leash from his ankle and trotted up the beach. It was getting dark now, so he didn't see who it actually was until she was right in front of him. They both seemed surprised.

"Maggie Keane. What're you doing down here at this time of night?"

"Looking for you. Why haven't you returned any of my messages?"

"Just been out of town a lot. And working. Stop by Eddie's sometime, you can usually find me there."

Greg turned to trot off. Maggie took hold of his surfboard leash.

"I prefer it down here in South Bay, by the beach. Have a seat."

He reluctantly laid his board on the sand, dropping down beside her. His hair and wetsuit were still soaked. The breeze was making him shiver, or was it Maggie? She had a knack for popping up at exactly the wrong time.

"I heard you had a new kitten. You ever date women your own age?"

He could hear the smile in her voice. She'd been blatantly coming onto him ever since they bumped into each other at a coffee shop last year. That was right around the time that everything went to hell. Greg tried to push the memories from his mind.

"It just sort of seems to happen that way—"

"I thought you'd learn your lesson after the last one"

That was a low blow, but Greg didn't respond. There was no point getting into a fight with a high school acquaintance that he barely remembered. Looking at her life now you might forget that she came home from D.C. with her tail between her legs after an embezzlement scandal. She spent all her time, these days, sipping mimosas and kissing up to the South Bay elite.

"Are you happy with your little bartending gig?"

It was more of a jab than a question.

"Pays the bills and keeps me busy."

"What if I told you I had a job offer that might be a little more exciting? Something that's right up your alley."

Greg squinted to look at her face. It was too dark to determine if she was serious or not.

"I'm listening."

"I've got a new business partner. Could be very lucrative, but I'm not sure how much to trust him. I was hoping I could hire you to do a little digging."

"Sounds like you need a private investigator."

"I need somebody I can trust. I'll make it worth your while."

The thought of getting paid for something he was good at did sound pretty appealing.

"How much digging?"

"You're the expert, so I'll leave it to you. All I want to know is if I can trust him or not. And that you'll keep this between us. If you can agree to those terms, I'll pay you twenty-five hundred dollars."

Maggie picked her phone up, punching out a message with her thumbs. She crossed her legs and stood up without using her hands. She was already disappearing into the gloom when Greg called out after her.

"What's the name?"

"I just texted it to you."

Greg's phone was back at the house, along with Kristen and a warm shower. He waited until Maggie was gone before he got up to jog home.

CHAPTER
SEVEN

Mark Lathrop. That was the name Maggie texted Greg the night before. He let it roll around in his head as he drove up the mountain Saturday morning. He'd made the trip so many times that he barely paid attention, speeding through the dangerous curves. The lush pines and stunning vistas were just a brightly colored blur out his window. It gave him plenty of time to consider what he'd found out about her mysterious new business partner. It wasn't much.

From what he could gather, Lathrop was a former Hollywood mover and shaker. His name used to pop up in entertainment industry trade magazines a decade ago, but nothing more recent than that. He was a hotshot talent agent back then, with a stable of rising film and music stars, until he quietly left the business. There were no news stories about the man, or the kind of business he was conducting afterwards. Whatever Lathrop had gotten into, he was successful enough to buy a multi-million dollar house on the beach in South Bay last year. He also owned a massive yacht, judging by the few pictures Greg found online.

Greg turned his attention to what trails he was going to search that day. He wouldn't be able to do any more research on Lathrop until he got home Sunday night, anyway. His phone got zero reception in the mountains, and there was no computer at his cabin. He parked the car and went in through the back door. His mountain bike was still there in the kitchen, unlocked and untouched. He pulled it outside and strapped his backpack on. His

Glock and a canteen were the heaviest things he carried with him on these trips. So far, the canteen was the only one of the two that he ever managed to empty.

Greg pedaled hard from the moment he climbed onto his bike. He had a lot of ground to cover in less than forty-eight hours. His first stop would be at Pete's Trading Post—a combination biker bar and mini market not far from his cabin. It was the only place to go for supplies, or a plate of food, outside of a little town called Deer Springs.

Greg had already been through Deer Springs a few times in his search, but came up empty handed. Pete's, on the other hand, was always the best place to get the latest local gossip. The place definitely had a seedy vibe, but they made decent burgers and a few cute waitresses.

He and Marco only went there a couple times in the previous months because it was too big of a temptation for his recently sober sidekick. The question of Greg's sobriety never factored into that decision, but was no more stable than Marco's. He'd already fallen off the wagon once in the last year, leaving him to question whether he really needed to be sober at all.

Greg was still wrestling with that thought when he arrived at Pete's thirty minutes later. He was already sweating and slightly winded. It always took him a few hours to get used to the thin air at this altitude. The smell of pine needles and wildflowers mingled together with stale beer and barbecue as Greg walked up. The parking lot looked like an import motorcycle dealership on the weekends. Guys of all ages would be strutting around in their colorful leathers, drinking pitchers of beer and smoking cigarettes.

The place was more of a Harley Davidson hangout when Greg's dad used to bring him and his brother here as kids. Back then, you saw more fat bikers beating each other to death with chains rather than wearing brightly colored helmets. Greg couldn't decide which version of Pete's he liked better as he took a stool at the bar and ordered coffee.

One thing that hadn't changed since the good old days was the music. ZZ Top, Bad Company and Led Zeppelin still ruled the jukebox, even if most of the clientele were still in diapers when those records had come out. It provided the perfect soundtrack for the motorcycle road races that filled every flat screen on the walls. A couple of young guys next to him started cheering when one of the riders lost control of his bike. It went cartwheeling off, while the rider slid along the slick black asphalt. The guy nearest Greg slapped him on the shoulder and started screaming in his face.

"Holy shit, bro! Did you see that?"

He was a black kid with short, kinky dreads and a lightly freckled face. There was a wide smile spread across his face. Greg wasn't sure how to respond. He was never one to sit around watching surfer wipe out videos, although millions of them were posted online.

"That was a pretty good one. You ever crash like that?"

"Hell no, but I lost a brother to an accident."

Greg knew a thing or two about losing a brother. The pain still felt like an open wound whenever he let himself think about it. Especially now that Officer Bob had reopened the investigation into Tim's death. It seemed more real up here in the mountains, the place where they had spent so many summers together as kids.

Greg cleared his throat to speak.

"Sorry for your loss."

"It's all good. It was a few years ago now."

Greg turned to face his new friend.

"You ride up here a lot?"

"Almost every weekend, unless I have to work."

"Oh yeah? What do you do?"

"This and that. Sales, mostly."

The kid smiled. Greg gave a knowing nod. He saw a small opening and decided to take it.

"You ever come across something called 'Grizzly Bear' in your line of work?"

The smile flickered, but only for a second.

"You a cop or something?"

"Nope. I'm a bartender. Place called Eddie's by the beach."

It wasn't a lie, but it felt like one. At least the kid seemed convinced.

"I've heard of that place. Punk club, right? That's cool. What's your name?"

"Greg."

"Tommy."

Greg went in for a handshake, but it ended up a fist bump.

"No offense, but what's a dude your age doing working at a place like that?"

"I work the day shift. Easier on the ears. So?"

"What? Grizzly Bear? I've heard about that shit, but I thought it was a rumor. Haven't personally seen any. You?"

"Nope. Just heard the rumors, too."

Tommy's friends started screaming again. The kid spun around to look up at the TV screen. Greg grabbed his coffee mug and went out onto the patio. He wanted to see what else he could find out.

A drunken speed-demon was doing donuts on his motorcycle in the parking lot. Thick clouds of rubbery smoke filled the air as Greg tried to navigate through the crowd. He'd almost reached the back when a waitress raced by with a tray of empty glasses. Her auburn hair was pulled up in a bun, exposing sunburned shoulders under a lacy halter-top. She had a small, black mole on her left cheek, like a 1920s starlet. Greg spotted the tattoo on her left shoulder blade, but couldn't make out what it was.

"Excuse me. Hey!"

She looked back with a sneer before disappearing into the kitchen. Greg tried to follow, but the crowd closed in behind her. He tried to squeeze through until a big hand was planted firmly on his chest.

"Where do you think you're going?"

He had thick grey hair tied back in a ponytail. A folded red bandana covered his entire forehead and most of his eyebrows. His beard was almost yellow where it sprouted from red cheeks and around his meaty lips.

Greg tried to squeeze by him.

"I need to talk to that waitress."

"You and half the guys here. You'll have to wait until she comes back out. This entrance is for employees only."

"Fair enough. You work here?"

"Try not to. I own the place."

He sized Greg up for a moment before disappearing through the same door as the waitress. Greg guessed that a guy like that could spot a former cop from several miles away. The chances were pretty slim that the waitress would be coming back out onto the patio anytime soon. He decided his best bet was to go back inside and try to catch her there.

It wasn't any easier getting through the crowd on the return trip. He finally made it out to the parking lot just in time to see the waitress climb onto the back of a motorcycle. She and the driver went screaming off down the road. They were both wearing helmets so Greg couldn't see their faces, but her tattoo was unmistakable. It was a bear paw, just like Kristen's. Greg could sense that he was getting closer to finding Magnus again, but it wasn't happening fast enough.

Greg turned to see the owner coming outside with a baseball bat in his fist. A couple of bartenders were right behind him. Greg took the hint and bolted for his bike. He doubted they would chase him if he left on his own, but he couldn't be sure. The wind felt good on his face as he sped down the mountain road toward the trailhead. It was time to resume the search for Marco.

᭡

IT WAS CLOSE TO dusk. Greg had been pedaling deeper into the forest all afternoon. He was making his way up a scrubby slope, trying not to think about the shooting pains in his thighs and calves, when he heard the gunshot. It was a single pop, far away and not easy to pinpoint, but it was unmistakable. He dropped his bike to the ground and crouched down to listen. When nothing happened for five minutes he climbed back on and pedaled to the top of the hill.

Greg pulled the map out of his backpack. He'd already pedaled around Grizzly Flats again in case there was any new activity. That was a couple of hours ago, and the search came up empty, as usual. Now he was further East on the Pacific Crest trail than he had ever gone before. Most weekends he would make it back to crash in the cabin on Saturday night, but he had a feeling that he might be sleeping outdoors tonight. He was glad his canteen was still half full and that he had trail mix and beef jerky to snack on.

He knew in his heart that there was a slim chance he would ever find Marco out here. A guy like Magnus was too smart to go and set up shop in the same neck of the woods, especially when so many people were looking for him. But he also knew that Magnus was probably desperate and low on supplies. Very few of the motorcycles had gotten out of Grizzly Flats the night of the raid, which meant that almost everything had burned. Even if they managed to stretch what they had with them for this long, there was a good chance that his men would turn up at Pete's, before long. Or maybe that's what the waitress was doing there, smuggling supplies to wherever they were hiding out. That meant Greg only had to find the trails that they were using to get in and out. Then he might be able to figure out, once and for all, if Marco was alive. He thought he owed his friend at least that much.

The sky was orange in the west where the sun was going down. A wide valley stretched out before him. There was a dry streambed that sloped downward, winding through a thicket of boulders, Manzanita and fallen trees. Definitely not the kind of terrain he wanted to ride down in the dark. He decided to make his camp for the night.

Greg fished his phone from the pack. The thing was useless for any kind of communication out here, but it was still a great camera. He snapped several shots, including a panorama of the entire valley below. His stomach was grumbling by the time he finished.

He wolfed down a couple handfuls of trail mix and took a big gulp of water before putting it all away. He still had the same amount of ground to cover the next day, so he had to ration his supplies. His leg muscles were seizing up, but he thought everything would be fine after he got a good night's rest. He just had to make sure not to get lost on the way back.

He hid his bike in the chaparral and slipped into a camouflage rain poncho he kept in his pack. Then he climbed the nearest tree. The lightweight nylon camping hammock he always carried made a good bed in a pinch. He tied the ropes between two thick branches and slipped inside. There was enough room in the cocoon for him on one end and his pack on the other.

Greg was always amazed at how the littlest noises sounded so loud in wide-open spaces. Every branch that fell was a bear ready to attack. Every twig that snapped was Magnus and his guards coming to find him. He finally tried counting stars to fall asleep.

He woke up several hours later, sometime before dawn. A strange noise had startled him, something that sounded like voices. Greg lay absolutely still in his hammock waiting to see if it was just a dream. He was about to write it off to an overactive imagination when he heard a woman laugh. It sounded like she was coming up the hill behind him, the same way he'd come the day before. Then he heard other people talking—at least two women and a few men.

Greg sat up and pulled the Glock from his pack. If these were people from Magnus's crew, then he knew they would be armed too. He eased back and tried to control his breathing. He could feel his heart practically beating through his chest as they came closer. Two girls arrived first, passing under the tree next to his.

"Nina. Hey, wait up. My flashlight batteries just went dead. I can't see anything."

"Use the ones from your vibrator."

"Who needs a vibrator when you've got five hot guys with you? That new recruit's really cute."

"I guess so, if you like them stupid."

"I'll take hot and stupid over the opposite any day."

They both laughed and kept moving. Greg did the math in his head. He was totally outnumbered, even if he got the drop on them. And he couldn't follow them in the dark and risk getting caught. That wouldn't be good for him or Marco. He'd just have to let them pass, but he hoped he'd overhear something useful from the guys. It felt like hours passed before they arrived.

"Is this the right way?"

"The map says to come over the hill and follow the stream, but I don't hear any water."

"We're in a drought, dipshit. Just head for the rocks over there."

"Damn, these packs are heavy. What's in them anyway?"

"No idea. Red said he'd shoot us himself if we tried to pick the locks."

"Stop complaining, you two. Magnus is gonna think we're superheroes when we show up with all these supplies. We'll have our choice of Ursulas for the next couple of weeks."

"I know, I know. How much further is it?"

"About another hour or so. Maybe a little more. But only if you stop slowing us down."

The voices started to fade as they made their way down the hill. Greg waited until it was silent again before he finally exhaled. His fingers cramped from gripping the Glock so hard. It was almost sunrise when he sat up to have a look around.

Greg was already on his bike and headed back to the cabin when the sun came up. Whenever he made a turn, he tore a small strip off of his rain poncho and tied it to a tree branch. It was a risk he had to take if he wanted to point the Sheriff's Department in the right direction.

CHAPTER
EIGHT

The new recruits arrived a little after sunrise. Marco watched all seven of them drop their packs and wait for praise from Magnus. The crazy son of a bitch immediately attacked them instead.

"You were supposed to be here two days ago." One of the guys stepped forward. He didn't look any older or more experienced than the others, but he had balls; Marco had to give him that.

"Red told us to wait. Said the Sheriff's Department was poking around again."

Magnus was practically growling now.

"You don't work for Red, do you? We almost died out here waiting for this shipment to arrive."

Magnus waved a couple of guards over. They set their guns down and turned the wheels on the combination locks. A few cartons of cigarettes tumbled out of the first one they opened, followed by bundles of cash. The kid who had carried that one shook his head in disbelief. Marco couldn't imagine what it felt like to miss such a golden opportunity.

The next few packs had mostly soap, toilet paper and toothbrushes; then came the freeze-dried military rations and cartons of cigarettes. It was obvious that Magnus was most excited about the seventh pack. He opened that one himself, unleashing a flood of pill bottles. A couple of them rolled across the dirt before Magnus quickly scooped them up.

Two of the guards grabbed the rest of the supplies and took them away. Magnus and his remaining crew turned to face the mules that had brought them the supplies.

"You girls look like you could use a nap. Why don't you head over to my tent and get yourselves cleaned up?"

A guard escorted the women away, which left only the five guys.

"As for you, breakfast will be ready in a few minutes. Go claim a spot in one of the tents and wait for further instructions. But don't get too comfortable. There's work to do."

They all started walking in the direction that Magnus had pointed. All except for the one who had been acting like he was their leader. He reached into his back pocket and pulled out a folded piece of paper.

"I've got a message for you. From Red."

Magnus took it from his trembling hand and unfolded it. His eyes went wide as he scanned the page. His face was contorted with rage by the time he'd reached the bottom.

"You look familiar."

"My name's—"

"I don't give a shit what your name is. Where do I know you from?"

"I lived at Grizzly Flats for a few months last year."

If Magnus recognized the kid, he wasn't letting on.

"I'm guessing you didn't read this message before you delivered it to me."

"Course not. He just said it was important and that I should hand directly to you."

Magnus waved the crumpled paper in front of his ashen face. "According to this, Red wants to do a little trading. Problem is, what he's offering already belongs to me."

The messenger's voice was shaky now, pleading.

"What? I swear I had no idea. Send me back with a message of your own."

"I'll send a message to Red, all right. Don't worry about that."

He took the kid by the collar and walked him over to the nearest guard.

"This one and the other prisoners should start breaking down the camp. We have to get out of here before sunset tonight."

Magnus motioned to where Marco and the other three laborers were sitting. The kid was still wailing as the guards led him away.

"I didn't do anything wrong!"

Marco shook his head in disgust, sure that he was going to die out there.

෨

It was after sunset when Greg made it back to the cabin on Sunday. He called the Virgil Heights Police Chief the minute his phone got signal again, close to the base of the mountain. Greg knew the Sheriff's Department would take the tip about Magnus more seriously if it came from somebody still on the force. The Chief agreed to call it in himself, promising to keep Greg posted if there was any progress.

Greg pulled up to the house in South Bay around midnight. Kristen wanted to chat because he'd been gone for two days. They had gotten really close in the last couple of months, to the point where Greg thought he might actually be starting to love her. But he still wasn't sure what to share with her when it came to Magnus. Being under the control of somebody as manipulative as that wasn't something that went away overnight.

On the other hand, Kristen never had a single good thing to say about her former boss. But Greg always noticed a different kind of fear in her eyes whenever she talked about life before Grizzly Flats. How she'd shoplifted her food every day, and broke into cars to get money for drugs—or worse.

Greg sighed. She climbed behind him on the couch and wrapped her legs around his waist. She was rubbing his shoulders and whispering in his ear.

"Did you find any new information about your friend Marco?"

"It's hard to say. I should have more information tomorrow. There is one thing I wanted to ask you about. Do you know that bar Pete's, the one that's up on the highway?"

"Of course. That's where Magnus did most of his major deals. Why?"

"Were any of the other girls—the 'Ursulas'—working up there? You know, to keep an eye on things for him."

"If they were, he never told me about it."

There was a slight edge to her voice now.

"I saw a girl there today. About your age, maybe a little younger. Her hair was dyed a reddish brown color. She has the same tattoo as you."

Greg reached behind himself and gave her a pat on the shoulder. She released her grip and leaned back against the cushions. He sat up to face her.

"Does she sound familiar?"

"Not really."

"She had a mole, right here on her left cheek."

He brought his finger up and lightly touched her face. Kristen twisted up her lips, as if she was giving his question serious thought.

"It's been a while since I've seen her, but I guess that could have been Mary. Except—"

"What? Did she escape?"

"No. She never lived at Grizzly Flats. Magnus just mentioned her once or twice. Did she look okay?"

Kristen's voice was full of concern, but something about her story didn't add up.

"She looked like a cocktail waitress at a biker bar…"

He heard the venom in his own words. It was obvious that she did too.

"Hm. I wish I could help you more."

"You still might be able to. Did you ever see Magnus doing deals with any Mexican businessmen? Maybe at Pete's?"

She bit her lip, giving the question serious thought.

"Not that I know of. It was always those bikers, but he did plenty of deals I didn't know about."

Greg was starting to think that his pet theory about the cartels was off the mark. He stood up and faked a stretch. He needed to get out of the situation before things got too heated. Kristen pawed at his thigh.

"Where are you going? I thought we could snuggle."

"Sorry. I need to get some sleep. I've got work in the morning."

Her disappointment filled the room as he walked away without looking back.

∿

"Jesus. You look terrible."

Greg didn't need Eddie to tell him the weekend had taken its toll. The bathroom mirror did a good job of that earlier that morning.

"You don't look so hot yourself."

"Just a little hungover, that's all."

Eddie took a sip from his coffee mug. Greg lifted a case of beer and lugged it over behind the bar. Whoever closed the place down the night before did a terrible job of restocking the reach-in coolers.

"Hey, Eddie. You know almost everybody in town. Ever met a guy named Mark Lathrop?"

"Name doesn't ring a bell. What's he do?"

Greg searched Eddie's face. Something didn't seem right about the old man. He'd already had a few health scares in the past year, mostly related to stress. It was one of the main reasons he decided to retire.

"That's what I'm trying to figure out. For a friend. You sure you're feeling all right?"

Eddie frowned in response.

"I'm fine, I'm fine. Let me ask around about—What'd you say his name was again?"

"Lathrop."

"Got it. I'll let you know what I find out."

"Sounds good, but do me a favor and keep it quiet."

"Sure thing. Hey, when are you going to take me hunting up at that cabin of yours? I used to be a pretty good shot when I was your age."

"One of these weekends, Eddie. Just give me some time to figure a few things out. We can take Chris and Junior too."

"You know where to find me."

Greg nodded and went back to work at the other end of the bar. He wished that Eddie would get a hobby, something to keep him from hanging around the bar all day. Junior was standing there when he looked up again. His reflexes really seemed to be slowing down now that he was no longer a cop.

"You scared the crap out of me."

"You have to talk to Chris. He just got suspended from school for coming to class stoned."

"Where is he now?"

"Over at the shop."

"Okay. Watch the bar for me, but listen—you probably shouldn't say anything to your father about what happened. Something's up with him."

Greg threw his bar towel down and walked over to the salon. Chris was slouched on the couch inside, thumbing through a surf magazine. He didn't look up when Greg walked in.

"Interesting article?"

"Huh? Oh, *heh heh*, yeah. Whatever. I don't even know."

His eyes were puffy and red. The smile on his face was wide and goofy. Greg didn't smile back.

"Heard you had some trouble at school today."

"I don't even care. I'd rather be at home anyway."

"What about your mom? Ever think about her?"

That sounded like something Greg's father would have said to him. Greg wasn't getting stoned when he was kid, but he still got into plenty of trouble at school, mostly for fighting. He was praying that Chris would choose a different path.

"You think she's happy about this?"

"I dunno. That's her problem."

"She works really hard. You might want to give her a break."

Greg waited a moment to let that sink in. He could see the wheels slowly starting to turn in the boy's head. It seemed like this parenting thing might come naturally to him. *The kid just needs a male role model now that his father's gone.*

The sense of accomplishment didn't last long.

"I've heard plenty of stories of stuff you did back in the day."

"From who? Your mom and dad?"

Greg regretted mentioning the boy's dead father the minute the words left his mouth. Chris wasted no time responding.

"Why does everybody around here have to die?"

Greg plopped down next to him. He dug his fingers into the arm of the couch and squeezed. It was a question he'd been asking himself for a long time.

"I'm sorry—"

Chris's eyes flooded with tears. He tried to fight them, but wasn't grown-up enough to have mastered that skill yet. Greg threw an arm around his shoulder and tried to correct the course of the conversation.

"You still surfing a lot?"

Chris wiped his nose on the sleeve of his hoodie.

"Whenever I can get somebody to give me a ride."

"You can call me any time."

"Until you take off again."

Greg pulled back, trying to keep his voice down.

"What's that supposed to mean?"

"You've been gone for, like, eight months. Everybody's gone."

"Come on, buddy. I'm back now—"

"Whatever. There are other people I can surf with."

Chris wiped his eyes and stood up. A suffocating silence filled the room. Greg looked around and thought about when the salon was still his brother's record store. He remembered the long days he'd spent there with Tim. Back when it seemed like nothing would ever change. Before death was a reality that had to be reckoned with daily.

It reminded him that he needed to follow up with officer Bob about J.J. He was so caught up in his own thoughts that he almost forgot he was supposed to be there for Chris.

"Where's mom?"

"I really am sorry I brought your dad up. That's not why I came over here."

Chris sucked the snot back up into his nose with a loud snort.

"My dad was an asshole." They both stood up and stepped into the parking lot. If nothing else, their conversation seemed to have cleared the cobwebs from the kid's head for the moment. Greg wished he could say the same for himself. Junior was waiting for them just inside the door of Eddie's.

"Go get your stuff from my car. Your grandpa's driving you home. And listen to me—no TV and no video games. Do you understand?"

Chris nodded and shuffled off. Greg noticed that he'd already perfected the round-shouldered, self-defeated posture that teenage boys so loved. Junior was leaning on the bar, looking at Greg.

"How did it go?"

"Good, I guess…"

Junior shook her head. She was clearly disappointed.

"That's too bad."

"What did you expect?"

"He really looks up to you, Greg. If you can't get through to him I'm not sure who will."

He reached over and put his hand on top of hers.

"It'll take time."

"For both of us."

"For all of us."

Junior slid her other hand over on top of his. Greg glanced down at the bar between them, happy that at least one thing in his life hadn't changed. Junior caught him looking and flashed a wicked grin.

"Don't forget you have a girlfriend waiting for you at home."

"You've got a dirty mind, Junior. We can be friends without sleeping together. Right?"

She changed the subject instead of answering the question.

"Speaking of sleeping. Are you still having those nightmares about the shooting?"

He wanted to ask which shooting she meant—the kid in the blue hat, his best friend Ricky or her ex-husband— but thought it was too gruesome a joke. A lie would have to suffice.

"Not that often."

They both let their eyes wander, each caught up in the memory of waking up beside each other. Greg felt a flush rise up on his cheeks accompanied by a sudden urge to relive old times. He pulled his hands back and stepped away from the bar.

"I should go."

"Yes, you definitely should."

∽

A SLOW DAY AT work is just what Greg needed to get his other job done. With Eddie's mostly empty, he was able to do a bunch of research on Mark Lathrop. There weren't that many details yet, and a lot of it was still guesswork, but it looked like Lathrop had moved out of R-rated Hollywood and onto the X-rated internet.

Putting the pieces together wasn't easy, so Greg kept digging. It seemed like Lathrop had gone to great pains to cover his tracks. Then, Greg stumbled on a photo taken at a Las Vegas porn convention last year. Lathrop wasn't mentioned in the caption of the shot because he wasn't the intended focus. But Greg spotted him in the background, holding a cocktail, and chatting with a well-known director who mostly served up wholesome American meat for fetishists in Asia.

It was looking like Lathrop had set up shop overseas, which would explain his sudden disappearance from U.S.-based trade publications. Greg was feeling pretty proud of himself for getting that far, but he still had more questions than answers.

He couldn't wait to see the look on Maggie's face when he told her what she had gotten herself into. Greg called her at the end of his shift and they agreed to meet at her place in South Bay. It was risky to be alone with her; he needed to get better at discretion if he was going to be a private investigator.

Kristen was in her usual position in the backyard when Greg stopped by to check on her. It was a pretty great way to be greeted every afternoon, no matter what Junior said.

"How was work today?"

"The first part was pretty good. Not sure about the second part."

"Please tell me you aren't going to see that horrible woman, Maggie. It's gross the way she throws herself at you."

"It's just business. Nothing for you to worry about."

"But I made us a special dinner."

"I'll keep my meeting short so we can still eat together. Probably around eight. That sound all right?"

"I guess."

He went inside to get changed when his phone rang. It was the VHPD Police Chief. Greg answered right away.

"Tell me you have good news."

"They sent a team out this afternoon. The place was deserted."

"That isn't possible."

"They said they found evidence that a large group of people had been there recently, which is odd for a location that's so far off the beaten path."

"Any clues where they might have gone?"

"I'm afraid not. I'll call you back if I get any updates."

Greg looked out the window into the backyard. He could see the top of Kristen's head over the back of the lounge chair. It was impossible to tell if she was involved in any of this. He definitely hadn't given her enough information to tip anybody off about the raid. Or were his questions about the waitress enough to make

Magnus paranoid? Whatever was going on, he had to figure it out quick. Marco's life might depend on it.

∽

MAGGIE'S HOUSE WAS ONLY a couple of streets away from Greg's. It was a medium-sized bungalow that had the tattered charm of another era. Greg was impressed as he walked up. There were still a few old beach houses like this one, scattered around South Bay, just waiting to be discovered and leveled. He took out his phone out to snap a picture of it and the door swung open.

She was standing there in a sheer beach cover up. The bikini underneath was smaller than most women her age could or would attempt. Her curvy figure was a perfect silhouette, framed by the door in the afternoon sunlight.

"Greg Salem, right on time. Are you always this punctual?"

"I've got plans later on. Nice place, by the way."

"Thanks. Felt funny paying millions for a tear down, but my realtor says it'll quadruple in value once the new house goes up. Come on in."

Greg walked up the steps, but Maggie didn't move. He slipped between her body and the doorframe, careful not to touch her as he passed. The wooden floors in the living room looked original, but had obviously been refinished. Same with the built in cabinets and exposed ceiling beams.

"Shame to see such a beautiful place destroyed."

"You really do live in the past, don't you, Greg? Drink?"

"No thanks. I have to—"

"Right. You have plans. Take a seat and tell me what you found out."

He sat on one end of the huge sectional sofa. She plopped down on the cushion right beside him. It looked like she had been at the beach all day, but she smelled fresh from the shower.

"Like I said on the phone, I don't have all the details yet. I just wanted to share what little I know in case that's enough to help you make a decision."

"Shoot."

Greg hesitated for a beat, savoring the moment.

"There's no easy way to say this, but from what I can tell Mark Lathrop's building some kind of porn empire."

Her eyes went wide as he finished his sentence. She brought her hands up to her mouth to cover a gasp. Greg basked in the glow of her shock and horror, eager to watch her squirm. Maggie started laughing out loud instead. She was practically doubled over, trying to catch her breath, when she managed to spit out a few words.

"No duh, Greg. What do you think we're partnering on?"

He was at a loss for words. It seemed like there still some things he had to figure out about Maggie Keane. She straightened up and almost pulled herself together.

"You didn't honestly think I would be a offended by that information, did you?"

"I guess I misjudged the situation."

"Oh, Greg. Don't apologize. It's my fault for not giving you more to go on before I sent you off to play detective. I got used to being vague from my years in D.C. Practically every conversation you have in that viper pit is being recorded."

She brought her hand up onto his shoulder and caressed his cheek. Greg wanted to pull away, but he was already pushed into the corner of the sofa. Maggie was showing no signs of slowing.

"Are you afraid your little kitten will find out? This can be our little secret."

"That's definitely part of it. She's already insanely jealous of you."

Maggie pulled back. She had a look of genuine shock on her face, mixed with triumph.

"Poor thing. Why on earth would she be jealous of a woman like me?"

"It's no big mystery. You're rich, powerful and, well, look at you."

The comment left his lips before he even knew what he was saying. He fumbled to bring the conversation back around to business again. Maggie beat him to the punch.

"Before I forget, here's the payment I promised you."

She handed over a personal check made out to him. The letters "P.I." were scribbled after his name. He liked the way it looked, but wasn't sure that he had earned her money yet. The amount was double what they'd agreed to.

"This is for five thousand…"

"Consider it a down payment on future services."

"So I should keep digging on Lathrop, then."

"Until I say stop."

"And what exactly do you want me to find out about him?"

"That's simple, Greg. I want to know how I can destroy him when the time comes."

CHAPTER NINE

Greg kept his eyes on the horizon, studying the waves. A new set was rolling in and he liked the shape of the first one. He turned his board around and started paddling. It wasn't long before the swell sucked him up into its momentum. He pushed himself up in a fluid motion that took him from laying flat to standing tall, in a heartbeat.

He shot down the face, carving to his right as the tip of the wave curled overhead. The sky was disappearing, replaced by a glowing green-blue wall of water that swallowed him up. He crouched down lower and lower as the water rushed in all around him. It wasn't a race that he was going to win so he let gravity take him down. The wave slapped the surface of the ocean with a thunderous crash. Greg went limp, tumbling and spinning like a rag doll as the water dragged him to shore.

He emerged from the whitewash with a smile on his face. His shoulders immediately relaxed as he climbed back up onto his board. He was paddling back out for more when he came upon a group of three other surfers. It didn't take him long to recognize Jeff Barrett's prison tattoos and dive bar physique. He didn't realize Chris was with them until after Barrett started talking. "Sup Salem? I thought you'd be bartending at Eddie's this morning."

Greg gave the boy a sideways glance, but tried not to overreact.

"And I thought you'd be surfing up at the tidal pools."

"Normally would be, but we're giving the kid some lessons today."

Barrett motioned to Chris. The boy dropped his gaze to the water. Greg found it funny how different Barrett was from himself, despite everything they had in common. The same neighborhood, same schools, same love of punk rock, but only one of them became a cop.

"We talking about surf lessons, or something else?"

"The hell's that supposed to mean? I thought you and I were straight these days."

"It's not the two of us I'm worried about."

"Dude! Salem's playing daddy now. Classic!"

Barrett and his buddy roared with laughter. Greg turned his attention to Chris.

"Your mom know you're out here with these two?"

Chris didn't flinch.

"Maybe."

"Well, maybe I'll be the one to tell her."

"Whatever, dude."

Chris dropped onto his belly and started paddling to catch a wave. Greg tried to follow behind him, but Barrett grabbed the front of his board and pushed it down. He slid forward and did a somersault underwater as the wave rolled by overhead. They were already gone when Greg climbed back up onto his board. He wanted to chase after them, but the ocean wasn't complying. All three of them were climbing out of the water when the next set finally rolled in.

Greg watched as they headed up the sand, stopping to talk with Kristen along the way. He guessed that Barrett was probably just hitting on the new chick. Any surfer in his right mind would do the same thing. Greg knew they'd be gone by the time he reached the shore, but decided to get on with his day either way.

Kristen greeted him with a hug when he walked up. Greg barely noticed.

"What were those guys talking to you about?"

"Nothing really. I think the big one wanted to get a closer look at me. Wasn't that your friend's son with them?"

"Yeah. That kid's making some bad decisions these days."

"God, Greg. You're wound up tight today. Why don't we go back to the house and make some bad decisions of our own?"

"Maybe later. I have to call Junior and then I need to stop by to see Officer Bob."

⚬❦

"Mr. Salem. I must have forgotten we had an appointment."

"Cut the crap. You know why I'm here."

"I do, but I'm not sure I have any news you'll want to hear. You like pancakes?"

They walked out of the BCPD station together and crossed the street. There was a little diner a few blocks down that was famous for its breakfasts. Most weekends there would be line of people around the block waiting to get in. Tuesday morning after eleven was less of a problem, especially if you were dining with Officer Bob.

They got seated right away. The waitress set two cups of coffee down on the table. Officer Bob told her to fix two of 'the usual', without even looking at the menu. Greg waited until she was out of earshot before he started in with his questions.

"Did you manage to track down J.J.?"

"We did. Had a long conversation with him yesterday, as a matter of fact."

Officer Bob took a sip of coffee, then set the mug down and added more cream.

"I told you not to get your hopes up when we reopened the case."

"We both knew that wouldn't be possible after twenty years. Tell me what he said."

"Apparently he was some kind of hotshot botany professor before his tryst with Quincy. Your friend J.J.'s got quite a story to tell. Said he was working on an autobiography."

Greg grimaced at the thought. The last thing he needed was to have his name dragged through the mud in some trumped-up tell-all book. The SoCal Sentinel was bad enough.

"I'll wait until the movie comes out. What did he have to say about Tim?"

The waitress arrived and set two plates down. Both were piled high with fluffy buttermilk pancakes. Officer Bob grabbed the syrup and gave a generous pour. He offered the bottle to Greg before shoveling food into his mouth. Greg nibbled at his, too disgusted by the older man's voracious appetite.

Officer Bob didn't speak again until his plate was clean.

"That's better. Now what were you asking me?"

"What did J.J. say about my brother?"

"Right. Well, naturally he claimed to have no knowledge about Tim's death. Said that Quincy must have misunderstood him, or wrote those lies about him on purpose. He doesn't have the highest opinion of her, as you can imagine."

Greg raised an eyebrow, acknowledging Officer Bob's sarcastic comment.

"Does he know she's dead?"

"Of course. He had plenty of interesting things to say about you as well."

"Like?"

"I'm afraid that's a police matter."

"Come on. You have to let me take a look at the transcripts."

"That's a privilege reserved for officers of the Bay Cities Police Department. We're hiring, by the way."

Officer Bob stood up and dropped a twenty onto the table.

"There is one thing that you might find interesting. It seems like Mr. Jacoby has turned back to music now that his teaching career is over."

"Which band?"

"No idea. Breakfast is on me, Mr. Salem. Have a great day."

Greg followed him out and headed for home. It was only a few blocks, but it went by in a flash. There was so much going on that he didn't know where to start. Finding Marco and bringing him home safe was still at the top of the list, but he couldn't shake the thought that J.J. knew something about Tim's death.

He had come back around to Mark Lathrop and Maggie Keane by the time he stepped into the house. Why was somebody with her money and connections getting into the porn business? He sat down to do some more research about Lathrop on the computer, but found himself typing "John Jacoby" into the search engine instead.

It didn't take much digging to find out the name of J.J.'s new band. They were called PRJ, short for Punk Rox Jukebox. From what Greg could tell it was a collection of punk rock sidemen from the eighties and nineties who traveled the West Coast playing cover songs in college town dive bars. He found it hilarious that the set list on their website included several Bad Citizen Corporation songs.

Greg clicked the "Tour Schedule" link. The current two-week run was scheduled to end in Orange County the following night. That was a show that he didn't want to miss.

◈

THE NIGHT SHIFT AT Eddie's was way different than the day shift. For starters, the crowd was younger by a decade or two, and much rowdier. Greg had only done it once, before he even officially worked there. These days they actually expected him to know how to mix cocktails and keep up with the endless flow of orders. Luckily, he had his new boss Junior there to help him— sort of.

"Keep up, old man. These drinks won't pour themselves."

Greg tried to snap her with a towel. She stepped farther down the bar, taking orders as she went. He followed behind her, picking up empties and snatching tips. It was a pretty good rhythm, but it didn't last long. They reached the end of the bar and she went out the side door to make a call. Greg turned around for a second pass when he saw a familiar face walking through the front entrance. He went over to take the man's order.

"Expanding your sales territory?"

Tommy's face lit up. He set his motorcycle helmet on the bar in front of him and stuck out his fist. This time Greg knew exactly what to do.

"Thought you said you worked the day shift."

"I like to stay up late sometimes and see what the kids are up to. Buy you a drink?"

"Light beer. Thanks."

Greg opened a bottle and set it down. Tommy gave a toast and took a look around. Greg could tell his new friend was disappointed by what he saw.

"Were you expecting something different?"

"It's just, I kept hearing about this legendary punk club from some of my buddies—"

"And it's just a bar?"

"Yeah. You could say that. Probably a different crowd when the bands play, right?"

"Depends on the band. It's mostly middle-aged white people, no matter how you slice it. So what brings you down to The Bay Cities? Business or pleasure?"

Tommy took a long drink, eyeing Greg over the end of his bottle.

"You sure act like a cop."

Greg took a step back and lifted his arms. His T-shirt sleeves hardly covered the tattoos on his biceps.

"Just another bartender, trying to make my rent. Which reminds me, there's work to do."

He went back to taking orders. Tequila was popular with this crowd, so he was mostly mixing margaritas. Junior came back behind the bar and tapped him on the shoulder. He turned to face her and felt the sting of her palm across his cheek. She was ready to slap him again when he twisted her arm and led her away. Most of the crowd was too drunk to even notice the commotion. He pushed her into the men's room and blocked the door with his foot.

"What the hell was that all about?"

"When were you going to tell me about Chris and Barrett?"

It had totally slipped his mind with everything else that was going on. She swung at him again, but he managed to duck her hand this time.

"Calm down. I meant to tell you. Did something happen?"

"A couple of cops picked him up outside a liquor store about an hour ago. He apparently tried to beat the crap out of the guy behind the counter. He pretty much destroyed the place in the process. They said he was practically foaming at the mouth when another customer called 911."

"What the hell is he on?"

"How should I know? They asked him what he'd been doing all day and he claimed to have gone surfing with you and Barrett."

"That was this morning, Junior. And for the record, we weren't surfing together. They were surfing and I tried to separate them, but they gave me the slip. Do you need me to get him?"

"You've done enough."

She pushed him out of the way and stormed off. He couldn't chase after her, even if he wanted to. The bar had already been left unattended for too long, and the locals were getting restless. It wasn't anything a round on the house couldn't fix. Tommy was still sitting in the same spot when Greg finally reached him again.

"Service in this place is terrible."

"Sorry about that. I had a little situation."

"Looked like that situation hurt. Is that your girlfriend or your wife?"

"My boss."

"You might want to think about switching jobs."

Tommy stood up and grabbed his helmet. Greg opened a new beer and set it down in front of him before he could leave. He still had a few questions he wanted to ask.

"Been up to Pete's lately?"

Tommy took the beer, but remained standing. The look on his face made it clear that he was still suspicious. That would only matter to Greg for a few more minutes, unless Tommy had some useful info.

"I get up there a couple times a week. Why do you ask?"

"Old friend of mine owns the place. Guy named Red. You know him?"

"Yeah...but I'm surprised you do. How'd you two get connected?"

"My family's had a cabin up there for years. Practically grew up in that bar."

"That so? Well then you probably know all the rumors about Red's—"

Just then a fight broke out near one of the pool tables. Glasses and tables were flying before Greg could get the bat out from behind the reach-in cooler. He slid across the bar and hit the ground running. Some locals already had the brawlers contained when Greg arrived.

"You're eighty-sixed! Don't bother coming back!"

They led the two drunks out to the parking lot with Greg close behind. He had seen plenty of brawls turn ugly once a helpful crowd got involved. Tommy was already speeding off on his bike when Greg got the situation under control. Whatever he was going to say about Red would have to wait.

Greg went back inside to clean up the mess. Junior was standing at the bar when he entered. She had a plastic sandwich bag in her clenched fist.

"I forgot I had this in my purse. I found it in Chris's room last night."

She slapped it into Greg's hand. He stretched the corners and let the baggie unroll. Inside were two of the biggest marijuana buds he had ever seen. Beside them were a small disposable lighter and a short brass pipe.

"Where is Chris now?"

Junior's voice started quivering.

"They're keeping him overnight at the hospital for evaluation."

She collapsed into his arms. He pulled her close, but kept staring at the baggie in his hand. Somebody had drawn a picture in the upper left hand corner with black marker. It was a tiny bear paw.

CHAPTER TEN

reg walked through the front doors of the VHPD the next morning. He stormed down the hall and straight into the Chief's office.

"I need you to run a test on that."

The Chief folded his hands and looked up.

"Well, hello to you too. You know, the polite thing to do when you're asking for a favor is to sweet talk me first."

"Sorry. I didn't get much sleep last night. Junior's kid got mixed up in drugs. It started with weed, but now he's moved on to something stronger."

Greg's mentor grabbed the baggy. He slipped his glasses on to take a closer look.

"I know you might be a little rusty since leaving the force, but this looks like weed."

"Test it for me. Please. I think it might be some kind of hybrid strain."

Greg sat back and waited for a response. The Police Chief gave him a skeptical look.

"You don't think this is that stuff that the bear-man claimed he was growing? You're starting to sound a little paranoid."

Greg stood up and snatched the bag of weed back. He turned it around so that the bear paw logo was right in front of the Chief's eyes. The older man squinted disapprovingly.

"Looks like something my grandson would draw. And he's two."

"Just test it for me. What can it hurt?"

"Last I checked the lab was for use by officers on active duty."

Two Police Chief's in my life, both feeding me the same bullshit lines.

"That's why I'm having you test it."

Greg laughed as he sat down again. The Police Chief groaned, dropping the evidence into the top drawer of his desk.

"How're you doing, Greg?"

"Pretty good."

Aside from the fact that I'm a bartender, my best friend's kid is turning into a dope fiend and a bear cult kidnapped my partner. Greg let his eyes wander around the room. He didn't really miss being a cop, but he missed the routine. Putting on his uniform in the morning, going through his case files, patrolling the streets. It was something he could rely on. These days it seemed like he was getting pulled in a hundred different directions all at once. He knew that something had to give, he just wasn't willing to consider what it might be until he had an answer about Marco.

The Police Chief rolled the baggy around in his fingers. He was buying time, trying to craft his next question. Greg sat in silence, waiting for the other shoe to drop.

"How's the girl?"

The official police reports from the raid on Grizzly Flats assumed all unaccounted for fugitives had escaped. Nobody but the Police Chief knew that Greg had actually taken one of them home with him. They purposely didn't speak about her much, so that he couldn't be implicated if it was ever discovered, but Greg saw that it was eating the old man up inside. He knew it wasn't about the law as much as it was about Greg's safety.

If it ever got serious and Greg truly needed the police's help, Kristen could present serious problems for him. Which meant he had to keep going it alone as long as she was around.

"She seems good," Greg said. "You'd never know she didn't grow up at the beach."

Greg realized that it sound like he was talking about his daughter or niece, not his girlfriend. He gave up and tried to change the subject.

"Have you heard anything from the Sheriff's Department recently?"

"I check in every couple of days, but I've got to be honest—that last false alarm really pissed them off."

"I get it, but that doesn't change the fact that Magnus and his crew are still out there. And Marco might be with them."

"You don't need to tell me again. I know you're thinking about your friend's safety, but what if—?"

"What?"

"We don't even know if he's still alive. And even if he is…"

The old man gave a frustrated shake of his head. Greg leaned forward to slam his hands down on the desk.

"Spit it out."

"What if he isn't being held against his will?"

"Why? Because he's got a history of drug problems?"

"And a pretty impressive police record. I'm just asking you to put your personal feelings aside and consider the possibility."

Cops are some of the least forgiving people on the planet.

Greg snorted, but he knew the old man was right. He was really sticking his neck out trying to find Marco this way. If he didn't have the Police Chief on his side, he pretty much wouldn't have anybody.

He stood up and pushed the chair back with the sole of his sneaker. Marco was the last friend he had who would join him on a suicide mission like that. The irony wasn't lost on Greg.

"Thanks, Chief."

"I'd stay out of the mountains for a little while if I were you."

"That an order?"

"Just advice. Take a break and clear your head. Might give you some new perspective. You seem like a powder keg these days."

"Let me know when you get the results on the weed."

"The minute I hear back from the lab. And Greg..."

Greg stopped in the doorway, but didn't turn around right away. The Police Chief reached into his desk and pulled out a plastic evidence bag with a tarnished handgun inside. Greg froze when he realized what it was.

"Is that—?"

"Yep. Thought you might want see it before it gets archived. Give you a little closure."

Chills ran down Greg's spine as images from that day in the alley flashed in his mind. He could see the kid in the blue hat falling to the pavement, his body twisting, and his arms flailing. The spreading pool of blood.

"Where did you find it?"

"Turned up in a drug raid last week. Dealer claims that Manny asked him to hold it for him, but he never came back to get it..."

"...Because you put him and the rest of the gang away."

"All in a day's work. He requested a meeting with you, by the way."

Greg's whole body contracted. It felt like he had been punched in the chest.

"The kid in the blue hat?"

"He has a name, you know."

"Don't say it."

Greg's reached out to steady himself on the edge of the desk. He spun around and lunged for the door. The Police Chief was yelling after him "Think it over. It might do you some good," as Greg raced down the hallway and stormed outside.

His head was about to explode from what he had just seen and heard. The gun that changed his life—haunted his dreams—was right there in an evidence bag.

Greg took greedy breaths through his nose as he walked across the empty street. It was obvious why the Police Chief was suggesting the meeting. He wanted Greg to get on with his life so that he might consider rejoining the ranks of the VHPD. Although, that was the furthest thing from Greg's mind at the moment. Why would the kid in the blue hat want to see me now?

His car was sitting right where it had been parked so many times before. The El Camino roared to life when he turned the key. He took the steering wheel in his hands, but kept his foot on the brake. There was still a lot of work to do on the Lathrop case, but he couldn't get himself to care: not when J.J. might have some information about Tim's death.

Greg threw the car into drive and took off for Orange County. PRJ was playing at Danny's Bar in Fullerton, not far from the state university. He wanted to get there early to catch J.J. before the show, so he didn't have to stay for the whole set.

He turned the radio on and flipped between stations. His fingers stopped moving when he heard his own name.

"...a former Virgil Heights police officer named Greg Salem, according to a new column in today's edition of the SoCal Sentinel. The controversy revolves around a lethal new strain of marijuana known on the streets as 'Grizzly Bear'. Sentinel gossip columnist Leslie Thompson says in her latest hit piece that Mr. Salem has declined to be interviewed on several occasions, leaving her to speculate that he might be behind this new designer drug..."

Greg turned the radio off and started pounding on the dashboard. The immediate release felt good, but not nearly enough to satisfy his mounting rage. He sat there for several minutes trying to calm down, but it wasn't working. He needed to talk to somebody to help him get out of his own head.

Greg grabbed his phone and started dialing. Kristen answered on the first ring. It felt good to hear her voice.

"What's up, sweetie?"

"Nothing. Just wanted to see how you're doing."

"On your way home?"

"Actually, no. I have some work to do tonight."

There was a pause before she responded.

"At the bar?"

"No, it's private investigation work."

"I should have guessed. Is she with you right now?"

Her voice was harder now, with a jagged edge of jealousy. An accusatory tone he'd never heard her use before. It wasn't helping Greg's state of mind like he hoped it would.

"Who? Maggie?"

She'd already hung up. He climbed in his car and started toward Fullerton; but first he had one more stop to make.

⮑

THE SOCAL SENTINEL OFFICE was on Hollywood Boulevard, not far from the tourist hotspots. Greg found street parking a few blocks away and walked down. Homeless people dressed like superheroes offered to take pictures with him for twenty bucks. He waved them off and kept moving until he reached the front doors of the building.

A sun-faded directory on the wall pointed him to the second floor. He was greeted at the front counter by a pear-shaped, middle aged man with a pronounced lisp.

"Can I help you?"

"I'm looking for Leslie Thompson."

The man narrowed his eyes. It clearly wasn't the first time somebody had come looking for their star columnist.

"Thompson's not in. I can take a message."

"When will she be back?"

"Hard to say with reporters. They're always on assignment."

"Well, if her main assignment is still Greg Salem, I'm right here. So I'll just wait."

Greg turned to look for a couch or a chair, but the room was empty. He dropped an elbow onto the counter and took out his phone instead. He could hear the man furiously typing on the computer keyboard behind him. Greg knew he wouldn't have long to wait.

The woman who eventually emerged was nothing like what he'd expected. She was almost six feet tall, with bright red hair that hung in loose curls from her head. The buttons on her fitted blouse strained against her bulging breasts. She walked right over and stuck out her hand.

"Mr. Salem."

Greg tucked the phone back into his pocket, and still left her hanging.

"Are you Thompson?"

She crossed her arms and cocked her head, sizing him up. Greg couldn't tell if she was annoyed or scared. She was about to speak, but he cut her off.

"I want to set the record straight on a few things you've written about me."

He took a step forward. She took a step back. The man behind the counter picked up the phone and started dialing. Greg guessed he only had a few moments before security arrived. He decided to make his point fast.

"I'm not some Hollywood star looking for attention or publicity."

"Okay..."

"So stay out of my business or I'll really give you something to write about."

"If you truly aren't looking for attention, then you wouldn't be here threatening a newspaper reporter."

"Take it however you want. Just leave me alone."

Greg spun to face the elevator. Two security guards exited when the doors opened. He let them pass before walking in and hitting the button for the lobby. He could see them talking to Leslie Thompson when the doors slid shut.

❧

THE EXCURSION TO *THE SoCal Sentinel* offices put Greg way behind schedule. What should have been a forty-five-minute trip down the freeway turned into two-and-a-half hours of stop-and-go traffic. It gave Greg plenty of time to stew.

Danny's Bar looked like any other hole in the wall from the outside. A live band was blaring through the wall where a couple of college kids were leaning to smoke cigarettes. The guy at the door carded Greg out of habit, but didn't even look at his birth date.

Greg pulled the heavy wooden door open and wandered inside. The place was pitch black, except for the well-lit stage where five guys were doing a passable version of "Institutionalized" by Suicidal Tendencies. He took an empty stool at the bar and scanned the stage. He wasn't even sure that he would recognize J.J.

these days. The last time they had seen each other was fifteen years ago when they were both blind drunk. That night had ended with a short fistfight and a long string of threats.

"What'll it be?"

The bartender was young, barely drinking age himself. His delicate mustache was carefully curled up at the ends, hardly covering his sneer. They were practically screaming at each other over the band.

"Club soda."

The kid put his elbow on the bar and leaned in. It was obvious he wanted to be heard.

"This is a bar. You want to sip on bubbly water, go somewhere else."

"Fine. You got Budweiser?"

"This is a bar in America, ain't it?"

Greg kept his cool until the bartender slammed the longneck down and wandered off. A thin film of sweat was forming on his upper lip and under his shirt. He hadn't taken a drink since the night that he and Marco got reacquainted. But he also hadn't been doing a very good job of keeping up with his meetings.

He was considering the bottle in front of him when the band broke into "Lady Killer" by The Vandals. Greg threw a five-dollar bill onto the bar and made his way to the stage empty-handed.

It was a healthy crowd for a cover band on a weeknight, but easy enough to maneuver. Greg was only half way there when he got a good look at the bassist. He was a little heavier these days, and his head was shaved clean, but it was definitely J.J. It looked like he might have spotted Greg too.

The final notes of the last song were still ringing out when J.J. stepped up to the mic.

"You're in luck tonight, because we have a special guest in the house. It's been a long time since we've played together, but I think we can still remember a few of the old songs. Give a round of applause for my friend, Greg Salem of Bad Citizen Corporation!"

There was a smattering of applause followed by a confused murmur. Heads turned, one by one, until it felt like the whole place was staring at Greg. J.J. didn't help the situation by announcing his name again and counting the band into a song from the first BCC record. That's when the crowd started yelling. Greg thought the music sounded clunky being played by a bunch of middle-aged guys, but he didn't know what else to do. So he jumped up on stage and started screaming.

The words came back without much effort, but the experience was surreal. This wasn't a crowd of lubed up BCC fans at Eddie's. It was a dive bar in Fullerton full of college kids who probably weren't born when his band broke-up.

They were kicking into their second song when Greg stepped to the edge of the stage. He wanted to make eye contact with the vibrating kids in the front row, watch the high-energy music pulsing through them like electricity, see their bodies twitching involuntarily as the relentless onslaught of sounds whipped them into a frenzy.

The place erupted when they ran out of songs ten minutes later. J.J. slammed his bass down and pushed Greg from the stage. They were through the back door and out in an alley before the crowd realized the show had ended. Greg was still winded.

"What the hell was that?"

A big grin was smeared across J.J.'s round face.

"You kidding? There's a whole new generation of kids that are really into BCC."

"What? How?"

"Welcome to the digital age. Everything old is new again. Might be time for us to get the band back together and cash in. Lord knows I could use some money."

Bad Citizen Corporation without Tim was always hard to stomach, but any reunion would have to happen without him. It didn't seem like a possibility at all with Marco missing. Or would he and J.J. be enough to make it feel like it used to? Greg didn't let himself dwell on the pipe dream too long before he got back down to business.

"That's not what I came down here for. I have some questions about Quincy McCloud…"

J.J.'s happy expression dissolved.

"…and my brother."

∽

J.J. TOOK GREG BACK to his motel room and told him everything he knew about Quincy. The place looked a lot like the one Marco used to live in, before it got condemned. J.J. swore up and down that he never slept with her. Greg was wishing he could say the same.

"She practically threw herself at me once she found out I used to be in BCC," J.J. said. "I'd get back from lecturing and she'd be in my office waiting for me, half naked and ready to rock."

"I kept telling her that it was too risky, no matter how tempting it was. And it was really freakin' tempting, Greg. That girl was a knock out."

J.J. claimed that she started making up lies when she realized he wasn't just playing hard to get. He knew he was screwed when rumors started circulating in the faculty lounge.

"There was something seriously wrong with that girl. You could see it in her eyes. She asked a million questions about you."

It gave Greg a certain sense of closure to find out more about the woman who had torn his world apart. Let him find a little forgiveness in his heart for her once he understood how deranged she truly was. But that wasn't why he'd come looking for J.J.

"So you're telling me that you don't have any information about Tim's death?"

J.J.'s lips started quivering and tears filled his eyes.

"Christ. No, all right? I was junkie, not a murderer. That whole period of my life is a long, blurry regret. I wish I could take it all back, every second of it, but I can't. And no, I don't have any info about Tim. If I did I would have told you a long time ago."

Greg could have kept pushing, but knew that J.J. didn't have the information he so badly needed in order to get on with his life.

"It's cool, J.J. I believe you."

They spent the next few hours trading war stories about the good old days. J.J.'s version wasn't quite as bad as the one Greg had been telling himself all these years. Some of it even sounded fun, the way that his old bassist remembered it. Greg was happy that J.J. had gotten sober too, otherwise he might have succumbed to the temptation to drink again.

He was getting up to leave when J.J. finally asked how Marco was doing. It was late, Greg was wiped out and he couldn't see any reason to lie. J.J. already knew how Quincy's story ended, so Greg told him how their old drummer helped bring her down. But that also meant explaining that Marco had been kidnapped, or murdered, by a would-be drug kingpin.

J.J.'s response wasn't what Greg expected.

"I taught botany. There's no way some marketing guy is fusing marijuana and coca plants together with somatic fusion out in the middle of the forest. If it was that easy somebody a lot smarter than him would have already done it. And they'd be really rich."

Greg thought J.J. sounded pretty convincing as an expert witness. Though, it wasn't much of a relief.

"Well, that's why I'm heading back up to the mountains first thing tomorrow."

J.J. was still in shock when he walked Greg to the door. They started to shake hands, but hugged instead, slapping each other's backs and promising to stay in touch. Kristen still wasn't picking up her phone so Greg texted her instead.

Hope you're okay. On my way home. Greg was still typing when he walked up to the El Camino. He was surprised to find J.J. waiting there for him.

"What's up, bro?"

J.J. only had two pieces of luggage, a small rolling suitcase and his bass guitar.

"Thought you might need some help looking for Marco."

CHAPTER ELEVEN

"**J**esus, dude. When was the last time this thing got emptied?"

Marco took the handle of the metal tub and dragged it out from under the outhouse. He and the kid who'd delivered the bad news about Red had been put on permanent latrine duty. Marco got the shitty job because of his latest escape attempt. The messenger, on the other hand, got every terrible job that Magnus could dream up. That's why Marco had befriended him.

The basin was full to overflowing, so they walked slowly across the camp. The last thing they wanted to do was spill any of the raw human sewage on their clothes. There wasn't a washing machine for a hundred miles or so, or a bathtub for that matter. So they took their time. Marco couldn't decide if the weight was worse than the smell.

"Has Magnus always been such a dick to you?"

"It wasn't this bad last time around."

There was an ease to the way his new partner carried himself out there, even under such brutal circumstances. A certain confidence that suggested he knew something the rest of them didn't. Marco guessed that he was either raised nearby, or had a screw loose. Whatever it was, Marco figured that he might be his ticket out of the Angeles National Forest.

They followed the dry riverbed to higher ground. The two of them had already dug the trench at the base of a huge, flat rock up above their new camp. It was the third location they'd been in since leaving Grizzly Flats, and the smallest by far. The plan was to dump the waste and cover it as best they could. After, they had to go back for the second tub. It was the only job that got them much distance from the guards, which meant Marco had plenty of time to ask questions.

"You ever think about taking off?"

"I probably would if I had anywhere else to go."

Marco pretended to think it over.

"You can always come with me, bro."

"No offense, man, but I'd do better on my own. You'd probably get us both killed."

Marco guessed he was right, but wasn't willing to leave it alone.

"Whatever, dude. All I'm saying is my buddy Greg could hook us up with a killer place by the beach."

"Sounds sweet. You really think he'll come back for you?"

Marco didn't doubt it for a second, but he didn't want to risk ruining the surprise.

"Not if I get out of here on my own first."

The dirt on top of the first pit was already turning to mud, and it needed another layer. They followed the same procedure as before and sat down under a tree to wait. It would have been peaceful if it weren't for the overwhelming stench. Marco saw an opportunity to keep prying.

"You've hung around with Magnus and his crew before. Why doesn't he just bail the Angeles National Forest all together?"

"He comes and goes whenever he feels like it. The biggest mistake you can make with Magnus is trying to understand his logic. Underestimate him and you'll probably end up dead."

"Like having guards follow me around all day, but leaving me free to escape at night."

"Actually, that one's easy to figure out."

The conversation was headed right where Marco hoped it would. His new friend didn't make him wait long for an answer.

"There's no TV up here, you're the next best thing."

"You calling me a clown? Whatever. He's gonna freak out when I actually pull it off."

His partner didn't seem convinced.

"It's trickier than you think. If the booby traps don't get you, the animals will."

Marco tried to laugh it off.

"Sounds like you've done your homework."

"Something like that. Were you serious about your buddy hooking us up at the beach?"

"Like a heart attack, bro. Say the word."

"Well, if you do get out of here, maybe I'll look you up."

Marco wanted to ask more questions, but couldn't risk pushing too hard. There was no telling how much of what he said would get back to Magnus. It was a relief when his partner was the one who kept the conversation going.

"I bet you followed the riverbed last night. Up that way as far as you could go."

Bulls eye. It led him straight to the bottom of a cliff.

"Maybe..."

"And I bet you'll try your luck in the other direction tonight."

"That might be my plan."

"All I'm saying is I wouldn't go down that way. Not unless you like bears."

"Which way would you go, smart guy?"

His partner didn't answer the question right away. He just stood up and looked over to the mountains where the sun was going down.

"It's going to be a beautiful sunset tonight."

Marco got the hint. He stood up and headed for the tubs. It was almost dinnertime and they didn't want to miss out; though neither had much of an appetite any more.

❦

IT WAS THE SAME as every other time. Marco waited for Magnus and the last of the guards to go to sleep before he took off. It probably wouldn't have mattered if he strolled right by them and waved goodbye, except for when he finally found a way out of this God forsaken wilderness. The guys around him were already snoring. Marco had gone back and forth since their conversation earlier that evening. Was his new friend actually telling him not to head down the riverbed, or covering his ass in case somebody else was listening? It was impossible to say, but Marco knew one thing—he hated bears. Whatever happened, he didn't want to run into any more of them if he could help it.

And just like that his mind was made up. He would head west, in the general direction of where the sun had set. If he could find Grizzly Flats, it wouldn't be hard to locate the Pacific Crest Trail and follow it to the highway. Marco knew from previous attempts that this was easier said than done.

He zipped up his jacket and pulled the hood on. It was the one item they'd let him keep from his backpack all those months ago, and it might come in handy. The weather remained pretty warm until sunset each night, but then the temperature dropped to freezing. Some nights it was only the cold that kept him moving as he stumbled through the forest in the dark.

Tonight was no different. Marco already knew most of the trails immediately outside of their current camp, so the first few miles were a cakewalk. Beyond that, things started getting tough.

Hills would get steeper. Boulders would get bigger. Trails would narrow and end.

And it wasn't like he had any breadcrumbs to leave behind. Every dead end or loud noise was another chance to doubt himself. Whenever that happened, a little voice in his head would start telling him to go back to camp, where it was safe. Except he knew that camp was only safe until Magnus decided it wasn't. That's when he started running again, chanting a pep talk out loud as he stumbled along.

"Run, motherfucker, run, motherfucker, run, motherfucker, RUN!"

It worked like a charm until it got him lost again. Only this time he felt like he was further from camp than he'd ever been before. That realization was both liberating and terrifying. Marco spun around in a circle, rubbing his hands together for warmth and trying to get his bearings in the dark.

He was gearing up to start running again when everything went to hell: a coyote howled in the distance; an owl hooted in the tree overhead, and something really big lumbered through the bushes behind him.

Marco stifled a scream and took off at a sprint. Whatever was in the bushes froze for a second and bolted in the other direction. But that didn't matter to Marco. His new plan was to keep running until he dropped dead or the sun came up. He made it to the top of the next rise before his adrenaline and lungs petered out at the same time.

He fell to his knees at first, huffing and puffing for air. Then he dropped down on all fours, crawling and grunting as he panted and drooled. He probably would have looked like some college kid on a bad mushroom trip if anybody was around to see him, but nobody was. Marco fell to his side and rolled onto his back. His eyes scanned the starry sky, flicking between the Big Dipper and the Little Dipper. They were the only two constellations he knew by name, other than that bad-ass Orion.

It seemed to take forever before his breathing returned to normal. Marco was going to need something more than a chant to get him moving this time. He sat up and took a look around. Another dry creek bed—Or was it the same one, dude?—that led back down from where he'd just come. His legs felt like they were made of jello when he stood up. The cold was nipping at his fingers and nose. Marco took a step in one direction, but quickly changed his mind and went the opposite way. That's when he saw the little strip of nylon tied to a tree branch.

He jumped up and yanked it down, turning it in his hands as if there was more to see. His energy was spiking again as he scanned the trees all around. Nothing else jumped out at him so he kept heading the way he'd been going. The next piece of nylon was at a fork in the trail. It led to the next one. And the one after that.

Marco got lost a couple of times on this scavenger hunt, but there was a certain logic to the way the clues were laid out. Every time he went too far without finding his next scrap, he simply retraced his steps until he found it. Grizzly Flats came into view a couple hours later. He had never been so happy to see a burned out marijuana field in his entire life, but he didn't linger. There was still a long way to go if he hoped to get out alive.

"Run, motherfucker, run, motherfucker, run, motherfucker, RUN!"

Marco imagined that every possible monster was chasing him along that last stretch of trail. Sometimes it was Magnus. Sometimes it was bears. Sometimes it was Officer Bob. Every time it was just enough to keep his exhausted mind from telling his legs to stop moving. He had no idea how much time had passed when the black shape of Pete's poked up through the gloom. The parking lot was empty and all the lights were out. Marco felt like he was jogging down the Las Vegas Strip, screaming to the night sky, "Civilization is a miracle!"

The winding mountain roads were almost always empty at this time of night. Marco made his way along the shoulder, following the dirt road that led to Greg's cabin. He hoped that the El Camino would be parked there, and the lights to the cabin would be on. It wasn't much of a surprise when his wishful thinking didn't come true.

Marco went around back and flung the door open, only to have it come bouncing back. His heart almost stopped. He wanted to bolt, but was too exhausted. He took the knob in his shaking hand again and slowly edged into the kitchen. The bike was waiting for him just inside, so the door must have hit the tire on his previous attempt. He went to the sink and gulped down a tumbler of water.

Marco considered grabbing one of the hunting rifles in the closet, but decided it wouldn't be much use on a bike. He reached into one of the drawers and pulled out a steak knife instead. It was small and mostly dull, but felt like a machete in his grip. He shoved it into his jacket pocket and wheeled the bike outside. It felt good to be going so fast with such minimal effort. *Let's see a bear catch me now.*

The wind blew his hair back as he sped from the dirt road and started down the hill. The bugs that flew into his teeth were some of the best he'd ever tasted. He only hoped the brakes would hold for the rest of this long night. The momentum he built going downhill got him half way up the next hill. From there he just stood up and pedaled.

He and Greg had watched serious cyclists conquer these mountains every weekend for months. Back then it seemed funny to watch groups of middle-aged bankers and realtors sweat and strain against gravity. Now Marco tried to picture how he looked in his filthy clothes, gritting his teeth as he pedaled for his life.

Anybody in their right mind would probably just assume he was homeless—and they wouldn't be far off. That was fine with him. Finding a place to live could take a back seat to staying alive any day.

With no other way to judge his progress, Marco started counting hills. He was just coming up over the top of his seventh one and crossing a long concrete bridge, when he heard a familiar buzzing sound. It was like a large mosquito at first, buzzing around his ear and threatening to suck his blood. But then it got louder. It didn't take long to figure out that a motorcycle was coming up on him fast.

Marco knew that he needed to pull off of the road and hide in some bushes, but the bridge provided no cover. He squeezed the brakes and took a look over the railing. It was a hundred-foot drop on either side. He could do nothing but pedal, praying he reached cover before the motorcycle arrived.

His ear was attuned to every turn the bike took in the canyons, shifting and revving through the curves. He could picture the leather-clad rider weaving with his knee inches from the asphalt as he leaned into the bends. Marco imagined the reflection of the yellow road lines snaking across his helmet's glossy black wind visor. The only thing he couldn't picture was the rider's face. Or maybe there would be two of them, one driving while the other swung an axe.

Marco shook his head and tried to clear the ridiculous thought from his mind. Whoever it was might not even be coming after him. Maybe it was just somebody out for a midnight ride. He was pumping his legs, shifting the bike wildly from side-to-side, when he neared the end of the bridge. Marco didn't dare look over his shoulder as he covered the last few yards

Soon they were side by side. Marco was trying desperately to speed up while the solo biker slowed down. Time stood still for a moment. The helmet turned and Marco could see his own gaunt reflection staring back. He was so transfixed that he didn't notice the leather boot come up, kicking the bike from beneath him.

Marco's handlebars twisted violently, sending him down to the pavement. The motorcycle slid to a stop and the rider flipped the kickstand down. Everything went silent for moment. The bike was standing in the middle of the moonlit bridge like some magazine glamour shot. Marco tensed as the mysterious rider ran back and knelt down beside him.

"There are a lot of people looking for you."

∾

"Wake up little man."

The cold water splashed across Marco's face. He opened his eyes and tried to take a look around, but his hair was in his face. That wouldn't have been a problem if it weren't for the ropes around his wrists. Marco let his chin drop, waiting for Magnus to start in on him. He was surprised to hear a woman's voice instead.

"What's your name?"

"Marco."

"You one of Magnus's men?"

He couldn't think of an answer that wouldn't get him killed. Either these people were planning to get some information about Magnus out of him, or they were going to take him back there themselves. Either way, Marco stood to lose.

"That dude's no friend of mine."

The woman in front of Marco squatted down, putting her hands on his knees. She had a soft touch and sweet smell, not at all like the girls back at camp. He brought his head up and she brushed the hair from his face. The guy behind him knocked it right back into place with a smack across Marco's ear. She leapt up.

"Jesus, Red! Leave him alone."

"I don't like him looking at you like that."

"You don't like anybody looking at me at all. Give me a few minutes with him."

"Alone? Hell no."

"Well then, can you at least stop hitting him?"

"You got a little crush on him or something?"

"No, but he'll be worth more in one piece."

She bent forward to look Marco in the eye.

"Do you remember how you got here last night?"

Memories of the bike crash came flooding back. They were accompanied by a series of phantom pains all across his body. Marco looked down and saw that his tattered shirt was covered in bloodstains. He wondered if the motorcycle rider was hovering nearby, or if he'd already collected his finder's fee and moved on.

"Where the hell am I?"

"Pete's. Do you know where that is?"

Marco nodded. He could smell bacon cooking now. If he was going to die in the back of a biker bar, he wanted that salty meat to be his last meal.

"Is the kitchen open?"

The woman stepped back. Marco gave her a quick scan. She was tall and thin with reddish-brown hair piled up on her head. She was wearing one of his favorite clothing combinations—high heels and a waitress apron.

"Red. Go get him some food."

"You kidding me?"

"Least we can do before we sell him back to Magnus."

"Get real, woman. We aren't selling him. We're trading him for you."

Marco heard aggravation creeping into the man's voice again. It didn't matter, because she seemed to be the one in charge. *Besides,* Marco thought, *I've got noting to lose.*

"I'll take two eggs, scrambled, with pancakes and bacon. And get me a cup of coffee while you're at it."

✑

GREG WAS EXHAUSTED FROM his night in Fullerton when he pulled up to Pete's the next morning. He reached over and took his Glock from the glove compartment. There weren't many motorcycles in the parking lot, probably because it was the middle of the week. So much for his plan to get lost in the crowd. He opened the front door and took a deep breath. There was nothing better than the smell of bacon cooking.

He took a stool at the bar and tried to look busy on his phone. There still wasn't any reception at Pete's, but he couldn't risk getting recognized by the bartender. Greg kept his eyes on the screen in his hand when he ordered the steak and eggs, and a cup of coffee. The bartender didn't seem offended at all by Greg's phone etiquette. He also didn't look familiar.

The TVs were showing the same sort of motorcycle races as the last time Greg was at Pete's. Or at least that's how it looked to him. He set his phone down on the bar and scanned the room. Most of the tables were empty and the jukebox was unplugged. The one face he hoped to see, besides Marco's, was nowhere to be found.

"You take cream with your coffee?"

Greg looked up, startled by the interruption.

"Excuse me? Oh. Black's fine."

The bartender set the mug down, giving Greg a strange look before heading back to the kitchen. Greg's hand checked the gun in his coat pocket. He half expected the bartender to come back with a gun of his own.

Greg turned his attention to the newspaper lying on the bar. He'd been avoiding *The SoCal Sentinel* since his visit to their office, but a headline caught his attention. He spun the page around and scanned the story.

LA Buzz: "Frankenstein' Marijuana Hybrid Rumored In ANF"

by Leslie Thompson, Staff Reporter

Rumors have been flying since a joint law enforcement raid left three people dead, resulted in dozens of arrests, and scorched several acres in the Angeles National Forest late last summer.

Sherriff's Department and DEA sources have been tight-lipped when asked about their excessive use of force, but an anonymous source close to the investigation has come forward to shed light on the situation.

"That crop the Forest Service and Sheriff's Department burned down was no normal marijuana field. It was something much scarier, a Frankenstein strain that, if any plants survived or if others exist, could have serious repercussions for decades to come."

At the center of the controversy is former police officer and punk rock legend, Greg Salem. The elusive Mr. Salem has been unavailable for comment, but performed an announced reunion with his legendary punk rock band, Bad Citizen Corporation, earlier this week. The show took place at a Fullerton club called Danny's Place in front of a sold out crowd.

Greg found it hilarious how the rumors took on a life of their own. Leslie Thompson's personal interest in him, however, was less funny. The waitress with the bear paw tattoo set his plate down right on top of the newspaper.

"Get you anything else? A warm-up, maybe?"

Greg tried to play it cool. He picked his fork up and poked the yolk on his egg. The snotty yellow liquid oozed out onto his pancakes. He pushed the plate back and cleared his throat.

"Sorry. I asked for over medium."

She snapped her gum while thinking it over. As if she already knew that he wasn't there for breakfast at all.

"Cook won't be happy about that."

"I'm not sure that's my problem. That egg's practically raw."

"Maybe you should tell him yourself. Come on."

Greg stood up, followed her around the bar and through the swinging kitchen door. He kept his eye on her tattoo as they walked. The big biker he'd met on his last visit was standing in front of the flat top griddle. He was wearing the same red bandana, Harley Davidson t-shirt and leather vest. The waitress tapped the cook on the shoulder.

"This customer's got a complaint."

Red spun around, a huge cleaver in his fist. Thick streams of sweat were running down his chubby red face. Greg slipped his hands into his coat pockets, bracing for a fight. The cook's voice was somewhere between a growl and a bark.

"What seems to be the problem?"

"I don't like my eggs runny."

Red laughed, pulling out a pack of cigarettes. He bent down and lit one on the stove without ever letting go of the cleaver.

"Yeah. You strike me as a guy who likes them hard."

"That might be true, but I'm guessing only one of us has been in a prison shower."

Red took a step forward, but Greg held his ground. The waitress just shook her head and wandered off into the storeroom. Greg waited until she shut the door before he went on.

"Let's cut the crap. I'm up here looking for a friend of mine."

"What makes you think I know anything about that?"

"I doubt much happens up here that you don't know about."

Red took a big drag, shoving the butt into a plate of food under the heat lamp.

"One thing's for sure. I know all about you. You're that ex-cop that likes to shoot kids."

Now Greg took a step forward. The two men were eyeballing each other via the pass-through, like husband and wife on visiting day. They were still staring each other down when the waitress came back out to grab the ruined plate of food. She took one look at the defiled pancakes and dumped the whole plate into the trash. Nobody said a word until she slipped back into the storeroom again.

"Nice ink on that waitress. You see a lot of bear paw tattoos around here?"

"I'd stop asking questions if I was you."

"And I'd start answering if I was you."

Red spun around and cracked two new eggs onto the flattop. They crackled and spat on a thin film of grease.

"Either show me a warrant or get out of my restaurant."

It was a cliché, but an effective one. There wasn't much Greg could do without a badge to back him up. At least not legally. He walked around and stuck his gun against the back of Red's head.

"Let me jog your memory. He's a thin guy, with long blonde hair. Looks like a junkie, talks like a surfer. You couldn't miss him around here."

"I'm telling the truth. I haven't seen anybody who looks like that."

Greg could see the cleaver slowly rising up. He shoved his barrel deeper into Red's neck and told him to drop it.

"I might not be a cop any more, but they'll still take my word over yours any day."

Red set the weapon down, bringing his hands up. This is where Greg would normally cuff him, but the Police Chief had taken those back along with the rest of his gear. So he told Red to get down on his knees instead. There was one more question Greg needed to ask, even though he knew it was a long shot.

"What about a guy named Tommy? He work for you?"

"Who?"

"Come on. Black guy with a big smile. Deals a little weed. I know you sent him down to The Bay Cities earlier this week to keep an eye on me."

"The only place I'd send a black guy is back to Africa."

Greg almost shot the racist fuck on principle, but the storeroom door creaked open before he had the chance.

"That's enough."

The waitress was standing there with a shotgun in her hand. Then the bartender stepped into the kitchen at the same moment with a familiar baseball bat. Greg lowered his gun, shoving it back in his pocket. Greg squeezed by the waitress, dropping a twenty on the bar before he headed for the parking lot.

"Keep the change."

༺

TOMMY WAS SITTING ON his motorcycle outside of the cabin when Greg pulled up. His timing was a little too perfect. Any chance that he had come into Greg's life by accident was completely gone.

Rocket from the Crypt's "On A Rope" came to a stop as Greg swung the door open. He and Tommy eyed each other while the wind rustled the leaves overhead in the trees. It was Tommy who finally stood up and ambled over.

"I was starting to think you weren't coming back."

"I might've hurried if I'd been expecting company."

Greg stood up, resting an elbow on the roof of his car. The band Fear was bashing through "Let's Have A War" on the stereo now. Tommy shook his head and smiled.

"You really do love that old punk shit, don't you?"

"Reminds me of happier times. What brings you out here?"

"Heard a rumor about your friend. Thought I should let you know as soon as possible."

"I'm listening."

"Word from my boys up here is that Red has him at the bar."

Greg was unsure whether he should tell him that he'd just come from there. He wanted to see exactly how much info Tommy would share before tipping his hand. In Greg's experience, salesmen didn't give anything away for free. Not unless they could double their investment by the end of the day. So he didn't respond at all. Tommy called his bluff.

"You can take the information or leave it. That's on you. Don't say I never did anything for you, though."

Tommy turned to leave. He was steps from his motorcycle when Greg finally spoke up.

"Thanks for stopping by."

"No problem, but I'd look into that rumor if I was you. That Red's an evil son of a bitch. No telling what he'd do to your friend if he doesn't get what he wants."

"Which is what exactly?"

"Grass, cash or ass. Red controls all three up here."

Greg shook his head. He couldn't risk Tommy being right about Marco.

"I just came from there. In the kitchen. I would have known if Marco was there."

"I'd go back. Take a closer look this time around. In all the nooks and crannies."

Tommy slid his helmet on and kicked the motorcycle engine to life. He rolled over to where Greg was still standing and flipped his visor up.

"I wouldn't go alone if I was you."

"You volunteering?"

"Maybe."

Greg shook his head. He still didn't trust him.

"Thanks, but no, thanks. I think I've got this handled."

"Whatever you say."

Tommy twisted the throttle and sent a rooster tail of pebbles and dirt into the air. The dust was still settling when J.J. stepped out of the cabin and onto the porch. He had a rifle in his hands and a baffled look on his face.

"What the hell was that about?"

"Looks like you might get the chance to help me rescue Marco after all."

CHAPTER TWELVE

Everything seemed normal at Pete's when Greg and J.J. drove by. A few motorcycles were scattered around the outside of the building and smoke was wafting from the chimney. The 'Closed' sign in the window was definitely unusual.

Greg went a few miles up the road before turning around. He killed the engine and slipped the El Camino into neutral, letting gravity do the rest of the work. No point in giving Red and his men any advance notice that he was coming back. The car glided into the far end of the parking lot, coasting to a stop behind some dumpsters. They parked next to an out-of-service phone booth that was more of an exhibitionist's outhouse these days.

The Glock was on the dashboard in front of Greg. J.J. had an old hunting rifle across his lap. They weren't exactly loaded for a siege, but they hadn't come empty handed either.

"I'm going to go down there and take a look around. I want you to stay hidden behind the car. Keep the rifle pointed at the front door. Understand?"

J.J. was so nervous that it looked like he might pass out. Greg knew he couldn't storm the place alone , but a queasy bass player wouldn't be much help either. He was starting to wonder if he should have taken Tommy up on his offer of help after all. "You don't have to shoot anybody. Just lay down some fire if you see me come running back this way. And try not to kill me in the process."

Greg forced a reassuring laugh. More than anything, he didn't want J.J.'s blood on his hands.

"Keep your head down and you'll be all right."

They both opened their doors and climbed out. J.J. got in place while Greg followed the edge of the parking lot to the back of the building. He hoped the kitchen door would be open so he could take Red by surprise. It was unlikely that anybody inside would start shooting if Greg could get a gun to Red's head again.

He reached up to try the knob. Unlocked. Greg cracked it open, ducking down to take a look around. The sound of meat sizzling and a cloud of foul-smelling smoke greeted him. Somebody was definitely standing in front of the flat top griddle, but it was hard to make out who it was. He pushed the door open a few more inches and crawled inside.

The smoke was thicker than he originally anticipated, which gave him a little cover. He moved quickly to where he hoped Red was cooking. Greg edged around a large stainless steel prep table and sprang. It was Red all right, face down on the flat top and close to well done. The butcher knife he'd used to threaten Greg earlier was sticking out of his back.

Greg reached for the knob and killed the flame. He badly wanted to vomit, could feel the bile rushing in from the corners of his mouth, but choked it back. Whoever had done this to Red might still be inside the bar. And they might have Marco with them.

He went to the swinging kitchen door, popping up to take a look through the round window. There were two more bodies laid out on the bar, head to toe. He caught his breath and took a closer look. It was a couple of the young bikers that he'd seen hanging around the place in recent weeks. He didn't know their names, but recognized their colorful leather jackets. It was two of the guys Tommy was hanging out with the day they met.

The door made a loud creaking sound when Greg pushed it open. He froze, waiting for thundering footsteps—or worse. When nothing happened, he pushed his way through until he was standing behind the bar. The bartender was slumped on the floor in the corner, the front of his T-shirt soaked through with blood. Greg kept moving forward into the dining room.

There was no sign of the waitress with the bear paw tattoo, or Marco. He did a quick sweep of the bathrooms and the small market, carefully clearing room after room. Everything was silent and still when he circled back into the kitchen. Red was in the same place Greg had left him, but the sizzling had mercifully stopped. He was about to go outside to call 911 when he remembered the little storeroom.

Greg inched over to the door. His heart was beating like a kick drum in his chest. He kept his back pressed against the wall, trying to listen over the high-pitched tinnitus whining in his ear. Greg swung the door inward, waving his gun back and forth as he entered. A few dusty shelves were pushed against the walls, but the room was mostly empty. All except for a single chair that was covered in coils of rope. A folded note was laying on the seat. Greg's name was written on the front.

He tore it open, reading the simple message several times to take it in:

> *The job offer's expired. You can kiss your friend goodbye. And your favorite Ursula.*
> —*Magnus*

There was a hand-drawn bear paw under the signature.

෨

THE EL CAMINO CAME barreling down the mountain roads. The wheels squealed as Greg powered through the curves. J.J. was gripping the dashboard as they went from seventy miles per hour to thirty-five in the blink of an eye, topping ninety in the straightaways. They reached the freeway in record time and made it to The Bay Cities off-ramp a little over three hours later. Eddie's went by in a blur as Greg tore up the pavement in his rush to get home.

Kristen was the first call Greg made after he finally got reception again. Then, when he got no answer, she became the second and third calls as well. It wasn't until after Greg had left lengthy messages, and texting until his thumbs were sore, that he finally called the police to report the horrific scene at Pete's. He and J.J. were long gone before the first cruisers arrived.

They screeched to a stop in the alley outside of the house. J.J. was right behind Greg when he crashed through the back gate, The two of them almost went through the sliding glass door at the back of the house.

"Kristen! Are you here?!"

They came around the corner into the living room and found her. She was sitting upright in a chair with her hands folded in her lap. Her eyes were round and wide and her skin was pale. Maggie Keane was seated in the love seat right across from her. She was the one who broke the silence.

"Hello, Greg. Who's your cute friend?"

Greg fell to his knees, letting his arms drop to his sides. J.J. stepped around him and took a seat next to Maggie. They were already making small talk when Kristen went over and helped Greg to his feet. She led him into the bedroom and softly closed the door.

"I think we need to talk."

He came out of his stupor long enough to see that she had been crying. He wanted to strangle her for ignoring his calls the last couple of days, but pulled her to his chest instead. She spoke in a soft voice as he ran his fingers through her hair.

"I'm pregnant, Greg."

✦

"I HAVE TO ADMIT I'm impressed. I never would have given you free reign to run around the mountains if I thought you might actually escape."

Marco grunted in response. It was the most he could manage with a balled up sock stuffed into his mouth. He was naked and his feet were in a bucket of water. Wires ran from the clamps on his fingertips to a car battery on the ground nearby.

Despite the distractions, Marco could tell that they were at a new location. Somewhere indoors. He had been brought there unconscious and there was still a bag over his head, but it definitely didn't smell like the forest. He thought he could even hear a TV playing in the background. It was a relief to know that he wouldn't necessarily become bear food.

There was something different about Magnus's voice too.

"Almost makes me think that maybe I chose the wrong guy to run my operation."

Marco tried to laugh, but it only produced a small snot bubble from his left nostril. He thought he'd probably be willing to sign up for the Marine Corp. at this point, if it meant he could stop getting his ass kicked. *If you can't beat 'em, join 'em.*

"I don't think you have half the brains of your partner, but you're persistent. I'll give you that. What do you say we bury the hatchet and start fresh?"

Marco's brain was screaming, "*Too soon! Too soon!*" But his head was nodding in agreement. He was willing to do whatever Magnus said after watching him sink a butcher knife into that biker's back. It wasn't the first time he'd seen Magnus kill, but it was the first time he'd seen him enjoy it. The look of sheer joy on his face as he dealt the final blow was enough to turn Marco into believer. Magnus was a crazy son of a bitch, but he'd sure as hell make a better boss than an enemy.

Magnus pulled the bag from Marco's head. It took a second for his eyes to adjust to the fluorescent lights. Magnus looked like a different person with new clothes and a fresh shave. Magnus leaned in until his face was only inches away from Marco's. He smelled of toothpaste and cologne. "One-time offer. What do you say?"

Magnus yanked the socks from Marco's mouth. Marco licked his lips and tried to swallow. It was hard to even form the words, but he managed to force them out.

"Does a bear shit in the woods?"

"Good choice, but we won't be living in the woods any more."

⛬

IT CAN ONLY BE bad news when the phone rings at three in the morning. But it wasn't like Greg was asleep anyway. The thought of losing Kristen to Magnus was bad enough, but now he had to worry about their unborn child too. Last night Greg was back up on stage in Fullerton and now he was at home thinking about how to support a family on bartending tips. *Jesus, I'll be sixty when the kid's in college. How the hell am I supposed to pay for that?*

He watched the vibrating phone dance across the coffee table, unwilling to pick it up. The number was unfamiliar and he wasn't in the mood for any more bombshells. He was relieved when it stopped just as suddenly as it began. Greg was waiting for a voicemail notification when the phone buzzed to life again. A different number this time, another one he didn't recognize. The news that was waiting for him on the other end was even worse than he'd suspected. He grabbed the phone before the fifth ring.

"This better be good."

"Sup, Greg?"

It was like hearing a ghost speak.

"Marco?! Where the hell are you?"

"Where I am is not important. It's who I'm with that you should be worried about."

Greg leapt from his chair and started pacing around the living room. J.J. was asleep out in his old garage apartment, but they could be back up the mountains before sunrise if necessary. Problem was that he had no way of knowing if they were even still up there. He would just have to hear Marco out, listening closely for any clues his partner might drop.

"Tell Magnus that if he lays a finger on you, I'll—"

"Take it easy, dude. I got the situation under control."

"Listen carefully, Marco. If you've got a gun to your head right now repeat after me: 'I'm fine.'"

"Dude. I'm fine..."

It was just as Greg had suspected.

"...No, wait. I mean it—listen. Nobody's got a gun to my head. I'm laying in a some huge ass bed with silk sheets, bro. And I've got a few friends to keep me company, if you know what I mean."

"Wait, what? Are you talking about Ursulas? Marco, I don't understand what you're saying. Is somebody listening in on the call? Tell me where you are. J.J. and I will come get you."

"What the hell's J.J. doing there?"

"It's a long story. We played a show last night in Fullerton."

The phone went silent. Greg guessed that Magnus had finally heard enough and decided to end the call.

"Marco? You still there?!"

"I'm here. Kinda bummed you two played a show without me, though."

"Are you kidding me? I've been looking all over the mountains for you. For months. Besides, it wasn't like we planned it."

"Who played drums?"

"Some guy from J.J.'s cover band. I never even got his name. It was a total fluke."

"Whatever, dude. It doesn't matter anyway. I was just calling to say that you can stop looking for me now. Everything's rad."

"You can't be serious, Marco."

"Oh, I'm totally serious. Like a heart attack. Catch you later, bro."

The line went dead for real this time. Greg fell back into his chair, trying to make sense of it all. He almost jumped through the ceiling when Kristen brushed his cheek with the back of her hand.

"Jesus Christ!"

"Calm down. I was just checking on you. Who were you yelling at on the phone?"

She still looked half asleep. A little dazed and a little helpless. The mother of his child. Greg wrapped her in his arms and squeezed, but not too tight.

"What made you decide to tell Maggie you were pregnant, of all people?"

She pulled her head back to look him in the eyes.

"It wasn't really my plan. Maggie called me."

"Why?"

"To tell me not to worry about you and her."

She lay her head back down on his chest.

"What else did she have to say?"

"Nothing much. She's not at all the person I thought she was."

Greg had his own opinions, but kept them to himself. He could tell that something else was on Kristen's mind from the hesitation in her voice.

"Are you going right back up to the mountains again?"

"It doesn't look like it. I think I've got bigger things to worry about right here."

Spring 2016—*The white van pulled up outside of the house in Studio City. It was early in the morning, but the crew was already assembled. They had three movies left to shoot at this location before moving on. The neighbors finally figured out what kind of movies they were making and complained to the police.*

The driver jumped out of the van and went around to open the sliding door. Mary was still in shock from what she had witnessed earlier that day at Pete's. She dropped both feet down to the pavement and straightened out her new dress. The driver had given it to her after the last outfit got splattered with Red's blood.

"Where are we?"

"Does it matter? We'll be here for a few more days, and then somewhere else after that. You ready to get back to work?"

Work. Mindless, mechanical sex with strangers in a front of a camera. Mary never used to mind it much when it was about the drugs. She just went through the motions back then, killing time between highs. But the thought of going back to that life now filled her with paralyzing dread. Red might have been a jealous boyfriend, but at least he had helped her get clean.

The driver grabbed Mary by the wrist, pulling her toward the house. She knew it was pointless to resist. The closer they got to the front door, the more she needed to get numb again.

"You got anything on you?"

He chuckled as they stepped inside.

"Some things never change. Come on."

They wound their way through the crowded living room. The crew was in the middle of a production meeting. Heads turned to watch her pass, followed by hushed whispers. She just kept her eyes on the carpet, pretending not to notice.

The driver kicked a bedroom door open and pushed her inside. Lines were already chalked up on the nightstand. She knelt down and snatched a rolled up dollar bill in her hand. It was just like riding a bike. The first line disappeared up her nose. A bloom of dark energy swelled in her chest, giving her the courage to speak up. "Why did you have to kill him?"

"Because he broke our agreement. He was supposed to get you cleaned up and keep you out of sight until I could decide what to do. Nobody told him to fall in love with you."

"I was up there for months. He never let me leave his sight. What did you expect?"

"Yeah, well I've been focusing on some other business opportunities. Now I think it's time to stop being such a silent partner in this porn empire I helped start."

She inhaled another line. Her renewed euphoria was already diminished, replaced by a familiar resignation. The insatiable hunger was back in control of her life.

He checked the time on his phone.

"Go ahead and finish what's there, but then it's time to earn it."

"And what if I say no?"

"Then I'll have to kill your friend, Kristen."

Mary polished off the last line. She stared at him with pure hate in her eyes.

"Fine. Let's go."

"Not so fast. I have a more important job for you this time."

Six Months Later...

CHAPTER
THIRTEEN

C hris reached for his towel, but it wasn't on the hook. This wouldn't be the first time he'd gotten into the shower at the rehab without it. The anti-anxiety medication they shoved down his throat made him spacey. He was soaking wet and starting to shiver. A leaky faucet was dripping into the sink nearby, tiny splashes reflecting off the floor-to-ceiling tiles in the cavernous bathroom.

He hated everything about this place, starting with the creepy doctor that ran it. But anything was better than doing time in juvenal hall for assaulting a liquor store clerk. That asshole was threatening to press charges until Officer Bob convinced him to change his mind. All it took was a promise of rehab and a check from his grandpa to pay for the damages.

Chris took a couple tentative steps forward, his eyes scanning the room for movement. He just had to make it to his locker. There wasn't an extra towel in his gym bag, but he could get most of the water off with one of his T-shirts. From there it was a short walk back to the closet in his dingy room. If he made it that far.

Chris was almost there when the first punch caught him in the kidney. The second blow came from the other side, landing on the back of his head. He grunted and fell forward, more from the wet floor than the beating. His head hit the metal door with a loud bang that sounded worse than it was. He tensed and waited for the third punch, springing to his feet when it came.

It was two of the older boys, just as he'd expected. They were in their late teens, but built like grown men. The bigger kid had an ugly round face that was covered in hideous acne scars. His slightly smaller sidekick was a new kid with a wispy mustache and a permanent grin. Chris threw an elbow into the smaller one's throat. He followed up with a cross to the jaw.

The bigger kid lunged, but his hands slid from Chris's wet body. Chris took a step back and let the momentum carry his attacker into the locker, just like Barrett had taught him. He grabbed his attacker's mop of greasy hair, slamming his face into the locker door. Chris's teeth were gnashing together when the attendants pulled him off.

Chris knew he should have felt ridiculous being escorted down the hallway naked, but it wasn't the first time he'd fought his way out of the showers. Every day was a life or death struggle at the hellhole where his family had sent him. The most troubled teenagers from every local high school living on top of each other, sharing information about how to buy, sell and use drugs. Faking their way through twelve-step meetings and group therapy all day, and beating each other senseless every night.Chris had only been there for a month, but it felt like an eternity. Nothing the counselors said made any sense to him, and he wasn't making any friends. Even with the three kids that shared his room. They all hung around together, playing cards and bragging about girls they'd hooked up with. Their fake friendship and ridiculous lies made Chris feel sick. So he kept to himself, pretending to read while quietly wishing them dead.

The best part of every day was when the attendants finally turned the lights out at night. That usually forced everybody to finally shut up and go to sleep. Chris did his best thinking alone in his bed. He came to conclusions that didn't seem so obvious when he was surrounded by other people and their stupid opinions.

That's where they were taking him now. It was supposed to be an afternoon of quiet reflection, but Chris had other plans.

❧

GREG CHECKED HIS PHONE again. If they didn't leave soon he would miss visiting hours at the rehab altogether. But Greg wasn't in charge, Maggie Keane was. Right now she was in a closed door meeting with her business partner, Mark Lathrop. They'd been in there for an hour already while Greg stood outside in the blazing Studio City sun. He was out there with the rest of the bodyguards and drivers. Technically Greg was neither, but sometimes he felt like it. *They both live in South Bay. So why in hell do we have to meet in the Valley?*

Maggie told him to come inside, but he didn't want anything to do with their porn shoots. Greg didn't have any hang ups about sex, but porn felt like a form of slavery to him. He'd watched too many of the girls coming and going with their plastic bodies and empty eyes. It might've made him quit if working for Maggie didn't pay so much better than bartending or being a cop.

Money was about the only thing on his mind with Kristen's due date looming. Less than a month to go and Greg Salem would be a father, whether he liked it or not.

It wasn't the kid that he was worried about. That part actually seemed like it might be fun. And it wasn't Kristen either. She'd only gotten more beautiful as the months went by. He really enjoyed helping her decorate the nursery, and arguing with her over names for their son.

Everything was fine, except for the timing. Not that there's a perfect time to get surprised with life-altering news. He was thankful that they had Junior to lean on, but she had her hands full with Chris. And he didn't want to bother Eddie because of his poor health. J.J. was doing most of the shifts at Eddie's L Bar these days, picking up where Greg left off, now that he was working for Maggie full time.

A few things about Maggie had changed too. Something about Kristen's pregnancy brought out a maternal instinct in her, or as close as she could come. Greg never got a straight answer out of either of them about how it happened, but she and Kristen became friends. That meant that Greg and Maggie became friends too. The three of them were spending so much time together that Maggie eventually gave him a full-time job. It was the kind of opportunity that could buy a lot of loyalty from Greg, and Maggie knew it. It didn't keep them from fighting like brother and sister, but it was better than before. Except when Maggie tried to act like a badass in front of Lathrop and his crew. That still got on Greg's nerves.

He thought he heard the door open, but it was just Mark Lathrop's driver getting out of the town car to stretch his legs. Greg checked his phone again and tried to calculate how long it would take them to get back to The Bay Cities at two on a Thursday afternoon. Every passing minute meant another fifteen stuck in traffic.

He was getting ready to go inside and drag Maggie out when the front door opened. She emerged from the dimly lit interior and recoiled at the sunshine. Greg could see the half naked actors and actresses traipsing around in the background before she shut the door. He immediately headed for the car, but she stopped him in his tracks.

"Not so fast. It looks likes we're going to be here for another couple of hours. At least."

Greg spun on his heels, walking over to where she stood on the porch. He wanted to get close enough that their conversation stayed private.

"I told you I had somewhere to be this afternoon."

Maggie started grandstanding for the assembled help.

"Well, change your plans."

"I can't. I'll come back and get you if you're staying, but I'm taking the car and leaving."

"Jesus, Greg. What's so important that you would want to strand me in the Valley?"

She practically started hissing when he stepped in front of her.

"You know I'm still your boss, right?"

"Only until I quit."

He walked over to the car and started the engine. Maggie was standing right where he'd left her, a defiant expression plastered on her face. Greg pulled over near the front door of the house and rolled down his window.

"What time should I come back for you?"

"Eight will work. But so help me God, if you're one minute late…"

Maggie spun with a dismissive flick of her wrist, disappearing back into the house. Greg sped off down the long, curving driveway and headed for the freeway.

⊰

THE TESTS CAME BACK on Chris's bag of weed a few weeks after Greg dropped it off in Virgil Heights. It was a potent, hybrid strain of marijuana that had been soaked in some kind of chemical compound. Most likely roach spray. It seemed like J.J. was right about somatic fusion after all—everything Magnus told Greg about Grizzly Bear was probably a lie. But that didn't keep other bear paw baggies from turning up all over Los Angeles.

The Bay Cities was ground zero. A high number of the lowlifes caught with them had gone on some kind of violent spree. And every one of them said they'd paid triple the usual street value for the chance to try the hottest new drug on the market. Several law enforcement agencies in Los Angeles teamed up to create a joint task force to investigate the lethal new weed, but denied all rumors of its existence whenever asked. The secrecy only drove the public's growing appetite for information.

Greg couldn't decide if he was thinking like a cop when he blamed himself for Grizzly Bear coming to his hometown. There were just too many coincidences to ignore, starting with Tommy. The guy was a self-professed seller who'd come into Greg's life right before everything went south. But Tommy wasn't the only person that sprang to mind whenever Greg tried to work through the possibilities. If anybody was capable of unleashing a get rich quick scheme on his hometown, it was Maggie Keane and Mark Lathrop. He tried to put the hateful thoughts about them out of his mind, but they never stayed gone long.

Redd Kross was in the middle of "I Hate My School" when Greg pulled up outside of the rehab center. It was an expensive residential facility in Venice with a tough love approach designed specifically for teens. Grandpa Eddie said he would keep paying until Chris was an adult if that's what it took. Junior and Greg both prayed that a prolonged stay wouldn't be necessary, but it was looking worse with each passing month.

Greg got out of Maggie's town car and reached into the trunk for his guitar. It was the same battered acoustic he used to play back in the early nineties. The case was covered in stickers for bands that had broken up when the first Bush was still president. Some of them were so faded and worn that you couldn't even make the names out any more. He grabbed the handle and made his way to the front door.

Guitar was about the only connection that Greg had with Chris these days. They'd spend hours together some weekends, strumming in unison without saying a word to each other. Which was fine with Greg. He knew what it was like to be young and full of rage. He also knew that music was one of the best ways to connect with other people, especially when talking seemed utterly pointless.

Greg never thought of himself as a guitar player, but he could fake it. He was just thankful that Chris mostly wanted to learn songs that he actually knew, including a handful by Bad Citizen Corporation. It had already gotten to the point where Chris knew those old punk songs better than Greg did.

Greg walked in and went to the counter. The woman seated there dropped her eyes and reached for the phone as he approached. Chris's doctor emerged from the doors to the left. He was tall and lean with thick blond hair. Two burly attendants flanked him on either side, arms folded across their bulging chests. The doctor lifted his clipboard, studying it for a moment. He had a way of stressing certain words when he spoke, as though he was consciously trying to annoy whoever he was addressing. It always did the trick on Greg.

"Hello, Mr. Salem. I'm afraid there's been another *altercation*. Is Chris's mother with you?" This was the same dance they did every time he came to visit Chris, especially when Greg showed up without Junior. The doctor had it in his head that Greg was a bad influence. It might have been because of his tattoos, or his checkered past. Or it could have been that Chris talked about him a little too often. It didn't matter much to Greg either way since he was listed as a legal guardian in Chris's file.

"What kind of altercation?"

"We have him *isolated* for now, but we have some serious concerns."

Greg slammed the guitar case to the floor. A stale note rang out from inside of it as he stepped forward. He was the closest thing Chris had to father, whether the doctor liked it or not.

"Is he all right? What happened?"

"He put another patient into the *infirmary* today. The boy needed five stitches in his forehead by the time Chris got through with him."

Greg wasn't surprised. Chris had gone through a growth spurt ever since he'd been admitted. Starchy food and physical activity had turned the pudgy twerp into a raging, hormonal teen. Mix that new found strength with the boy's endless well of anger and you got a recipe for disaster. But none of that mattered to Greg at the moment.

"I want to see him right now."

"Fine, but I'm warning you.

He was practically walking on the doctor's heels to get him moving faster. A TV blared in one of the rooms as they passed, loud rap music thumping from another. Greg felt a chill run down his spine the deeper they went into the facility, as if his entire body was telling him to grab Chris and run. They took several disorienting turns before reaching his room. It was a little too quiet for Greg's comfort.

"When's the last time you checked on him?"

The doctor looked over to one of the attendants.

"Fifteen minutes. Maybe a little longer."

The second attendant slid a master key into the lock, twisting the handle on the door. It swung open in a silent, swooping arc. Greg's eyes fell on the bed first, the bare mattress covered in stains and the blankets shoved to one side. The attendants were already pushing past him before he noticed the dangling feet right above it. Chris was hanging from a sheet attached to an overhead light.

His limp body folded and fell as they grabbed his legs, pulling him down to the cold linoleum floor.

One of the attendants took off running down the hall, screaming as he went.

"Code blue!"

Greg didn't move as he watched the doctor go to work on Chris's lifeless body.

❧

IT WAS ALMOST EIGHT when the emergency room doctor finally emerged. Greg listened in as he explained the situation.

"We're very lucky they discovered him when they did. From what we can tell he'd only been up there a minute at most. There are still more tests to run."

Junior and Eddie were both speechless. so Greg inserted himself.

"Is he awake?"

"Yes, but I'm afraid he isn't ready for visitors. Are you his father?"

"I'm a close family friend. What kind of tests?"

The doctor turned to face Junior when he answered Greg's question.

"He was really only up there long enough to cut off the flow of oxygen, but we need to be sure there wasn't any permanent cerebral damage. It's still early, but I'm expecting a full recovery."

Eddie let out a long, slow breath and collapsed into the nearest chair. Greg caught a whiff of stale whisky on the old man's breath. It was becoming his signature scent.

Junior squeezed Greg's arm and tucked her face into his neck. He wanted to hold her like that forever, close his eyes and pretend that nothing had ever changed.

His phone buzzed repeatedly, like an angry wasp trapped in his pocket. He did his best to ignore it. The doctor lingered for a second, waiting to see if there were any more questions before eventually slipping away. There was a brief moment of calm before Greg's phone started up again. Junior released her grip and stepped back.

"You should probably get that."

"It's just my boss."

Eddie stood up and walked over. Greg noticed that he'd developed an old man's shuffle in the last few months.

"You can always come back to work at the bar."

"Thanks, Eddie. We'll see."

"Anything would be better than that guy who replaced you."

Greg held his phone up to reveal a screen full of missed calls and text messages.

"I guess I should go deal with this. Keep me posted on Chris. And call if you need anything. I'll come right over."

He hustled into the elevator, checking his phone on the way down. Maggie's first text message was a simple: *'Where the f r u?'* That had come an hour before. The most recent one was brand new, and a little more involved: *'U r so fired. Drop the car at my house and leave the keys in the mailbox. Goodbye.'* He didn't bother reading or listening to the dozen messages that came in between. He typed *'Will bring it over in the morning.'* and moved on.

Greg had his hand on the town car's door handle when he heard footsteps. A television reporter was rushing towards him, her camera crew in tow. Greg thought he recognized her from the media mob on the mountain, but he couldn't be sure. They were all starting to look alike. He was thrilled that she didn't have red hair.

He only managed to get the car door open a crack before they cornered him. She shoved her microphone in his face, barraging him with questions. Her suffocating perfume stung his nostrils.

"Is it true that there has been another overdose?"

Greg turned his head, flinching as the cameraman shined a blinding light in his eyes.

"I'm sorry. I think you've got me confused with somebody else—"

"Don't be modest, Mr. Salem. Is it true that you came out of retirement to join the task force investigating this lethal new street drug?"

Greg clinched his fists. There were so many things he wanted to say, but the camera made him nervous.

"What? No. I don't have anything to do with any Grizzly Bear special task force—"

The reporter was practically salivating as she landed her next question.

"But you do admit that Grizzly Bear exists?"

She wasn't nearly as dumb as he'd assumed. And she had him right where she wanted him. Greg knew he needed to do something fast, say something smart, but the most he could manage was "No comment." He yanked the door open, forcing his way into the town car.

The reporter was pounding on the window. He started the engine and sped off.

CHAPTER FOURTEEN

reg was only vaguely aware that Christmas was around the corner. It was mainly because Kristen had developed a craving for eggnog. He'd already cleaned out all the local liquor stores before wising up and ordering online. The six cartons came packed in a Styrofoam container filled with dry ice. They'd gone through three shipments in the last four weeks.

Kristen was still in bed when he brought her breakfast on a tray. He had to set it on the comforter beside her because her belly was too big to fit underneath.

"Your cinnamon eggnog waffles, and a decaf eggnog latte to wash it down."

"I could get used to this service."

"And I could never smell eggnog again and be happy about it."

She giggled and tore into a waffle with her fingers. He liked to watch her eat now that she had put some weight on. Her face was fuller and she seemed to savor every bite, whether it was eggnog muffins or eggnog cheesecake. She always did a good job pretending not notice him staring at her. It took a minute before he could tear himself away.

"Enjoy your breakfast. I'll be back in a little while."

"Going back to the hospital?"

"Not until this afternoon. I have to take Maggie's car back, and then I'm going surfing."

He didn't have to look to know she was disappointed. It stopped him in his tracks.

"You'll be fine without me for a couple of hours, right?"

"I guess, it's—"

She caught her breath. Greg went back to the bed and sat down beside her. There wasn't much he could do in these moments, so he held her hand and waited. It was hard to tell if she sensed his impatience, or if she even cared. He did his best to hide it anyway. Her tone was cold when she finally spoke again.

"Can't Maggie wait?"

"Not really. I mean, I'm pretty sure she fired me last night."

"After what happened with Chris? Let me talk to her for you. I'm sure she'll get over it."

Greg clamped his teeth in imitation of a smile. He'd only lost his job the night before, but he was already stressed out about supporting his new family. Eddie's L Bar was still his standby, unless he committed to becoming a private investigator full time. Both options seemed less appealing by the minute. Going back to being a cop wasn't even a consideration.

"Let me handle it."

Kristen eventually went back to picking at her breakfast. That's when Greg made his move. He kissed her on the cheek, jumped up and headed for the backyard. It crossed his mind to wake J.J. up and bring him along, but he reconsidered. His old bass player had been crashing in the garage apartment since starting the bartending gig. Greg thought he would appreciate another couple hours of sleep after closing down Eddie's the night before.

Greg grabbed one of the surfboards that was leaning against the back gate and stepped into the alley. Maggie's town car was parked behind the El Camino, right where he'd left it the night before. Greg swung the back door open and laid his board across the leather seat. It took a little maneuvering to make it fit with the door closed. *What's a little sand and wax between friends?*

His plan was to drop the car off before walking to the beach for a session. But not until he'd begged Maggie for his job back. She was probably drunk when she fired him anyway.

He wanted to go surfing more than anything else. A new swell had rolled in over the last couple days and he looked forward to blowing off some steam. He hadn't been out in a few days, but it felt like an eternity. Greg climbed behind the wheel and wound through the maze of narrow beach streets that twisted around South Bay.

Greg pulled into her garage ten minutes later. The classic beach house that he'd so admired was completely gone. Every inch of available space had been filled with a boxy, modern monstrosity that looked like a high-end motel from the outside. Four sheer walls climbing to whatever heights the zoning laws allowed. It obscured her neighbor's beach views for blocks in every direction. He thought it was a minor miracle that she'd gotten so much done in less than a year.

Greg unloaded his surfboard and left it leaning against the house. He wanted to make one more sweep of the car to be sure that there wasn't anything of his he'd forgotten. There was no way to know if Maggie would even be in any condition to speak. She was a good drinker, but terrible at dealing with hangovers.

He was locking the town car up when he heard the kitchen door squeak open. Greg looked up expecting Maggie, but found Mark Lathrop instead.

One hand was tucked into the pocket of a plush bathrobe, the other was holding a mug. His jet-black coif was perfect as always, but the bags under his eyes told a different story. Greg didn't want to know anything about what he and Maggie had done the night before. He would pay good money to avoid learning any of the details, money he didn't have.

If Lathrop sensed his discomfort, he didn't let it show.

"Interest you in a cup of coffee?"

His voice was even and smooth, but his eyes flicked around the garage. It seemed like he might be looking for something or somebody.

"I was actually about to go surfing. Maybe next time."

"The waves aren't going anywhere. Come on. It won't take long."

Lathrop stepped aside, motioning to the door. He was being friendly, but it didn't seem like he was asking. Greg guessed a couple of his goons were champing at the bit just inside the kitchen.

"Where's Maggie?"

"She's a little tied up. But that's actually what I wanted to speak with you about."

Lathrop hit the garage door button on the wall. The friendly twinkle in his baby blue eyes turned cold. Greg listened to the door slam shut behind him, sure that he was out of options. That cup of coffee was sounding better by the moment.

Greg could smell last night's cologne on Lathrop as he squeezed by him. Much to his surprise, there was nobody waiting for him in the kitchen. Lathrop went straight to the cupboard and pulled down a mug.

"How do you take it?"

"Black's fine."

"I'm a little surprised that a man of your age can handle it without a little cream. How old are you anyway, thirty-six? Thirty-seven?"

He filled the mug, setting it down on the counter. Greg climbed up onto a stool and took a sip. The coffee was way too hot to drink.

"Forty. You?"

"Thirty-six, if you can believe that. Hollywood ages you, especially your skin. The good news is that if you have enough money you can always buy new skin."

His smile was almost blinding as he raised his mug.

"To new skin."

Greg did the same, but didn't repeat the toast. He gave the room a casual once over while waiting for Lathrop to play his hand. There was no sign of Maggie that he could see, and it was starting to worry him. It wasn't like her to stay out of sight for this long with Greg in the house. She might be pissed off, but he wasn't willing to let some psycho billionaire harvest her skin.

Greg decided he had nothing to lose.

"Is there something you wanted to discuss, Mr. Lathrop?"

"Call me Mark."

"No need to get friendly. I'm not staying long. I'd like to see Maggie, though."

"Fine."

Lathrop slammed his mug down hard on the granite countertop. The coffee was still sloshing around as he went to find her upstairs. Greg guessed he only had a few minutes, so he jumped up to take a look around. He followed the flow of the open floor plan into the living room. There were two wine glasses on the coffee table beside an empty bottle. Maggie's dress from the day before was in a small pile on the cold wooden floor; a balled up wad of Lathrop's clothes were right beside it.

He went through the dining room on his way back to the kitchen. It didn't look like any of the gleaming furniture had been used yet. *Must be nice to have that kind of money to waste,* he thought, pushing his way through the service door. Greg climbed back up onto his stool, grabbing the untouched morning paper. He wanted to appear oblivious when Lathrop came back.

The bottom headline on the front page caught his attention.

LA Buzz: "Hero Cop' Confirms Existence Of 'Grizzly Bear'"

by Leslie Thompson, Staff Reporter

Former Virgil Heights police officer, Greg Salem, has confirmed the existence of the lethal street drug commonly known as 'Grizzly Bear.'

In a brief television interview that hit the airwaves late last night, Salem, the 'hero cop' who saved a woman and her son from a serial killer in The Bay Cities last summer, accidentally let slip that he is involved in a joint law enforcement task force assigned to investigate reports of the toxic marijuana strain.

Greg's mind raced. Leslie Thompson might only be doing her job, but it was making Greg's life impossible. He was so startled by Lathrop's reappearance that he almost fell off from his stool.

"No dice. She's in the shower. But honestly, she's still so pissed off at you that I doubt she'll come down anyway."

Greg flipped the newspaper over, pushing it away. He set his coffee mug down on top of it for good measure. Lathrop took his seat across the counter from Greg to continue their conversation. He motioned to the newspaper instead.

"Anything interesting in there?"

"Same shit, different day."

"Talk about a dying business. I haven't looked at one of those things in years."

Greg nodded, relieved that he was off the hook about Thompson's latest column—at least for the moment. He hoped that everybody else he knew shared Lathrop's opinion about newspapers. The TV piece from the hospital parking lot was of greater concern. Luckily, Lathrop moved on.

"As I was saying. I understand you might be in the market for work. I'm sure by now you understand the nature of my business."

"Yep. Internet porn. Mostly in Asia."

"It's more than that, but fine for the purposes of this initial conversation. You have to diversify these days. So what do you think?"

There were a lot of things Greg could have said in response. Being a smartass seemed like the best choice.

"Are you asking me to star in one of your films? I don't do the kind of bondage scenes you're so famous for."

"They're all actors, Greg. Total pros. Nobody actually gets hurt in the making of our films. Aside from a few broken hearts from on-set romances."

Lathrop waited for a laugh. He went on when Greg didn't oblige.

"I was actually thinking that you could head up my security detail. Make sure that only the right people have access to me, and the wrong people…go away."

"I'm not sure my references are very solid."

"What? Because of Maggie? She's supposed to be a silent partner anyway."

"How's that working out for you?"

"Believe me when I tell you that I have other partners that are much bigger pains in the ass—but not by much."

This time they both laughed, at Maggie's expense.

"Think it over, Greg. We could really use you on the team."

Greg stood up. He really wanted to make sure that Maggie was all right.

"I will. Tell Maggie I said hello."

"I bet she'd like it better if you told her yourself. Ain't that right, Maggie?"

Lathrop yelled to her, waiting for a response. He acted surprised when nothing came from upstairs.

"She must still be in the shower. We had a long night, if you know what I mean."

Greg knew, but wanted to keep the image out his head. Lathrop's game still wasn't clear.

"I'll show myself out."

Greg headed for the front door, but veered left to the stairs instead. He didn't think he would get very far, but at least wanted to gauge the response. Lathrop jumped up and screamed.

"I said she doesn't want to see you!"

Two of Lathrop's goons made their grand entrance at the top of the staircase. Greg had been in the room with the two goons on several occasions, but never got their names. It didn't look like that was going to change today. Lathrop was suddenly standing beside him, a smug smile on his face.

"Don't worry, boys, he was just leaving."

Greg hesitated, waiting to hear Maggie's voice. It was a real relief when she stepped out of the bedroom.

"I guess I'm not the only one who won't take no for an answer."

She was leaning in the doorway, wearing a tiny satin robe that barely covered her naked body. There was a towel on her head and her cheeks were flushed. Puffy eyes told him that she'd been crying, but her voice was calm and steady.

"Did you bring my car back in one piece?"

"Yes. Are you okay?"

She nodded and blinked to avoid making eye contact.

"Don't worry about me, Greg. You're the one with no job and a kid on the way. Focus on what's important."

"Sure I can't get you to change your mind?"

"It's too late for that. Besides, you make a better bartender than a bodyguard. Stick to what you know. And take care of Kristen, she's been through a lot."

Maggie traded glances with Lathrop before closing the bedroom door behind her. Greg went back down the stairs, slipping through the garage door without another word. Lathrop was right on his heels.

"Sorry about that. She has quite a temper."

"Not the first time I've seen it."

"My offer still stands. I'll make it worth your while."

Greg tried to look like he was seriously considering the offer. He would say almost anything to get out of there.

"Let me think it over. I'll get back to you."

"Sure thing. Give me a call and we can discuss it in more detail. Maybe even talk it over on my yacht. Bring your girlfriend too."

∽

GREG WAS RELIEVED WHEN he finally made it into the water. He only had two days to dig up all the information he could on Lathrop. At that point he would either make a very informed business decision, or give Maggie the information she needed to destroy her partner. Greg had his work cut out for him.

He could see the stand-up paddleboard recovery group, SUP Sober, holding their weekly meeting out past the break line. He wanted to paddle over and say hi to his old friends, but gave it a second thought. It seemed like drinking was always in the back of his mind these days. He'd managed not to act on the impulses so far, but only barely. He was what people in the program would call a 'dry drunk,' a ticking time bomb waiting to explode. The situation with Marco wasn't helping.

Whatever had happened up in the mountains, whatever pressure his sidekick was under, Greg couldn't find a way to forgive him. They had been through too much together to throw it all away. And for what? To work for a guy like Magnus? It killed him to think that Marco was partially responsible for the poisonous crap that was hitting the streets: The drugs that almost led Chris to take his own life.

Maybe Greg had been completely wrong about their last conversation. He had relived that phone call many times in his head since that night. Trying to pick out certain words, little clues that could lead him to where Marco was still being held captive. But it always brought him to the same terrible conclusion. If Marco was still alive, it was only because he truly had gone to work for Magnus.

It was too much for Greg to think about with everything else going on. Marco was a survivor who would probably outlive all of them. Greg dropped down on his board and paddled to catch a wave. Whatever the SUP Sober group had to offer was behind him now. He was barreling his way to the shore to make some big decisions.

J.J. was sitting in the backyard when Greg walked in. A bong was on the table in front of him.

"Please tell me you aren't out here getting stoned where the neighbors can see you."

J.J.'s voice was raspy and his eyes were red.

"They wouldn't care anyway."

"Go in the garage if you have to smoke that crap."

J.J. stood up, trying to get the last word in as he left.

"Go to hell, Greg."

Greg slapped him across the side of the head before heading for the house. J.J. was right behind him, bitching and moaning as he walked.

"My goddamn ear is ringing."

"You're lucky I didn't snap your neck."

"Some things never change."

J.J. mumbled it loud enough for Greg to hear. Greg knew he should let it go, but there was no turning back once J.J. got under his skin. It was like having a little brother that he never wanted.

"What did you say?"

"Nothing. Forget it."

"No. Tell me. What hasn't changed?"

"You and this tough guy routine, punching your way through the world like some angry little toddler. Same exact thing you've been doing since we were in the band."

"Well, at least I wasn't a junkie."

"Right, Greg, but I cleaned up. And you're still exactly the same."

Greg leaned forward, his hands tightening into fists. His eyes were on the bong in J.J.'s hand. In that moment it became a symbol of everything going wrong in Greg's life. The urge to break it in half was overwhelming.

"You call that getting clean?"

"It's just a little weed."

Greg imagined landing one punch and watching J.J. go down. But he would never forgive himself once it was over. If anything had changed, it was that regret had crept in.

They were stuck in a standoff—rage-filled Greg and round-shouldered J.J.—when Kristen waddled up in a hurry.

"That was Junior on the phone. She said you need to get down to the hospital now."

⚜

BARRETT WAS STILL IN the waiting room when Greg and J.J. rushed in. Junior was seated across from him, arms folded and a scowl on her face. Greg looked around for Eddie, but the old man was nowhere to be seen. Barrett laughed when he saw that the reinforcements had arrived.

"Classic. Greg Salem to the rescue."

Junior opened her mouth to talk, but Greg beat her to the punch.

"What are you doing here, Barrett?"

"Heard the news about Chris. I came to make sure he was all right."

"Well thanks for your concern, but I think we've got it handled. You can go now."

Barrett stood up. It was looking like Greg might get the fight he was looking for after all. He couldn't wait.

"Chris called and told me to stop by. That's the only opinion I'm concerned about."

Junior could no longer control her anger. She leapt from her chair, catching Barrett with a straight arm to the jaw. He recovered fast and threw her hard into the wall. Greg had him in a headlock before he could follow up with a punch. J.J. was already down at the nurse's station yelling for them to call for security.

Barrett was flopping like a fish on the line, but Greg kept his arms locked tight. They went through a few rows of chairs, slamming hard into the side of a vending machine. Greg's grip slipped a little on impact and Barrett managed to wriggle free. He spun around and threw a jab into Greg's gut. Greg came back with an elbow to the nose. Barrett's blood was everywhere when hospital security arrived and pepper sprayed them both.

Greg's vision went blurry. Every inch of skin on his face felt like it was engulfed in flames. He tried to stay upright, but all he could manage to do was roll around on the ground, clawing at his own face. Barrett was doing the same when Junior snuck up and gave him a couple of rib-cracking kicks. She was rearing back for a third when the guards brought her down too. J.J. was the only one of the four of them still standing when the police sirens rolled up.

The first voice Greg heard was the last one he expected.

"Mr. Salem. I see you're up to your old tricks."

"Just arrest me and get it over with."

"My pleasure."

They threw cuffs on Greg, Barrett and Junior before leading them outside. J.J. stayed behind in the waiting room to give his statement. After that he was supposed to stick around until Eddie came back. Greg knew the old man could bail them both out, but he wanted somebody there to explain what had happened. It wasn't worth the shock to Eddie's fragile health to come back and find the place torn up and empty. Especially while his grandson recovered from a suicide attempt in the next room.

They all reached the station around the same time in three different cars. Officer Bob insisted that Greg ride alone with him. He fully expected a lecture, but neither of them said a word the whole ride. It wasn't until they got into the police station that the older man finally spoke up, barking orders to the officer behind the front desk while pointing at Junior and Barrett.

"Get these two into separate holding rooms. We need to get some information from them before we let them go."

"What about him?"

Officer Bob turned to look at Greg, almost surprised to see him standing there.

"He's coming with me."

They made the familiar walk together and assumed the usual positions. Greg's hands were still in restraints, but at least they weren't behind his back. Officer Bob kicked his feet up onto the desk, leaning back in his chair. It was clear that he had something he wanted to get off of his chest.

"I heard you joined a joint task force."

Greg could feel his blood pressure spiking. A flush of heat spread across his cheeks.

"Come on. We both know that isn't true."

"I know it's not true because I checked on it, through the proper channels. I was wondering if you knew too."

Greg felt like he was fifteen years old again. He was more than happy to play the part.

"I have no interest in coming out of retirement, but thanks for asking."

"Even as a private investigator?"

"I'm no P.I., but I do have a family to support. Anything wrong with me working?"

"Nope. As long as you have a license."

"Like I said, I'm not a P.I. Just helping a friend out with some of her business affairs."

Officer Bob grimaced. Greg knew he was about to find out the real reason he was being questioned. Whatever was going on, it was about more than a fistfight at a hospital.

"I assume we're talking about Maggie Keane. How long have you known her?"

"We went to high school together."

"And you're working for her now?"

"I was. Until last night."

Officer Bob brought his legs down and leaned across the desk. His voice barely above a whisper.

"When's the last time you saw her?"

"I was at her house this morning. I stopped by to drop her car off. Is everything okay?"

Officer Bob cleared his throat.

"There's no easy way to say this, Greg. Her body washed up near the pier about an hour ago. A couple of fishermen found her."

Greg wanted to jump up and find Lathrop, but it would be hard to strangle him with his hands in cuffs. Besides, Officer Bob hadn't mentioned anything about murder quite yet. The older man stood up and went over to a small refrigerator in the corner. He unlocked Greg's cuffs, handing him a bottle of water. Greg took a drink and considered his options.

"What the hell happened?"

"Hard to say. The medical examiner has the body right now…"

CHAPTER
FIFTEEN

A patrol car dropped Greg off at the hospital sometime after sunset. Officer Bob was keeping Junior and Barrett for questioning, but only long enough to let them cool down. Greg warned him that it might take a while. Officer Bob said he was happy to put them up over night if that's what it took.

Bad Religion was blazing through "We're Only Gonna Die" when the El Camino shot from the hospital parking lot. There was no doubt in Greg's mind what he needed to do now, despite the promises he'd made back at the police station. Maggie might have been a shallow, money-hungry backstabber, but she was also a friend. A local.

All of that only made the guilt worse. He couldn't shake the idea that she might be dead because he hadn't picked her up from Studio City. It was because of him that she had taken a ride home with that scumbag Lathrop.

And who was he? Just some rich kid from Hollywood slumming it down at the beach. At least that's what Officer Bob told him. The BCPD had been watching Lathrop ever since he came to town and started throwing money around. Which is really saying something in South Bay, where beach bonfires are lit with hundred dollar bills.

Everything that had been building up inside of Greg for months was spilling over now. He couldn't predict what he would do once he tracked Lathrop down. He guessed at least one of them would end up in jail, the hospital or the morgue.

It made him sick to think about their conversation in her living room. How they'd laughed about what a pain in the ass Maggie could be when she only had a few more hours to live. But why? *Did she finally dig up enough dirt to destroy Lathrop? Or did something else get her killed?*

A cold chill ran down Greg's spine. He flashed back to the conversation he'd had with Lathrop that morning. To the very last thing that Maggie's likely killer had said—"Bring your girlfriend too." It hadn't sounded like a threat at the time, but Greg wasn't so sure now. He wasn't willing to chance it.

Greg stepped on the gas and sped toward home. He needed to put Kristen someplace safe until Lathrop was found. She would be devastated when she got the news about Maggie, so he couldn't tell her yet. He didn't want to scare her, and he definitely didn't have time to comfort her. But where could he take her? Greg was running out of friends fast.

He parked his car behind the house and dashed through the back gate. Kristen wasn't in her usual spot on the lounge chair. He took a few steps toward the house, listening carefully as he walked. He was relieved when she came into view through the kitchen window. He was greeted by the most amazing smell as he walked inside. Kristen was in a maternity dress and apron, pulling something out of the oven. He walked over and took a seat at the kitchen table. The scene of domestic bliss was almost enough to make him forget the terrible news he'd been given about Maggie, but not quite. He tried to play it off, sure that he wouldn't be winning any acting awards.

"Hey, sweetie. I baked you some brownies."

"It smells incredible. Hope it isn't a recipe you learned at Grizzly Flats."

"Very funny. I just thought you could use a little pick me up, with everything that's going on. You seem a little…off. I'm going to give some to Junior too."

"When did you talk to her?"

The words came out faster than he intended. If she noticed the edge in his voice, she didn't let it show.

"A few hours ago. Looks like they're sending Chris home earlier than expected."

"I heard."

"That kid's a handful and she has two businesses to run. I told her I would come stay there for a few days, to help out. If that's okay with you?"

Greg couldn't believe his luck. He tried to act surprised while being extremely supportive of her generous offer.

"That's great. I was actually headed over there to drop a guitar off for Chris."

"That's weird. Junior didn't mention anything about a guitar."

"She wouldn't have. I was going to surprise him with it."

"That's sweet of you. I'm sure he'll be thrilled. When are you going?"

Greg stood up, anxious to get Kristen stashed at Junior's.

"Let me grab the guitar from J.J.'s apartment. Get your things together and I'll drop you off too."

He walked across the backyard, using his spare key to unlock J.J.'s door. The room was much darker than he used to keep it, thanks to the heavy curtains nailed above the windows. It smelled like dirty socks mixed with another, skunky odor. Greg shook his head and went to the closet, carefully pushing J.J.'s clothes aside.

Greg still had a couple of electric guitars on some shelves back there. He found the one he was looking for, a Les Paul Custom, and yanked it from its perch. The case was in his hand when he spun around again.

His eyes had finally adjusted to the gloom enough that he could make out the contents of the room. J.J. only came to town with a couple of items and hadn't acquired much since then. Almost everything else in the apartment had been Greg's, except for the familiar bong. That was definitely a new addition.

He went over to take a closer look, finding a baggy beside it. He spotted the bear paw logo and almost dropped the guitar.

※

WITH KRISTEN AT JUNIOR'S, Greg could finally turn his thoughts back to Maggie and Lathrop. His first stop was Eddie's. He wanted to fill J.J. in on what happened and find out how early they could leave for The Valley. The BCPD were already keeping an around-the-clock watch on Lathrop's house in South Bay. Other than that, the house in Studio City was the last place Greg had seen Maggie and Lathrop together. He suspected that Lathrop might still be there wrapping up the shoot, or hiding out.

He slid the El Camino into a tight spot right next to five motorcycles. The place looked busier than usual, which was a bad sign if he wanted J.J.'s help. He took a step inside and spotted him mixing a round of margaritas for a gang of race-ready young bikers. Greg did a quick scan of their faces, but didn't see Tommy among them. He took a stool at the far end of the bar, waiting for J.J. to finish up.

It was strange not seeing Eddie there, but that's who was picking Chris up. Junior had been banned from the hospital since the fight with Barrett. Greg hoped the old man was sober enough to drive.

His eyes wandered to the TV. He was glad to see a cable news show instead of a local station. The last thing he needed was to watch a clip of that terrible night at the hospital.

"Hey, man. What's up?"

Greg turned, following the hand on his shoulder to a familiar freckled face. The last time he'd seen Tommy was that night outside of his cabin.

"What brings you down from the mountain?"

"Man, I don't hang out up there anymore. Not after what happened with Red."

"Yeah, that was pretty horrible."

"I only had to read about it. You're the one who had to see it with your own eyes."

Truth was that Greg hadn't given much thought to Red or Pete's since that day. Something about the whole gruesome scene flicked a switch in his head. Made him numb to the death that swirled around him like whirlpool. Even now the images that flashed in his mind felt like somebody else's memories—a B-movie horror flick that Greg had already watched a thousand times before.

Tommy swung around, taking the stool next to him. Greg could tell from his glassy eyes and permanent grin that he'd had a few drinks, and maybe some weed too. Which was fine with him. He knew from experience that alcohol could act as a truth serum, if you caught the drinker at the right moment.

J.J. wandered over and set Tommy's margarita down. Greg asked for a cup of coffee. He started the impromptu interrogation with a couple of softball questions.

"So you a beach rat now?"

"Nah. I was just out for a ride with my boys. Told them I knew a place down here."

Greg looked over at Tommy's friends. All in their mid-twenties, with baby faces hidden under three-day stubble.

"You and your crew heading somewhere later, or is Eddie's your home for the night?"

"See, there you go again with all those questions. Only now I know you were actually a cop."

Tommy slapped the bar, almost knocking his drink over. Greg smiled knowingly. His life was becoming an open book thanks to *The SoCal Sentinel*.

"You never asked me if I *was* a cop. You asked me if I *am* a cop."

"Typical cop word games. But at least that explains how you knew so much about Grizzly Bear before almost anybody else."

Greg took a sip of his coffee. It tasted like it had been brewed several hours ago and left to burn on the hotplate. But people didn't come to Eddie's for the coffee. He grabbed a couple creamers and stirred them in with a straw. Lathrop's comment about being too old for black coffee was still ringing in his ears when Tommy spoke up again.

"So what made you want to quit working at this fine establishment?"

"I've got a son on the way, so I needed to find something that pays better."

"Congrats, man! Let me buy you a shot."

Tommy tried to get J.J.'s attention, but Greg waved him off. He needed to get the conversation back on track.

"No, thanks. You still in sales? I wasn't the only one who had heard about Grizzly Bear, if memory serves."

"Only thing I heard was rumors. Now that shit's on the news every other day. And so are you. How's it feel to be famous again?"

"I wouldn't know, since I never was to start with."

"You're hilarious, man. I'll catch you later."

Tommy patted Greg on the back and stood up. Greg had one more question. He knew it was a long shot, but he had nothing to lose at this point.

"You ever heard of a guy named Mark Lathrop?"

"Lathrop? No, man."

Tommy was wobbly at best, but managed to make it back over to his friends without spilling a drop. Greg watched J.J. make another sweep of the bar before he waved him over.

"What time do you get off tonight?"

"Around seven. Why?"

J.J.'s furrowed brow reinforced the skepticism in his voice. Greg pretended not to notice.

"I'm going to need your help with a case tonight. Can you get somebody to cover the last couple hours of your shift?"

"I don't know, man. I really need the cash. Besides—"

"'Besides' what?"

"I was thinking about going to see a movie."

"A movie? Jesus. I said I need your help with an important case."

Greg could see the beads of sweat forming on J.J.'s forehead. He was talking under his breath, clearly trying to pump himself up.

"Say whatever you have to say."

"I didn't move to town so I could play cops and robbers with you."

J.J. was rushing his words. His spit was flying everywhere. Greg had been impatient when he walked into the bar, but now he was furious.

"What are you talking about? You helped me look for Marco."

"That's because it was Marco. I'm not some tough guy you can pull into a gunfight whenever you feel like it. I'm a bartender, and a bass player. That's it."

"And a stoner, apparently."

It was a low blow, but he had it coming. Greg was starting to remember why J.J. used to get on his nerves so bad back in the BCC days. His personality always had a way of sucking all the energy out of almost any situation.

"For your information, I have a prescription."

"And a history of addiction."

J.J. folded his arms to stand his ground. Greg gave him a dismissive wave.

"Whatever, dude."

Greg pushed back from the bar and stood up. Tommy and his friends were hanging around the pool table now, but Greg wasn't in the mood for goodbyes. He stomped off to the side door, stopping to take a parting shot.

"Marco would be there for me in a heartbeat. Wouldn't even give it a second thought."

"Last time I checked, I'm not Marco."

CHAPTER SIXTEEN

reg pulled up to the house in Studio City later that night. He grabbed his Glock and stepped out into the crisp night air. All the windows on the house were blacked out.

He brought the gun up, working his way along the bushes that lined the driveway. The only sound was the hum and whir of the Ventura Freeway down below. He kept his back to the front wall of the house, ducking beneath the windows on his way to the porch.

Greg reached out and gave the doorknob a twist. Locked. He had never been around to the back of the house before, but he knew there was a large pool with a small waterfall and adjoining hot tub. Maggie and Lathrop had discussed it in front of him when they were trying to decide where to shoot a particular scene. Maggie had flirted with Lathrop by mentioning how much she liked a man who could go under and hold his breath for a long time.

Greg used the same careful procedure as before, slowly making his way to the far corner of the house. The property took a steep downward turn a few yards beyond that, an ivy-covered hill dropping off to the neighbor's property below. He could see the entire valley from where he stood. A sea of twinkling orange lights that stretched to the bulging black mountains in the distance.

He followed the sound of running water until he was standing in front of the pool. Large slabs of polished concrete lined the patio under his feet as he scurried for cover behind a row of lounge chairs. The entire back wall of the house was made of glass, giving

Greg a clear view of the mostly dark interior. The only light was coming from a cracked door somewhere deep inside.

Greg was almost certain the house was empty, but stayed low as he crossed to take a closer look. He gave the sliding glass door a light tug. It slid away from the frame without making a sound. Greg stepped inside and stopped to listen. There was a faint sound in the distance, something mechanical, like a noisy air conditioner or refrigerator. The rhythmic squeaking got louder as he moved forward.

He knew exactly what the sound was by the time he reached the bedroom door. And he also knew that whoever was inside the room would be too occupied to pull a gun of their own. He took a deep breath and threw his shoulder into the door.

The woman's back was slender and milky white. Satin sheets were bunched up where she ground away on the man beneath her. She was wearing a Santa hat and nothing else.

"Freeze! Nobody move!"

She screamed and collapsed forward with a groan. Her partner groped blindly for the nightstand. Greg bounded forward, grabbing the handgun that was sitting there. Then he ripped the covers back and pulled them down to the end of the bed. There were no more weapons hidden there, only the two naked bodies he already knew about.

"You want to join in or something? Three's the magic number."

The woman was high as a kite, her eyes practically spinning in her head. Greg stepped back, gun up.

"Keep your hands where I can see them."

He might not be a cop any more, but these two didn't have to know it. Lover boy's hand recoiled and the woman started mumbling curses under her breath. Greg didn't see the bear paw tattoo on her shoulder until he took a final step forward.

"You. On top. Roll over to your side so I can see your face."

They were both cursing now, but she did as she was told. It was the waitress from Red's.

"I know you. What's your name?"

"Ursula."

"Give me you're real name, or I'll—"

"Mary."

Greg became suddenly aware of the lighting equipment and cameras scattered around the room. There was a large, faded stain on the carpet near the bed. He didn't want to imagine what kind of fetish porn resulted in that much of a mess.

"Who else is here?"

"Nobody. Location got burned by a couple of nosy neighbors. The crew moved on this morning."

"What about all this gear?"

Greg motioned to the room.

"I was supposed to be right behind them with the rest of the cameras. But he got behind me instead."

She gave lover boy a playful slap, getting a smile in return. He was either too stoned or too stupid to realize he was in serious danger of getting shot. She leaned to her left, but froze when Greg tracked her with the barrel of his gun.

"Take it easy. I just want a cigarette."

"No more sudden moves."

Lover boy stayed nice and quiet. She took a drag off her smoke, pulling the sheet up in feigned modesty. Greg knew he had to keep up with the questions if he wanted to find Lathrop.

"Where's your boss?"

"Haven't seen him since he split last night. Took that mean bitch with him."

"Was my friend with them? The one you and Red were keeping in the store room at Pete's."

Greg held the gun up at an angle to indicate Marco's height. Mary shook her head, trying to look innocent.

"I have no idea what you're talking about."

"Then tell me this. What the hell happened up there?"

She laughed. A billowy puff of smoke escaped from between her red lips.

"I was already on my way down here by then."

"You seem really broken up about it."

She dropped her cigarette into a half empty beer can. It sizzled and died.

"That's what happens when you deal with animals."

∽

CHRIS WAITED PATIENTLY. HE waited until his mother checked on him for the fifteenth time, until he heard his grandpa finally say goodbye a little after midnight. He lay perfectly still as Kristen brushed her teeth in the bathroom, flushed the toilet and settled into the squeaky cushions of the couch where she was sleeping. He waited until the entire house had been absolutely silent for a full hour, and then he got out of bed.

His clothes were still in a pile on the dresser. He carefully slipped out of the pajamas his mother insisted he wear and quietly got dressed. His wallet and phone had both been confiscated, but he wasn't going to need them anyway. He went over to the window, turned the lock and slid it up slowly.

Chris felt a chill as he crept through the grass outside his mother's bedroom. He could hear her inside, turning the pages on her book and trying to keep herself awake. There was no way that she would ever understand why he had to do what he was doing.

How completely his world had been shattered that night up at the tidal pools.

He went around the corner of the house, emerging into the front yard. Their family used to spend so much time out there together. Digging in the garden with his mom. Throwing a baseball with his Grandpa. He hoped that they would someday understand that he wasn't like either of them.

Chris headed for the street, skirting the glow of the streetlights. The last thing he needed now was for somebody in the house to see him wandering down the sidewalk. He'd be back in that awful rehab before he knew it.

The van was waiting half a block down on the left. The headlights stayed off as it started rolling toward him. He broke into a jog to meet it as the side door slid open. Chris jumped in. He already had a pipe and lighter in his hand when they passed by his house.

CHAPTER
SEVENTEEN

Lover boy was still in the bed when Greg took Mary outside. She didn't resist much, but she wasn't going peacefully either. So far he'd gotten very few answers out of her.

"How do you know Kristen Raines?"

That question stopped her cold.

"Now there's a name I haven't heard in a long time. How's she doing?"

"Better, now that she got away from that crazy bastard Magnus."

"Lucky girl. She gets the handsome cop and a brand new life."

"It could happen for you too. Just tell me where we're going."

He opened the passenger door of the El Camino, waving her inside. She plopped down into the seat as he locked the door, slamming it shut. Her head was already leaning against the glass when he climbed in to start the engine.

"This hunk of junk got a heater in it? I'm freezing."

"Maybe you should wear more clothes."

"First time a guy's ever said that to me."

Greg twisted the key and the engine responded. He turned to look at her before throwing the car into gear.

"So, where to next?"

"How should I know? You're the one waving the gun around."

"It's simple. Tell me where the crew took the gear."

"If you're trying to get me killed, shoot me yourself."

He was considering it when the back window blew out. The cab of the El Camino was instantly filled with a spray of glass pebbles.

Greg pushed her down to the floor where she curled into a ball. He could see lover boy advancing across the driveway, a revolver in his outstretched arm. Greg slammed the car into reverse and stomped on the gas pedal.

"Hold on!"

Lover boy had no time to react. The rear bumper caught him in the knee. There was a loud *thud* followed by louder howling. Greg stomped on the brakes and slammed the El Camino into park. The engine was still running when he jumped out and went over to where the guy was writhing around on the ground. The silent act was gone now, replaced by a string of angry curses growled from behind a clenched jaw.

"You broke my leg!"

"And you broke my window. I'd say we're even."

Greg knelt down to study his mangled knee. The skin was torn open and bits of bone were showing through. He had to call 911, but wanted to get some info first.

"Where did your crew take the gear?"

"Your mom's house…"

Greg stood up to give him a kick when he heard the passenger door slam. Mary was sprinting from the driveway to the street on foot. He looked down at lover boy again and considered finishing what he'd started, but jumped into the El Camino instead. *Sure would be nice to have some backup right about now.*

Mary was running right down the middle of the street at full tilt. He pulled up behind her and flicked his high beams. The downhill momentum carried her another few yards before she finally slowed to a stroll. She was sitting on the ground when he got out to grab her. She looked helpless in the glow of his headlights.

"Where the hell do you think you're going?"

"Some place where I won't get killed. Might be a nice change of pace."

❧

J.J. SET THE NEW margarita down and removed all the empties. Tommy's friends took off one by one until he was seated at the bar alone. The crowds were heavy earlier in the night, but thinned out about an hour ago. It was close to midnight when the only other table of customers settled their tab and left. Tommy lifted his glass and took a sip.

"Is it always this dead during the week?"

J.J. was wiping down the bar and flipping chairs onto tables. He tried every trick in the book to get his last customer to leave so he could go home. He looked up, but kept working.

"Depends. Crowds are usually bigger on the weekends."

"That when Greg used to work?"

"Day shift mostly, but not any more. Is he a friend of yours?"

"You could say that. We met up on the mountain."

J.J. stopped what he was doing and leaned on the bar. He studied Tommy's face for a second, racking his brain to place him. The light bulb went on when Tommy smiled.

"You're the guy on the motorcycle. From up at the cabin."

"Nailed it. What's Greg doing for work now that he hung up his apron?"

"I guess you'd call him a P.I. I prefer to call him a 'dick.'"

J.J. picked up a rack of clean glasses, stacking them behind the bar. Tommy took his phone out and started pushing buttons. He set it down again when J.J. turned around.

"Must be weird."

"What's that?"

"All these news stories about him. Seems like the kind of dude who prefers to fly under the radar."

J.J. laughed as he opened the register and started counting the cash. Tommy didn't understand the joke.

"What's so funny?"

"Everybody seems to have that impression of Greg. Cracks me up after what I've been through with him."

"Sounds like you've got some stories to tell."

"Let's just say that I knew him before he was a hero cop. Or whatever kind of amateur private eye security guard he is now."

J.J. nodded his head, proud of his own insult. Tommy nodded in agreement.

"I'd love to hear all about it. Can I buy you a drink?"

"No thanks. My drinking days are behind me. Should probably close up anyway."

J.J. closed the register and started turning off the neon beer lights. Tommy reached into his jacket pocket, pulling out a plastic baggy.

"You got a lighter?"

It wasn't an offer that J.J. had to give much thought to.

"Now you're talking."

⁓

LOVER BOY WAS GONE by the time they got back to the house. Greg followed the trail of blood until it disappeared at the edge of the property. He'd either gone over the fence and tumbled to his death, or he was hiding somewhere nearby. Greg didn't have time to look for him, so he dialed 911 from a phone in the house and reported a break in. He knew the police in a neighborhood like this would take a burglary seriously. That would keep lover boy out of commission long enough for he and Mary to crash the next shoot unannounced, whether she liked it or not.

Mary seemed antsy once he hung up the phone. She was clutching his arm and almost dragging him to the car.

"Let's get out of here."

"What's your rush? You got a problem with cops?"

"Not really, but they always seem to have a problem with me."

"We can leave as soon as you tell me where we're headed."

She turned, placing her palms on his chest. Her lips were parted slightly as she stood up on tiptoes and tried to kiss him. He couldn't help thinking that she had been with another guy less than an hour before. It didn't slow her down at all.

"Let's just go to a hotel or something. We can have a good time."

Greg pushed her back until there were a few crucial inches between them. The utter disappointment written all over her face was no match for the look of disgust on his.

"I'll pass, thanks. All I want is an address."

"And you'll let me go?"

"As soon as I'm sure you're not lying to me."

"Fine. Let's get out of here."

Mary didn't have an address for the next shoot location, but she claimed to know the way. Greg followed her instructions carefully as they crawled across the perfect grid of streets that covered the Valley. John Doe and Exene Cervenka from X were crooning about "Los Angeles" in the background when she pointed out a wrought iron gate. A short driveway led to a suburban McMansion covered in twinkling holiday lights.

"That's the place."

He leaned over her and squinted to take a look. If they were shooting porn inside, there was no way anybody would know from out on the street.

"I don't see any vans or trucks."

"They stopped hanging up the neon 'Porn Shoot' signs too. Turns out the neighbors prefer something a little more subtle."

"Very funny."

Greg parked and they both climbed out of the car. He was walking to the gate when he heard her shoes clicking away behind him.

"Where do you think you're going?"

"I got you here, so I'm taking off."

"Not yet."

He flashed the gun to remind her who was in charge, even though he knew he would never use it on her. She brought her hands up to rest them on cocked hips. Greg cut her off before she could start complaining again.

"Let's go."

The wall was low, but covered in a thick hedge. Greg pushed her up first, listening as she struggled through the dense branches. He waited until he heard her land on the other side before following her path. She was still brushing off the grass and leaves when he dropped down beside her.

"Are there security cameras?"

"Even if there are, nobody's watching them. It's just an expensive rental."

They crossed the square lawn under cover of a shadowy tree. He pushed her along until they reached the garage. Greg took a peek through one of the small beveled windows built into the door. Two white passenger vans and three or four motorcycles were parked inside. The back of one of the vans was covered in faded band stickers. A small European sports car was crammed in there too.

"What does Lathrop drive?"

"Depends on the night. If he's driving himself, it's probably a little blue convertible."

Bingo. Greg only had one more question.

"What's the best way to get in?"

"Pretty much nobody uses the front door around here."

They walked along the garage, following the path to a stone porch. An American flag dangled in the still night air where it hung by the unlocked door.

The high-ceilinged living room was empty and dark. Greg grabbed Mary and pulled her in there to listen. It was mostly silent except for a couple of men having a conversation about sports in the kitchen. It could have been Lathrop's bodyguards, or a couple camera operators on a coffee break.

He took two careful steps in that direction before Mary tugged at his elbow. She was motioning with her head to the staircase. A glaring light was coming from the second floor, which meant that the shoot was probably happening up there. From Greg's experience, Lathrop was never far from the action. He was the kind of guy who probably liked to flirt with the actresses between takes, to remind them of who was boss.

Greg took the first few steps before he realized that Mary wasn't with him. He looked back over his shoulder to see her standing down below. She was mouthing the word "sorry" and backing away. Greg knew then that he'd been set up.

Two armed men were moving fast behind her. He turned and started jogging up the stairs, only to find two more goons waiting on the landing. It was like a repeat of the situation at Lathrop's, but with different players. Greg thought about jumping over the banister, but knew that he was trapped. He set the Glock down at his feet and brought his hands up.

Mary faded into the darkness below. The two men came up the stairs and shoved him forward. It felt ridiculous to be escorted by four security guards when he wasn't even resisting. They led him down a long corridor lined with framed family photos. It looked like the occupants of this house were a typical family of four: mom and dad and two teen daughters. He wondered if they had any idea what kind of movie was being filmed here, or if they were only worried about how to pay for college in a few years. Greg could relate.

They reached the master bedroom at the end of the hall and stopped. One of the guards gave a light rap on the door before pushing it open. They stepped aside to let Greg go in alone. He wasn't sure what he would say to Lathrop when he saw him again, or what he might be tempted to do. Anything outside of listening was going to be a suicide mission.

The door clicked shut behind him. Greg walked up to the edge of the large sleigh bed and looked around. He thought he might be alone until a man emerged from the bathroom. He was slimmer than Greg remembered and his beard was shaved clean, but there was no mistaking Magnus Ursus.

"We meet again."

Greg was stunned as Magnus went on.

"Surprised to see me?

"I probably shouldn't be. Where's Lathrop?"

Magnus smiled, tilting his head to the door.

"Around here somewhere."

"You're his other partner."

"I was, until very recently. Let's just say there's been a hostile take over."

"So you're the one who told him to kill Maggie?"

"I thought that might get your attention."

Greg edged forward, every muscle in his body tensed and ready.

"If you wanted to see me so bad, you could have called."

"You think I survived this long by doing things the easy way? Have a seat before you do something stupid."

Magnus extended an upturned hand, indicating two chairs in the corner. They flanked a small round table with a chessboard on top. Greg shrugged and did as he was told. Magnus wandered over to join him.

"You play?"

Greg surveyed the chiseled marble pieces between them and nodded.

"I'm no expert, but I know the rules."

"Then we're already off to a better start than the last time we met."

Magnus smirked, reaching for the black queen. He held it in his palm and studied it with an intense gaze. Greg watched as he closed his fingers around the figure and shook it lightly in his fist. It seemed as though he'd made up his mind about something important. All Greg could do was wait to find out what it was. Magnus released a jagged breath, shifting his gaze to Greg.

"A lot has changed in the last few months."

"Does that mean you aren't hiding from the cartels any longer?"

Greg was trying to get a rise out of him, to create a level playing field, but Magnus ignored his question.

"It means that we've made significant progress on Grizzly Bear."

"I'm all ears."

Magnus seemed to relax at Greg's last response. He sat back, bringing his elbow up to rest on the table. His face transformed from ferocious to friendly in a heartbeat.

"We can circle back around to that. I understand congratulations are in order."

"For what?"

"Your baby boy."

Greg dug his fingernails into the end of his chair. It was bad enough that Magnus knew about their child at all, but they had barely told anybody what the sex was. Whoever was keeping an eye on Greg for Magnus was doing a bang-up job. Greg was starting to think that he knew why his new friend Tommy was showing up so often.

"You two have a name picked out yet?"

The tension was building too fast. Greg felt like he was about to erupt. He needed to get control of himself if he wanted to get out of there alive.

"I'm leaning toward Marco."

"It would be just like you to name your son after one of your lowlife *bros*."

"I'm not in the mood for your games. Where is he?"

Magnus set the chess piece down on the table again.

"We'll get around to that, but first I want hear about my girl."

"Kristen?"

Magnus sat forward, lowering his already quiet voice to a hiss.

"Call her what you want, it won't change who she is."

Greg got a close up view of the new Magnus and it made his skin crawl. He might not look as scary in a suit, but his gaze was twice as menacing. His piercing eyes danced and darted. It took everything in Greg to not reach up and knock that hard stare right off of his face.

"Whatever she is, it's none of your business now."

Magnus jumped up and went to the nightstand by the bed. He shook a couple of pills into his hand from a prescription bottle. Swallowed them dry.

"You've got balls, Greg. I offer you the opportunity of a lifetime and you turn me down flat. You have any idea how much money you walked away from?"

"I'm not interested in selling poison to kids."

Magnus went over to the window. He pulled the curtains apart to inspect the yard below.

"That's all a matter of perspective. I sell a revolutionary new strain of weed in the form of Grizzly Bear. You sell anger and disaffection in the form of your music. The two go hand in hand."

"There's no comparison. I make music—or at least I used to. You soak weed in roach spray and pretend like you're some kind of mad scientist."

Greg walked a fine line pushing somebody this unpredictable, especially given the circumstances. But he needed to keep Magnus talking.

"I'll admit that was a cheap trick, but things are evolving very quickly now. We've had some important breakthroughs recently."

Greg didn't take the bait. Magnus was clearly agitated when he came back over to stand next to the table.

"Like it or not, the real Grizzly Bear is about to flood the market. And once it does, nothing will ever be the same again."

"We'll see about that."

"Who's 'we,' Greg? Don't tell me those rumors about you and the task force are true. Because that would be fantastic."

"I'm only here for Marco."

"Well, you're in luck because he's very close by."

CHAPTER EIGHTEEN

Marco and Lathrop stood up when Greg walked into the room. They looked like two lost children waiting for their dad to come home from the war. Marco's eyes bulged as he tried to make sense of his unbelievable luck.

"No way."

Greg smiled, but clenched his jaw when he noticed the scars on Marco's face. Whatever had been going on for the last eight months didn't look fun. But at least his partner was still alive. Greg just had to find a way to get him home in one piece, without getting killed himself.

First things first. Greg stepped past Marco, driving a fist into Lathrop's jaw. His neck snapped and he went down to one knee.

"That was for Maggie."

Bloody drool was dangling from Lathrop's quivering lip.

"It wasn't me, I swear. You have to believe me...I loved her..."

Magnus walked in before Greg could throw another punch. Lathrop shifted his terrified gaze, stumbling back to his chair. Greg looked Marco in the eye.

"You doing all right?"

"Better now, bro."

Magnus kept moving forward until he was shoulder to shoulder with Greg.

"What a beautiful reunion. Too bad it won't last."

Marco was getting antsy, shifting his feet and rolling his shoulders. Greg hoped his friend wouldn't do anything stupid before the time was right. He kept his eyes on Marco while responding to Magnus.

"What do you want? Name it."

"I want my girl back."

"You're insane. No way I'm giving up the mother of my child."

"She belongs to me. Either I get her back or you'll understand how it feels to lose somebody close to you."

Greg shuddered. Loss was something he understood a little too well. But he wasn't willing to let Magnus have the satisfaction of hearing him say it. He threw an elbow instead.

Magnus ducked, launching a shoulder into Greg's gut. The two of them slammed into the wall on the far side of the room. A lamp shattered on the wood floor as they tumbled and skidded. Magnus recovered first, diving at Greg to land a few solid blows. Marco stepped forward, drilling his foot into Magnus's rib cage before heading to the door. This was the moment Marco had been waiting on, planning for.

Momentum carried Marco straight into the first bodyguard that came rushing in. A pistol flew from his hand and clattered away. It was within Greg's reach, but he needed both hands to defend himself against hurricane Magnus. Marco slammed his forehead into the man's nose and stepped over him. The next bodyguard suffered a similar fate, but not before catching Marco in the throat with his fist.

Marco was doubled over, gasping for air when the third guard stormed in. He brought the butt of his gun down on the back of Marco's head, knocking him straight to the floor. His attention turned to Magnus and Greg as they rolled around trading punches. He leveled his weapon and tried to take aim, but there was no clear shot. Lathrop swung a wooden chair into the man's chest and the gun went off with a loud pop. Lathrop dropped, clutching at his shoulder.

Magnus jumped to his feet, pulling Greg up by the shirt with him. They reached the nearest bodyguard and Magnus held his empty hand out. A handgun was placed there in response to his silent command. Magnus pointed at Marco's motionless body first. Greg froze.

"We need to evacuate. Now. Get him down to the van. Wait for me there."

The bodyguard studied Lathrop with a confused look.

"What about him?"

Magnus was shoving Greg out the door when he answered.

"Get somebody to carry him out, or finish him off yourself. I'll trust you to make the right decision."

Lathrop started wailing. He fell to his knees, pleading for his life. "You have to save me, Greg! Please…"

Greg pulled away from Magnus and spun to face Lathrop. The one-time Hollywood hot shot looked like an abused animal now—scared, alone and waiting to die. Greg was torn between mocking him, saving him and killing him.

"Is that what Maggie sounded like? Out on your precious yacht."

Magnus stepped in before Lathrop could answer.

"I'd love to see how this drama plays out, but we're running out of time."

Lathrop collapsed to the floor when Greg and Magnus turned to leave. They wound through the small crowd starting to form in the hallway. Your usual collection of film crew miscreants, with backwards baseball hats, stained T-shirts and three-day stubble. The few women who popped their heads from the bedrooms were either totally naked or well on their way. Nobody seemed troubled at all that Magnus had the barrel of his gun pressed against the back of Greg's head. Business as usual.

Magnus guided Greg down the stairs and out through the front door. They were standing in the driveway together when Magnus finally lowered his weapon.

"My offer still stands."

It took Greg a minute to understand what Magnus meant. He knew it was no use arguing with a lunatic, but Magnus was also an egomaniac.

"You're surrounded by beautiful women. You don't need her back."

"Love is a many splendored thing. Two days, or your friend dies."

Magnus turned to leave, but Greg grabbed his shoulder.

"I won't give her up without a fight."

"Forty-eight hours before we come and take what's mine. You get any of your old friends from the police force involved, Marco pays the price."

Checkmate.

❧

JUNIOR WAS FRANTIC WHEN she came out of Chris's bedroom the next morning. She ran for the couch to wake Kristen up, but she was gone too. Her blankets and pillows were neatly folded and piled in the corner. It was like she was never there, except that her phone was still plugged into the wall charger. Junior was checking the rest of the house when somebody started pounding on the door.

Greg was standing there when she went to answer.

"Where is she, Junior? I keep calling, but she doesn't answer."

He pushed by her to survey the living room. A Christmas tree was standing in the corner, but nobody had taken the time to decorate it yet. His eyes came to rest on the couch. Junior grabbed his elbow and spun him around.

"Jesus Christ, Greg. What's going on?"

"Where is she?"

"I don't know! And I don't know where Chris is either, if you care at all."

It was the first thing she said that actually registered. It felt like the wind had been knocked completely out of him.

"What do you mean he's gone?"

"The place was empty when I woke up."

He ran back out the front door with Junior chasing after him. The El Camino was still idling when they both arrived. Greg climbed in, putting the car into reverse before he even noticed she was in the passenger seat. "You have to stay here in case she—in case either of them come back."

"I know, but...but..."

"Spit it out, Junior. I have to go *right now*. The clock's ticking."

"Don't hurt him, Greg. Don't hurt Chris if he has anything to do with this."

Greg reached over and took her in his arms. She was too overwhelmed to even cry. He was too wound up to do a very good job comforting her. Somehow it still felt right. They stayed like that until she finally pulled away.

"You have to go find her."

"I'll find both of them. You can't let yourself think Chris had anything to do with this."

Junior was back on the porch when Greg sped away. He could see her standing there in his rearview mirror. The knots in his stomach got tighter as she shrank into the background.

❧

THE BACK GATE WAS open when Greg pulled up to his house. He clipped a couple of trashcans sliding to a stop before he jumped out of the car. Kristen wasn't in the backyard so he kept moving into the house. Both bedrooms were empty; the same with the living room and kitchen. There was no sign of a struggle, and all of her clothes were still in the closet.

Greg had no idea where else to look. She'd barely left the property since moving in. The only other place he could think of was the beach, but she rarely went there on her own: Only to sit on the sand and watch him surf. He decided it was worth a try anyway.

He was flying across the backyard when J.J.'s apartment door flung open. Greg stopped, even though he knew not to expect any help from his former bass player. Part of him was surprised that J.J. was still living there after their heated conversation yesterday. He turned around to face his tenant, but was greeted by Tommy's puffy, hung over face instead.

Tommy squinted as he looked up at the sun in disbelief.

"What time is it?"

"Close to eight. What are you doing here?"

"Closed Eddie's down last night. Way too drunk to drive. Your boy told me I could crash here."

"He's not my boy, but I'm glad you made it home in one piece. Or somewhere safe, at least. Now go back to bed."

"Ain't happening. I've been awake since the last time you came crashing through here."

"Wait. What do you mean? This is the first time I've come home since last night."

"Hell if I know. I heard a bunch of loud noises a couple hours ago. Sounded like a big truck pulled up in the alley. People were talking. Doors were slamming."

"What time was that?"

"No idea. It was still dark out. Too damn early, if you ask me."

Greg pushed past Tommy, searching the apartment for any sign of Kristen. J.J. didn't even stir the whole time Greg was digging around. Tommy looked much more alert when Greg brushed by him again on his way out.

"Man, you really are a terrible landlord."

"Do me a favor, tell J.J. to keep his mouth shut."

Greg slammed the gate behind him and ran down to the beach. A strong offshore breeze was blowing and the waves were choppy. There were only two or three die-hard surfers out in the water, his kind of people. He also spotted a couple of paddleboarders climbing out of the water down at the shoreline. Greg reached them right before they started the long, slow slog across the sand. They all recognized each other at the same moment.

"Greg. How are you?"

It was Shelia and Pete from the SUP Sober group. Pete went in for a handshake.

"Long time, no see. What brings you down here in your street clothes?"

Both of them smiled. Greg was only barely aware that he was still wearing the same outfit as last night. At that moment it was impossible to pretend like he cared.

"I'm looking for my girlfriend. She's hard to miss since she's eight months pregnant."

Pete was doing all the talking for the two of them now.

"I heard you were going to be a daddy. We're so stoked for you."

"Thanks. Listen, I'm kind of in a hurry. You haven't seen her around, have you?"

"No, sorry…"

"That's okay. Take care you guys."

"…but Junior's son was out here this morning."

Greg wanted to believe that Chris had shown up to attend the SUP Sober meeting, that at least Junior's nightmare was over. But he knew it was only a daydream.

"What time?"

"Must have been close to six. We tried to say hi, but he paddled away. Didn't seem like he had gotten much sleep last night, if you know what I mean."

"Was he alone?"

"He was with Jeff Barrett."

Greg was lost in thought all the way across the sand and down the alley to his house. He had gone to the beach on a mission to find Kristen and ended up with a lead on Chris. Calling Junior to let her know was the right thing to do, but with Barrett involved that would only mean more trouble. The more Greg thought about it, the angrier he got.

He was jogging into the backyard when he remembered that there was one other person he could always trust. They hadn't spoken in a few weeks, which must have been some kind of record for them. He tried to catch his breath as he pulled the phone from his pocket, finding the name in his contacts.

"Chief. It's Greg."

"It's about goddamned time you called. I was getting worried that this joint task force was going to your head."

"Very funny. What's new?"

"Another day closer to retirement. You calling to set up that meeting with the kid in the blue hat?"

"Nope. I actually want to take you up on your offer."

"I'm getting old, so you'll have to refresh my memory."

"I need you to look somebody up for me. Name's Kristen Raines."

❧

GREG WAS SITTING AT his kitchen table, trying to come up with a plan. He had given his old Police Chief all the information he had on Kristen. Or, at least, everything she'd told him. It would be up to the police database to let him know what was true and what wasn't.

Until then, he still had Chris to worry about. He could definitely handle Barrett on his own, but things would go much smoother if he had back up. Especially if he heard back about Kristen and needed to shift gears.

Greg went to refill his coffee when somebody knocked on the door. He got up to check the front door, but nobody was there. Then he heard it again, coming from the backyard. Tommy gave Greg a head nod when he opened up. He looked only slightly better than the last time they spoke.

"I'm taking off. Thanks for letting me crash here."

"Better than crashing out there."

Greg didn't even get a smile in return for his lame cop joke.

"You should be thanking J.J., not me. Is he awake yet?"

"Not even close. Dude snores like a bear."

Tommy was backing away, but Greg stopped him. "Is your motorcycle over at Eddie's?"

"Man, I hope so. I really don't like leaving her in strange places over night."

"Why don't I give you a ride? It's a long walk from here."

"That would be great. Especially since I can't find my wallet."

"Cool. We need to make a quick stop on the way."

CHAPTER
NINETEEN

eff Barrett was in his usual spot on the beach despite the season. Greg and Tommy crossed the sand, trudging toward him. Greg had taken the time to switch into board shorts and a hoodie, but his new friend was still dressed in his motorcycle leathers. He hoped the extra padding would come in handy if the situation turned ugly. They didn't see the second beach chair behind Barrett's until they got closer. Greg almost couldn't believe his eyes. Chris was dressed like Greg in board shorts and a hoodie, along with wrap-around shades. Barrett sat forward and gave Tommy a once over.

"Sup, Salem? I see you got smart and finally brought some back up."

"At least my back up can drink legally."

Chris barely looked up from the tablet computer in his lap. Barrett didn't flinch.

"I'm teaching the kid the ropes. Trying to share some of my success."

"You know it's a school day, right? Not sure the district would agree with this apprentice program you're running. Or his mom."

"You and I barely ever went to class and we turned out fine."

"I guess that's a matter of opinion, when it comes to you and me. Not really your call when it comes to Chris."

The boy lifted his chin at the mention of his name. Greg couldn't read his expression through the sunglasses. Barrett tried to laugh it off, but he was starting to sweat.

"Am I supposed to care about your opinion?"

"No, but I'd be worried about Junior if I was you. After all, her son's a runaway. That means she can probably press charges if she wants to."

Barrett looked over at Tommy, as if for affirmation. Greg had Barrett right where he wanted him.

"Let me ask you something. You got a thing for little boys?"

Barrett stood up, ready for a fight. Greg took a step back to brace himself for the attack. He barely made it out alive the last time the two of them fought on Barrett's home turf. They started circling each other, fists raised and heads bobbing. That's when Tommy finally stepped in.

"Why don't you sit back down?"

"Feel free to make me."

There was a brief moment when everything was perfectly still. Only the sound of the waves breaking in the background and the seagulls overhead. The next thing Greg knew, Barrett went crashing through his beach chair. Chris barely managed to get out of the way before the big man ate sand. It happened so fast that nobody even saw Tommy move.

Greg grabbed Chris by the wrists, tugging him up from the chair. The kid was in shock and felt like dead weight in Greg's grip. It took them a while to reach the car because Tommy struggled to walk across the sand in his biker boots. Greg didn't mention the fight until Chris was buckled in the middle of the El Camino's bench seat.

Greg was facing Tommy over the roof of the car.

"Thanks for your help."

"No problem, but I wouldn't mind a heads up next time."

Greg nodded in agreement.

"You were like a motorcycle Ninja back there. What the hell was that move?"

"Little something I learned in my line of work."

ॐ

GREG TRIED TO FIND out where Chris had been all night, but the kid didn't say a word the entire ride from the beach. He just kept his head back, watching the world go by outside the car window. A world that he'd inherited far too soon when the people around him started dying. Greg tried to tell him that he knew how he felt, but Chris wasn't listening. Greg wouldn't have listened at that age either. He turned up the stereo and let Steel Pulse's "Drug Squad" do the talking instead.

Junior bolted from the house and took Chris into her arms. She was crying, screaming and smiling all at once. Greg and Tommy watched through the car window until the they disappeared inside.

Greg took Tommy to Eddie's, as promised. They drove in silence for the first few blocks. Greg tried to picture the kind of adult Chris would turn out to be. Ghosts from his own past swirled around his head. The property values might be skyrocketing in his old neighborhood, but the problems remained the same. Greg wondered if his own unborn son would face them too.

He was so deep in thought that he almost didn't hear Tommy talking.

"You wanna get a cup of coffee or something?"

"Maybe next time. I've got a few things to take care of today."

"Cool. Let me know if you ever need any more help from the 'motorcycle Ninja.'"

Greg spun the wheel and pulled into Eddie's parking lot. Tommy was genuinely relieved to see his motorcycle still leaning on its kickstand. He reached for the door handle, jumping out before the El Camino stopped moving.

"Thanks again, Tommy. You really saved my ass."

"No problem, bro. Be safe."

Greg's phone buzzed. He answered while watching Tommy unlock his helmet and slide it on. It was the Police Chief in Virgil Heights.

"I checked on Kristen Raines for you. Not done yet, but I found some info that I thought you might want right away."

"What do you got?"

"You ever heard of a place called Deer Springs?"

"Yeah. It's a little town up near the cabin."

"Well, according to her colorful police record, that's where Kristen grew up."

"Thanks, Chief. Gotta go."

"Wait! Don't tell me your heading up there again. You're already in way over your head. You should have let the police handle this in the first place. Now it might be too late."

"It's never too late."

"Same thing goes for meeting with the kid in the blue hat. It's never too late."

Greg sighed, but the Police Chief didn't let up. He was like a broken record.

"It'll give you some resolution. If you won't do it for yourself, do it for him. What's the worst that could happen?"

"Fine. Set it up."

Tommy was already on his bike, revving the engine, when Greg approached.

"Change your mind about that coffee?"

"No, but I might need a Ninja after all."

✌

GREG DIDN'T TELL TOMMY everything that was going on, just enough to pique his interest. They agreed to meet at Greg's cabin and regroup there before moving on to Deer Springs. Tommy had offered to call a few of his other motorcycle friends, but Greg thought the reinforcements would be overkill. Just because Kristen grew up in Deer Springs, it was no guarantee that it's where she was hiding now.

He watched Tommy tear out of the parking lot and up the boulevard. Greg went inside Eddie's for a quick conversation before following him up the mountain. Eddie was seated in his usual spot at the corner of the bar, reading the paper and sipping from his mug. Greg could smell that it was more whisky than coffee these days.

Eddie wasn't slurring, but he clearly wasn't sober either.

"Surprised to see you here."

Greg tried to soldier on.

"Wish I could say the same. You heard from Junior this morning?"

"No. Should I have?"

Greg didn't know exactly how to answer that question. Should his daughter have called him in a time of need? Yes, absolutely. Would he have been any help in his current condition? Doubtful. If Eddie sensed Greg's disappointment, he didn't seem to care.

"You're in the paper again this morning."

Eddie opened up to an inside page and handed it to Greg.

LA Buzz: "Greg Salem Investigating Beach Cities Murder"

by Leslie Thompson, Staff Reporter

A former police officer at the center of the ongoing 'Grizzly Bear' controversy has gone rogue, according to sources close to the situation.

Greg Salem, rumored to be on joint law enforcement task force charged with investigating the recent drug epidemic, is reportedly now working as an unlicensed private investigator.

His current case involves the murder of a South Bay socialite and former Washington D.C lobbyist named Margaret Keane and her business partner Mark Lathrop.

Spokesmen for the Bay Cities Police Department declined to comment on this story, but sources say that Salem was a previous employee of Keane's. Information about the nature of her business was not available at the time of publication.

Greg set the paper down on the bar and stood. The only people that knew he was digging up dirt on Lathrop were Eddie and Kristen. Greg looked over at the old man, trying to figure it out. *Eddie might be turning into a drunk, but he would never betray me.*

"Call your daughter, Eddie. And pull yourself together."

Greg brushed past J.J. on his way out the door. They didn't say a word to each other.

Black Flag's "Damaged" guided him up the freeway ramp headed north. Traffic on the 405 was the irrational stopping and starting that he'd grown up with. He cut through downtown, watching the new high-rises shoot skyward, while sitting in bumper-to-bumper traffic. The congestion eased as he wound through the foothill communities and made his way back into the Angeles National Forest.

It seemed like another multi-million dollar golf community was climbing further up the mountain every time he came through there. He guessed it wouldn't be long before LA's last wilderness was gone all together. It was no wonder that mountain lions, coyotes and bears were getting spotted more and more in these neighborhoods, swimming in the pools and snatching pets from backyards. *Magnus was a lunatic, but he might be right about one thing—the California that Greg knew and loved was disappearing fast.* Greg reached the turn off for his cabin about three hours after he left. A light dusting of snow was coating the ground at this altitude, but it wasn't going to stick. He didn't hear the gunshots until he got closer. He could see Tommy pinned down behind his motorcycle as he pulled up. Somebody was inside the cabin taking potshots out the front door. Greg reached over to the glove compartment for his Glock, but found it empty.

He was cursing Magnus out loud when he hit the gas, pulling between Tommy and the cabin. He swung the passenger door open and yelled for him to climb in. They were both staying low in the cab when Tommy leapt in. Two more bullets ricocheted off the front bumper of the El Camino before the last shot rang out.

Dust and snow swirled in the shafts of light that poked through the trees. Birds were already chirping again as Greg motioned for Tommy to be quiet and listen. They could hear two female voices in the house. It sounded like they might be arguing with each other, but it didn't mean that they were alone. Greg reached up and slid the car into reverse, letting it roll backwards slowly. A little collision with a tree was way better than taking a bullet to the head.

Greg counted to ten before peeking up over the dashboard. Kristen was standing on the porch with a hunting rifle when he did. She lifted her free hand and gave him an enthusiastic wave, as if he was coming home from a weekend business trip. He slapped Tommy on the shoulder to let him know the coast was clear.

Kristen dropped her weapon, running across the gravel to Greg. He tumbled out of his door and jumped up to meet her, trying not to squeeze too hard. Tears streamed down her cheeks as she brought her hands up to his face.

"Oh my God, Greg. We didn't know he was your friend. We thought Magnus sent him. I can't believe you're really here."

She was in hysterics and couldn't stop talking or smiling.

"What are you doing up here, Kristen? You had me really worried."

"She said that Magnus had you. I thought you were dead, so…"

Greg pushed her back by the shoulders so that he could see her face. He almost couldn't get a word in.

"How did you know that Magnus had me?"

"…she told me to leave everything behind and hide. I thought your cabin would be the safest place for us. I knew you'd find me here if you were still alive. I was sure of it."

Greg looked over Kristen's shoulder to the cabin. The screen door swung open and a woman emerged. She had been mouthing apologies the last time he saw her. Now Greg had some questions for Mary.

CHAPTER TWENTY

Marco had definitely smuggled drugs from Mexico before, but never on a yacht. The luxury cruiser used to be Lathrop's pride and joy, Magnus and his crew appropriated it after his partner's death, like modern day pirates. He'd even had Marco paint over the old name, free-handing a new one right on top of it. The only thing missing was the Jolly Roger.

Not that Marco got to benefit from any of the amenities. The plan was for Magnus and his men to sleep in the comfort of the spacious cabin, while Marco made his bed in a dingy that was stored up on deck. He hoped the fitted canvas would help protect him from the wind and rain. It wasn't exactly The Ritz.

There weren't any bears, but there were sharks. It was something that Magnus had been reminding him of since they arrived a couple of hours ago. Anytime Marco wasn't loading their gear onto the boat fast enough, Magnus would threaten to slit his wrists and throw him overboard. Marco didn't put much stock in the idea that sharks could smell blood, but he also didn't want to bleed to death in the ocean and drown.

He knew from experience what Magnus was capable of. Had the scars to prove it. It was enough to help him keep his mouth shut for once.

Not that it mattered any more. Marco didn't have any fight left in him after Greg's last rescue attempt. He was resigned to the fact that Magnus would keep using him up until he was too broken or beat up to work any more. Any deal that psycho made with Greg was all lies. Magnus didn't intend to let Marco live no matter what his friend managed to deliver.

Truth was that Magnus was just the latest in a long line of near death experiences for Marco. He'd survived a dozen close calls before in his life, and he might scrape by again if his luck held out. But if he didn't, one thing was clear in his mind—Greg Salem was going to keep on living. Somebody had to have the life that they were promised as kids, and Greg had always been the best candidate.

Marco was clean and sober for over a year now, which gave him lots of time to think. It all seemed so ridiculous looking back. The unnecessary fights with police, the bad drug deals, scraping by in the name of being free. The punk rock attitude that was charming in his teens had lost its sheen after twenty-five years of rough living. Danger was a real thrill when he was still a kid, but these days it was pathetic. Nobody wants a forty-year old rebel in their life, and if they did they were damaged too.

So Marco had a new plan. He was going to keep his head down, only doing as he was told. Just keep his mouth shut and obey orders. It was the best way to be sure that he would still be in one piece when Greg came back. And when he did, Marco was going to do whatever it took to protect him. Or die trying.

◈

Greg got Kristen alone while she was in the shower. He was leaning against the sink, trying not to yell above the sound of running water. Tommy and Mary didn't need to hear this conversation.

"Why didn't you tell me about her?"

"I didn't want my screwed up past to scare you away. Okay?"

Kristen was instantly defensive, but Greg kept the pressure up. There was too much at stake to keep tiptoeing around the truth. If any of them were going to survive, he needed to know everything. Right now.

"Stop trying to protect me, so I can protect you for a change."

"Fine, Greg! Mary was about the only real friend I had growing up. We've known each other since we were in grade school."

"In Deer Springs?"

"My mom moved us around a lot when I was kid. I kind of lost track of Mary after junior high. Well, until..."

The shower curtain rustled again as she rinsed her hair. He guessed she was buying a little time. Greg was too impatient to wait.

"He's going to come for you. For both of us, and Mary might be helping him."

"Stop saying that. It isn't true. It's more complicated than you think."

"Was she one of *his* girls too? Neither of you have anything to be ashamed of."

Greg's clothes were getting damp, but he couldn't tell if it was steam or sweat. Kristen pulled the curtain back so hard that she almost tore it from the metal hooks.

"I'm not 'one of his girls.' Okay? I mean, I'm his girl, but not like that."

"Explain it to me then. We're running out of time."

Kristen's voice was softer now, resigned.

"He's my dad. Happy now?"

Greg brought his hand up to rub his neck. Nothing she'd said was making sense.

"Who else knew about this? Besides Mary."

"The only other person I told was Maggie. I don't even know why, it just sort of came out when we were chatting. She had that effect on me."

Is that why Magnus killed her? There had to be more to it than that. "Tell me everything you know about your father."

"His real name's Tom Schulte. He came around once or twice when I was a kid, but I barely remember him."

Greg finally had a name, but nothing was adding up. He turned around and let the tap run in the sink. Cold water felt good on his face. It helped him think through all the information he was absorbing as Kristen went on.

"My mother told me he died when I was ten or eleven. I never cared enough to question her about it."

"But that's when you guys started moving around all the time?"

"I guess so, yeah."

Kristen turned the shower off, reaching a hand out. Greg passed her a towel and watched her dry off.

"Where's your mother now?"

"Probably on her sixth husband, if I had to guess."

She grimaced, swinging her hair up into the towel on her head.

"I didn't see him again until after I graduated high school."

"At Grizzly Flats?"

"That's where he took me eventually. I didn't want to go with him so he threatened to kill my mom. I guess he could tell I didn't care—"

"So he used Mary against you instead?"

"He showed me horrible videos of her doing porn. She looked like some kind of zombie. He said he'd kill her if I ever left him…and…"

Greg could see that she'd finally had enough. He wrapped his arms around her and held her tight. It was staggering to consider the number of ways that parents could mess their kids up.

"It'll be okay. You and Mary are going to be safe."

She sniffled and wiped the tears from her eyes.

"I'm only worried about our son. That's who he's really after."

❧

"IF YOU LEAVE THIS house, don't bother coming back."

Chris froze in his tracks. He'd heard similar threats from his mother before, but there was something different about her tone this time. A mental and emotional exhaustion made her sound even older than she actually was. He knew that if he walked out the door everything would change forever. There was no way she would ever kick him out of her life completely, but he would be on his own. He looked over his shoulder while reaching for the doorknob.

"I love you, Mom."

Chris opened the door, stepping out into the cool night air. His mother was slamming things around inside the house now, furious and disappointed. He was torn between taking off and turning around to comfort her like he had so many times before. The soft click of the door shutting behind him was the sound of his childhood vanishing. Now he was just another troubled teen tripping toward adulthood. He stepped down to the lawn and headed for the sidewalk.

He was half way there when his grandpa appeared out of nowhere. The old man must have been hiding behind the garage, waiting for him.

"What the hell are you doing here?"

"Get back in the house, Chris. Now!"

"No thanks. I've got plans."

All Chris wanted was to get in the van with his friends and leave. Eddie reached out to grab the collar of his grandson's shirt. The boy swung his arm, swatting the old man's hand away. Eddie had few drinks in him and almost lost his balance, but managed to stay upright. His shoulders were squared and he held his chin high.

"You a tough guy now? Is that it?"

"Get out of my way, grandpa. *Please.*"

"You want me out of the way so bad, then move me. Otherwise you're going back in the house with your mother. Where you belong."

Eddie reached for his shirt. Chris responded with a jab that sent the old man to the grass.

"Keep your hands off of me!"

Chris could see a thin trickle of blood on his grandpa's upper lip as he stepped over him. He shook his wrist a few times to work out the pain before stepping into the van. The door slammed shut as the driver hit the gas. A gangly kid with bad acne and blue hair was sitting in the front seat, shoving weed into a brass pipe. He handed it back to Chris as the van lurched forward.

"What the hell was that all about, dude?"

"Nothing. Where's the lighter?"

The driver fished one from the pocket of his flannel shirt, tossing it into the back seat. Chris caught it and quickly flicked the flame. The smoke expanded in his lungs and eased his racing mind. Nobody spoke again for another few blocks, until they passed by Eddie's on their way down the boulevard. A crowd of punks was gathered out front, smoking cigarettes and waiting for the show to start. It was the passenger who finally broke the silence.

"You think we'll ever get to hang out in there?"

The smartass in the driver's seat answered before Chris could.

"Not if this jackass keeps beating up the owner."

He flashed a grin in the rearview mirror. Chris ignored him, studying his own reflection in the glass window. It was depressing how much his face looked like his father's. The reflection never looked like Greg no matter how much Chris squinted his eyes, or how hard he wished that it did.

They pulled into the parking lot near the freeway ramp five minutes later. They slowed to a stop and all three of them threw their doors open. The driver and passenger went around to the back of the van while Chris spun the dial on a combination lock. He rolled the metal door up, stepping inside the rehearsal studio. There was nowhere else in the world that he would rather be.

His band mates were still loading their gear in when Chris went over to his new Marshall half stack. He'd bought it with the money he made working for Jeff Barrett. He plugged the chord into the base of the Les Paul Custom Greg had given him and brought his hand down across the strings. The amp roared to life, sending shivers down his spine.

∾

GREG WAITED AROUND THE corner of the cabin, listening. Tommy was sitting on his motorcycle, talking to somebody on the phone in a hushed voice. There had been a couple times during the short conversation when Greg thought he'd heard his own name, but he couldn't be sure. The ringing in his ears was the worst it had ever been.

Whoever Tommy was talking to, the conversation sounded dead serious. Greg peeked his head around the corner to see if he could hear better, but the discussion was almost over.

"…I'll call you with an update first thing tomorrow morning… I'll be fine…No, listen to me. We've got him right where we want him…Okay, bye."

Greg tried to drop back into the shadows, but Tommy spotted him.

"What're you doing out here?"

"Getting some fresh air. I was starting to get a headache from listening to Kristen and Mary in there."

It was a good cover story, but it was also true. Greg had probably heard Kristen's voice more in the last hour than he had living with her for the last eight months. He was thankful that Tommy seemed to buy it.

"It's always like that when they're with their friends. You can never get a word in."

"Were you on the phone? My reception is terrible up here."

"Yeah. Letting my girl know that I wouldn't be coming home tonight."

"You tell her you were staying in a cabin with a porn star?"

"I might have left a few select details out."

They both laughed, but it didn't relieve the tension. Greg was seriously wondering if he'd invited the enemy into his camp. If so, Tommy was playing his cards close to his chest.

"You really think this Magnus dude will try to come take her?"

"Hard to know for sure, but he seemed pretty serious about getting her back."

"Guess that means we're in for fight."

"Probably so, but not for a day or two. We should go in and try to get some sleep."

They walked inside and sat down on the floor in front of the fireplace. Mary was sprawled out on the ratty old love seat, with her legs dangling over the end. Kristen was moving back and forth in a sturdy wooden rocking chair. Greg couldn't remember the last time two women had been there at the same time.

He put his hand on Kristen's belly and gave it a rub.

"What was it like growing up out here?"

Kristen and Mary answered at the same time. Kristen said "Quiet." Mary said "Boring."

"Do you two ever agree on anything?"

Mary spoke up first.

"Is there a difference between 'quiet' and 'boring' that I don't know about?"

Greg found it hard to argue with her logic, but that didn't mean he trusted her. Even now, quietly sitting in front of the fire like they were a happy family, he couldn't be sure who was on his side. He had less than forty-eight hours to find out for sure.

"Hey, Mary. You sure you'll be able to take Magnus out if it comes down to it?"

"You questioning my loyalty?"

"You already sold me out to him once."

"I figured you'd squirm your way out of there. Besides, if it's between some ex-cop and one of my oldest friends, I'd make the same decision again in a heartbeat."

It wasn't exactly the answer he was looking for, but it would have to do for now. The big question was this—should they stay and get ready to fight, or head back down the mountain to look for help? Greg was still wrestling with that when Tommy stood up, raising his arms in a giant stretch.

"I'm calling it a night. Are we taking turns on guard duty or what?"

Greg raised his hand.

"Sure. I'll take the first shift."

"Perfect. Come wake me up when it's my turn. Goodnight, ladies."

Mary didn't even wait until he was gone.

"He's really cute."

"…And he has a girlfriend."

"Who cares? So do I."

She swung her feet to the floor and went to the bedroom she was sharing with Kristen. Greg was supposed to crash on the couch, but he knew he wouldn't be sleeping much. He got up to grab the rifle that was leaning against the wall. Kristen held a hand out and he helped her up. She gave him a peck on the cheek and shuffled off behind Mary.

Greg pulled the rocking chair across the living room and out onto the porch. The sky was awash with stars as he set the rifle across his lap and settled in for a long night. As a kid, the darkness of these mountains used to fill him with terror. These days it felt like the only place other than the ocean where he could truly clear his mind.

He was worried about Chris and Junior. There hadn't been time to given them much thought since arriving at the cabin, but now the morning was replaying in his head. And so was that night up at the tidal pools. Was that really a year ago?

It was hard to watch the two of them struggling to keep their family together with less and less support from Eddie. The money he gave them was nice, but it didn't make up for what he was turning into. Especially when Junior needed him the most.

And Marco. The guy was no saint, but he'd had enough punishment for one lifetime. Greg started rocking faster as he pictured the fresh scars on Marco's face. He could feel the bile and anger building up inside as he imagined what Magnus might be doing to him right then. Greg would never forgive himself until he'd brought his friend home alive.

He heard a loud crash that brought him back to reality. It was on the far side of the El Camino, in the darkest part of the property.

Greg stood up and took cover behind the rocking chair. The butt of the rifle was tucked into his shoulder and his head was tilted on the sight. The only thing left to do was wait.

It was a full minute before he heard another sound. Louder this time, and closer. He swung the barrel slowly across the yard, looking for something he could take aim at. The darkness all around him bubbled and bloomed as his imagination filled it with monsters. That's when he saw the two glowing eyes staring back at him.

The black bear was down on all fours, but wasn't moving. Greg could hear it sniffing the wind, trying to make sense of its surroundings. He grunted a couple of times and lumbered toward the cabin. Greg banged the butt of the rifle on the wooden porch. When that didn't work he started shouting too.

"Go away, bear!"

The bear stood its ground, staring him down for another second or two. It didn't take off for the trees until Tommy bashed through the screen door. He had one of the other rifles in his hand, but was only wearing boxer shorts. Greg let him get as far as the steps before repeating something that Marco had said to him on the day that everything went to hell on the trail.

"Dude, bears!"

Tommy skidded to a stop before bolting back to the porch. Greg raised his rifle in the air, squeezing the trigger. He prayed that all bears spooked as easily as the one he'd just seen.

CHAPTER TWENTY-ONE

Marco grabbed the brick of weed and put it in the lifeboat with the others. Then it was back down the stairs to the galley where the rest of the shipment was stashed in the walls. One-hundred pounds of commercial grade bud in all, grown in Paraguay and routed through some existing associates that Magnus had in Mexico. Marco wasn't allowed to leave the boat when they docked south of the boarder, but he learned a lot by being a fly on the wall.

For one, Magnus spoke passable Spanish, especially when it came to a specific kind of business negotiation. It also seemed like his boss had a checkered past down there. Marco overheard two of the chain-smoking Mexican gunmen say how amazed they were to see that Magnus had come out of hiding at all. Which might explain why the yacht was back on the ocean as soon as the shipment got loaded.

Marco guessed Magnus could easily get a hundred and fifty thousand for it at the current street value, but that was before they treated and packaged it up as Grizzly Bear. From there the profits would only climb.

Not a bad for a two day trip, but first they had to get it to shore without getting busted. That's where Marco came in. It was actually a pretty genius plan—he had to give Magnus credit for that. A guy with his experience was the perfect mule, especially out on the ocean. Marco was also the perfect fall guy if everything went sideways.

That meant Magnus could pull into the harbor without a worry in the world. Meanwhile Marco would be bouncing along in the dark trying to keep from capsizing. The goal was to land the lifeboat along an empty stretch of beach in front of a massive sewage treatment plant. Magnus had arranged for two of his guards to meet Marco there to load the delivery into their van. The final destination was a facility near the Van Nuys airport.

The bomb that Magnus had mounted on one of the lifeboat's benches was his insurance policy. If Marco didn't arrive within the delivery window, Magnus could detonate it from his phone.

"We might lose the shipment," Magnus said. "But it would be worth it to know that you were shark food."

None of it mattered to Marco. He was biding his time until Greg came back to get him. That's when he would take his revenge on Magnus and anybody else who got in the way. What form his revenge took depended on the day that he dreamed it up. At the moment, while he was bringing another couple bricks up the stairs, strangulation sounded pretty good to him. Up close and personal. With his bare hands.

"The hell are you smiling about?"

Marco looked up to find Magnus leaning on the lifeboat. He went to the other side and loaded his bricks from there.

"I asked you a question."

"Whistle while you work. Spoonful of sugar. All that bullshit, dude."

"Just so we're on the same page: you know what'll happen if you or that shipment goes missing, right?"

Marco smiled before heading back down to the galley for another load. Magnus screamed after him from the top of the stairs.

"I'll kill everybody you know, starting with your friend Greg."

It wasn't a long list, but Marco got the point. Especially when Magnus showed him a picture of Maggie Keane during her last few seconds on earth. Her wrists were bound together and a gag was shoved deep into her mouth.

"Lathrop let her get too close. Then she stuck her nose in my personal business, so this is what happened. And you saw what happened to him. Ruin this delivery for me and you're next."

Marco only had a few more trips to make and then it would be show time. They were currently somewhere along the far side of Catalina Island seeking cover from the Coast Guard. Marco's solo journey began when they rounded the peninsula. Thirty miles of rough water in a lifeboat loaded down with enough weed to land him in prison for several lifetimes. It was going to be a brutal trip for sure, especially considering the cold weather and wind chill. But it was still a better alternative to the universal death sentence that Magnus was promising.

Thankfully his tormentor was gone when Marco came back up on deck. He guessed Magnus was up on the bridge, getting ready for his grand entrance in South Bay. It was a good thing Marco didn't get seasick or he might blow chunks just thinking about it.

He finished loading the lifeboat a little early. Magnus rewarded him by reiterating his threats. Marco nodded, giving a stiff salute as they lowered him down to the water. He pulled the ripcord on the outboard engine and twisted the accelerator. Watching the yacht and its crew disappear was a dream come true, except Marco had different dreams now. At the moment they involved lighting Magnus on fire and watching as his ashes blow away in the ocean breeze.

Marco pointed the bow to shore, slapping along on the rolling swells. The cold wind cut through his threadbare clothes as snot ran down his face. A blue nylon tarp was duct taped tightly around the product to protect it from getting wet, but Marco was already soaked after only ten minutes. He felt the salt water stinging his cracked lips, running his tongue across the deep crevices. Everything tasted like blood to him these days.

❦

IT WAS EARLY IN the morning on the third day. Tommy was asleep in the rocking chair on the porch. The rifle had fallen off of his lap and lay at his feet. It was still there when a bullet split the doorframe behind his head. He sprang from his seat and ran inside the house, remembering at the last second to grab the gun off the porch.

Greg had been fast asleep on the couch, but was standing beside the front window when Tommy ran by. He went straight for the back door, exactly according to the plan they had cooked up. Mary was in the living room throwing greenwood into the fireplace to send as much smoke up the chimney as she could. They knew that Magnus and his men would benefit from the cover out there, but it also might come in handy if they had to evacuate the cabin.

Kristen was in her bedroom where all the mattresses had been flipped up to cover the windows. Strategically placed holes the size of baseballs had been painstakingly bored into the material to let her return fire as necessary. A dresser was pushed in front of the bedroom door from the inside, pinned in place with the bedframe. She had two rifles and ten boxes of shells. If there was one good thing about this situation, it was that these two women had been raised in the mountains and knew how to shoot.

Greg ventured a peek through the curtains and almost got his nose blown off. The shot came from over behind the El Camino, which was parked about fifty yards away. If this was a Hollywood movie, Greg would have loaded his car up with explosives that could be detonated with a smartphone. But this was real life and

Greg didn't know the first thing about building bombs. However this played out, it was going to be a good old-fashioned gunfight.

"I told you we'd come!"

Magnus didn't need a bullhorn this time. His voice was loud enough to carry across the short distance between Greg's car and the cabin.

"And you know what we're here for."

Greg had to scream to be heard. Luckily he'd had plenty of practice at that.

"You came a long way for nothing."

"We'll see about that."

"Where's Marco?"

"Already dead. You're next."

There was a brief moment where it seemed like this might turn into a stand off. Then the bullets started flying again, blasting every window and chewing up the outside walls. Everybody inside dove for cover behind the nearest piece of furniture. Greg thought there were four or five men out there, from the sound of things. All of them armed with handguns.

Greg spoke up, but kept his voice down this time.

"Everybody all right?"

Mary and Kristen both responded immediately. Tommy took a minute, but said he was fine when he finally chimed in. Greg could hear a quiver of fear in his voice.

"Stay calm, Tommy. We need you to keep your head in the game."

"What kind of psycho stays calm in a situation like this?"

Greg heard Mary giggle in the living room and thought it was a good sign. They'd survived the first attack, even though he knew it was just a warm-up for the main event. Things would be different once Magnus got impatient.

Luckily, the four of them had discussed this in advance. Going on the offensive was the only real option. Greg gave the signal and they all got back into position, waiting until Magnus started speaking again. That way they would know where to aim through the smoke.

"There's more where that came—"

Shots rang out from every corner of the cabin. It pained Greg to hear the bullets ricocheting off of the El Camino, but he tried to maintain perspective. He prayed that at least one of them had hit their intended target. He got his answer as soon as it got quiet.

"That's going to cost you, assholes!"

Greg heard the first shot and dove for cover. Two more rang out, but it sounded like they were coming from hunting rifles. None of the bullets were striking the cabin this time. Greg crawled to a shattered window, pulling the curtains back. He could see Magnus and his men facing out into the thick forest that ringed the cabin. Somebody else had opened fire on them, creating a golden opportunity for Greg and his team. He brought his rifle up and started firing.

Magnus and his men were caught in crossfire and couldn't decide which way to run. Their only option was to head back down the road the way they'd come. From there they could either regroup and fight their way back to the cabin, or get back into their cars and leave. He hoped they would take option two, but he wasn't holding his breath.

The four of them in the cabin didn't stop firing until Magnus and his men disappeared from view. It looked like one of them got hit and was lying out in the open, flat on his back. His chest heaved and his head rolled angrily from side to side. The cop in Greg wanted to rush over to see if he could be saved, but that was somebody else's responsibility now. He went around the cabin to check on his own crew instead.

Mary was back at the fireplace adding new wood. He looked at the bear paw tattoo on her shoulder and had a moment of doubt, but let it pass. No point in worrying about something he couldn't change. *She would have shot me by now if that was the plan.*

"Everything okay in here?"

"Define 'okay'. Last I checked people are out there trying to kill us."

He moved on to the kitchen. Tommy was on the ground with his back against a cabinet. There was a large wet circle spreading on his right thigh.

"Jesus. Did you get hit?"

"Broken glass. I'll be fine."

Greg reached over to grab a dishtowel. He tossed it to Tommy.

"Put some pressure on it to stop the bleeding. I think that one's going to leave a scar."

"It'll make a good story some day. Who the hell called in the reinforcements?"

"No idea, but I'm not complaining."

Greg went over to Kristen's bedroom last. He should have been the most concerned about her, but she was so heavily fortified that it put his mind at ease. The room sounded silent as he started knocking on the door.

"Kristen, are you all right?"

"I'm fine, but…Greg, you have to see this."

He went back to the living room and eased the curtain open again. Two gunmen had emerged from the woods and were moving toward the injured man. It was hard to make out the shadowy figures thanks to all the smoke clinging to the ground and swirling around. One of them looked like a hobbling old man. And he was wide out in the open where Magnus could easily pick him off.

"Kristen, cover me!"

Greg threw the front door open and sprinted across the gravel. The closer he got, the better the visibility.

"Eddie! J.J.!"

"I told you I was a good shot."

"Get back into the woods before—"

Several shots cracked the temporary silence. Magnus and his crew were coming back for a second round, just like Greg knew they would. Eddie slumped off with J.J.'s help, barely making it back to the edge of the forest before the real shooting started. That left Greg alone and exposed with only smoke to hide behind. He dove for the El Camino and rolled beneath it.

Greg heard the footsteps pounding his way. Then he saw their feet. White puffs of frozen air escaped from his mouth as he tried to lay still. It was no use. Magnus would eventually realize that nobody from inside the cabin was shooting. Once he figured that out, all bets would be off.

Then Greg heard a familiar sound in the distance. It thundered off the mountainsides, shaking the trees as it came closer. A beautiful, rhythmic whirring that sent Magnus and his men into a frantic retreat. It wasn't long before the helicopter was right overhead. Greg looked up expecting to see a golden Sheriff's Department star, but found a TV news logo instead.

He cackled manically. The media he hated so much had saved his life.

Magnus and his soldiers drove off in a hurry, taking their wounded with them. Tommy tore from the front door of the cabin with his helmet already on. He ran around back where his motorcycle was hidden and sped off down the driveway. The chopper overhead noticed the action through the dissipating smoke and turned to follow after him. Greg listened to the revving engines and spinning blades as they sped away.

Eddie and J.J. came out of hiding and stood beside Greg in the fading smoke. He looked over to where Kristen and Mary shared a hug on the porch. Nobody spoke a word, but their eyes said plenty. They all knew that this war was far from over.

～6～

MARCO WAS CHILLING OUT at the processing facility in Van Nuys when Magnus stormed in. He walked straight up to him, grabbed a fistful of hair and drove his knuckles into his nose. Blood exploded across his face, blurring his vision as he resisted fighting back. Magnus wasn't impressed, dropping Marco to the floor with a right and several kicks to the ribs.

"Greg Salem is a dead man."

Marco was rolling on the ground, bracing himself for the next round. His arms were up over his head and he was trying to make himself as small as possible. Magnus took one look at the pathetic scene at his feet and stepped back.

"Get up. I said, GET UP!"

CHAPTER TWENTY-TWO

The sun had already set when the El Camino glided down the Bay Cities off ramp. Greg was behind the wheel; Kristen was beside him with her head on his shoulder. Mary was riding shotgun. The plan was to stop by Eddie's on the way back to South Bay so Junior could see with her own eyes that everybody was safe. They were barely through the door when she charged over to smother them with hugs. It wasn't anything that out of the ordinary, except that Mary had never met her before.

Greg managed to pry himself between them so he could ask about Chris.

"Where is he now?"

"We honestly don't know, but he'll come home when he's ready. Right?"

Greg knew that it could go either way. The best he could do was offer to help.

"I'll go find him. Try to talk some sense into him."

"Good luck. I hope he listens, but I'm not so sure. Might be a few years."

He gave her shoulder a squeeze. She braved a smile, trying to change the subject.

"What happened up there today?"

Greg told her everything, up to when the Sheriff's Department finally showed up. That was long after the action was over, and mostly in response to the news helicopter. Junior knew the rest of the story because Eddie and J.J had beat Greg back. And because they'd all watched the action unfolding on the TV behind the bar.

The news chopper had followed Tommy down the mountain as he chased after Magnus and his men. There wasn't much that Tommy could do unarmed and alone on a motorcycle, but he managed to stick with them—at least until they started shooting at him. He hit his brakes to avoid the bullets and laid his bike down. It slid out from under him and skidded along the pavement for a few hundred feet with Tommy right behind it.

Convinced he was hit, the chopper swung back around to cover the carnage while Magnus and his men got away. They hovered there for two or three minutes, focusing the camera on Tommy's unmoving body. That was the scene playing out again and again when Eddie grabbed the TV remote and turned it off. There were some groans from the assembled customers at the bar, so Junior bought a round of drinks to shut them up.

It looked worse on the screen than Greg had imagined. More terrifying even than the radio reports he'd listened to all the way home. Greg looked at his phone again to make sure that he had read Tommy's text message correctly. *'Alive and well. Spending the night in the hospital. You good?'*

Greg was exhausted. He let the girls do a quick toast before escorting them to the car. Eddie tried to protest, so Junior ran interference to let them escape. Mary was the only one of them drinking, but managed to down her whole beer before they got outside. She was fast asleep when they pulled up behind the house in South Bay ten minutes later. Kristen guided her inside to the bedroom while Greg stopped by the garage to see J.J.

There was no response to his knocking, so Greg went in. A suitcase was on the bed and J.J. was busy filling it.

"You really leaving?"

"Looks like it." J.J.'s tone was neutral, but his body language screamed a different story.

Greg took a seat at the end of the bed and tried to get through to him. "You saved our lives today. I owe you for that. We all do."

"I'm no hero."

He shoved a few dirty T-shirts into the suitcase, on top of his crumpled jeans. The only thing left to pack was his bass guitar. It was leaning in the corner next to Greg's acoustic. Greg suddenly wished that they had played together more often while J.J. was living there. Now was definitely not the right time to suggest it.

"I'm probably the only one around here who knows how you feel. People have been trying to make a hero out of me for as long as I can remember."

"You don't have the slightest idea what you're talking about."

J.J. took a step back and blurted out what was eating him up.

"It was me, Greg. I'm the one who told them what you were doing. The one who was spying on you this whole time. I mean, not on purpose, but still…"

Greg jumped up instinctually. J.J. flinched, waiting for the punch that never came.

"How is that even possible?"

"I didn't know. I thought they were BCC fans at first. We'd get high and they'd start asking questions—"

Any exhaustion Greg felt was being eaten alive by the adrenaline coursing through his veins. He wanted to rip his old bass player apart with his bare hands, but not before he got the information he needed.

"Who, J.J.? Tell me who, Goddamn it."

"Some girls I met down at the beach. Weed dealers."

"Were they young?"

"I don't know, man. Yeah, twenties or whatever. Not underage or anything. I thought they wanted to party with me."

"Did either of them have any tattoos?"

"Now that you mention it, one of them had a—"

"Bear paw on her left shoulder? No shit. What else? Tell me everything about them."

"One of them said her dad had a yacht. You should have seen it. Thing was unbelievable."

"All yachts have names. What was it called?"

"Oh man. I know this…It's the…the…"

J.J. brought a palm up to his forehead and pounded, as if he could beat the answer from his hazy memory. Greg was ready to jump in and help when J.J. finally came up with it.

"The Ursula."

"Where is it now?"

"They have it moored off shore, about a mile out. We took a dinghy from the harbor, but you can probably see it from the pier. Thing's huge."

The perfect hiding place, with plenty of escape options. It would also explain why Maggie washed up on the shore instead of turning up in a shallow mountain grave. Greg had a strong suspicion that if he found that boat, he would find Marco.

⌁

GREG SPRINTED ACROSS THE moonlit beach in a full body wetsuit. The surfboard under his arm banged against the serrated scuba knife strapped to his bicep. He took a last look at his iPhone before flinging it onto the sand. The thing would never survive the trip and it wouldn't do him any good when he got there.

Kristen and Mary were already in bed when he'd made his decision. He considered waking them up, but left a note for Kristen on the kitchen table instead. It explained what she should do if he didn't come back. There was bank account information, the deed to the cabin, and a telephone number for the Police Chief in Virgil Heights. He'd also left a P.S. that said he liked the name Greg for their son, but fully trusted her with the decision.

The icy water was black as Greg charged in. He climbed onto his board and paddled for the small triangle of lights on the horizon. He tried not to think about everything that might be wrong with this plan as he torpedoed through the breaking waves.

His arms ached and his hands were tingling by the time he made it out past the breakers. The gloves and booties were helping, but the cold still felt like it was crushing him from the outside. It would have been an easier trip on his stand-up paddleboard, but it also would have taken him longer to get down to the beach. And he would have been an easier target for gunfire once he got closer to the yacht.

Every minute mattered now that he thought Marco might be close by. Nothing would stop him until he knew for sure. He kept paddling and tried not to think about the sharks that had haunted his dreams since childhood.

Greg looked over his shoulder and was disappointed by the progress he'd made. The lights of South Bay danced on the sloping hill behind him, like stars in the mountain skies. The yacht bobbed in and out of view as Greg got closer. He gritted his teeth and paddled harder, the surfboard gliding across the choppy surface. It wasn't long before he was close enough to see the deck was empty, at least on his side of the yacht. Lights glowed through the cabin windows, but there was no movement inside. The boat was either empty, or they were waiting for him.

He had less than fifty yards to go when a glimmering fish jumped out of the water, bouncing off the tip of his board. Greg leapt back and uttered "Jesus!" a little too loud while he thrashed in the water. There was a small commotion along the rail of the yacht.

Two silhouettes were leaning over, trying to locate the source of the noise. His heart was racing as he climbed on his board and forced it down with all of his weight. He was a dead man if they saw the light reflecting off of it and started firing into the water.

It felt like an eternity before they finally gave up and went back inside. Greg waited a few minutes before paddling forward. He rolled from his surfboard and swam the remaining distance to the dive platform. The name of the yacht was painted there in thin, curving letters.

Music was playing somewhere inside, below deck. Greg took his gloves off and inched along the mounted lifeboat, stopping to take cover. Somebody was definitely smoking nearby. He peeked around the curve of the small vessel and saw a man standing near the bow. The slight ocean breeze blew his hair to one side as he looked out over the water. A cherry burned brightly on the cigarette pinched between his lips. The handle of a gun stuck out from the back of his jeans.

Greg clenched the knife in his fist and got ready to attack. He knew there would only be one chance to take him out quietly and grab his gun. After that, Magnus and anybody else onboard would be on him. He tiptoed forward to get within striking distance and sprang.

The guard heard the noise and tried to turn, but a moment too late. Greg landed a solid punch to the man's jaw and sent him sprawling to the deck. He reached for his gun, but Greg knocked it loose with a swift kick. The gun clattered and slid away in the scuffle.

The guard grabbed both of Greg's ankles and yanked his legs out from under him. Greg landed hard on his back, but managed to hold onto the knife. He brought it up in front of him as the guard clawed at Greg's eyes. He slammed his forehead into the guard's nose, finishing him with a punch to the throat. Greg found the gun and scurried back to the lifeboat. He couldn't be sure if anybody inside heard the scuffle, so he knelt down to wait and catch his breath.

Greg was standing up to make his way into the cabin when he felt an arm wrap around his neck. It was tight as a vice and instantly cut the flow of air to his lungs. He managed to bring the knife up at an awkward angle, but still made a clean slice. His attacker cursed as Greg spun away. He was still gasping for air when he recognized the voice.

"That hurt, dude!."

Greg almost couldn't believe his eyes. Marco's body was still inside the lifeboat, but his head and arm were hanging out. Blood was dripping from his latest wound. There was a pained smile on his face.

"About time you showed up."

"Are you all right?"

Greg stepped forward, but Marco brushed him off. He dropped out of sight for a second beneath the canvas cover. A filthy T-shirt was tied around his forearm when he climbed out a few moments later. The two of them stood there taking each other in.

Marco still had his junky physique, but ropy muscles bulged from under his leathery skin now. There were more cuts on his face than the last time Greg had seen him, and his eyes had grown colder. But under all of that, he was still Marco.

"Aren't you freezing?"

"You can get used to almost anything."

Greg slapped the side of the lifeboat.

"You know how to put this thing in the water?"

"Hell yes. I'm practically a pro, you just flip those levers over there. But I'm not going anywhere yet."

"What's that supposed to mean?"

Marco held his hand out for the gun. Greg hesitated.

"We could still get out of here pretty easily if we bail now."

"Not until I settle this. You can wait here, or leave without me if you want. I'll find a way back to shore on my own."

"How many more are there?"

"Magnus and one other guy."

Greg wrestled with it for second. There was nothing legal about to happen, but part of him knew that it had to end like this. *Who the hell would miss Magnus any way?*

"You sure this is what you want to do?"

"All I've been thinking about for months, bro."

Months. Greg could suddenly feel every second of agony that Marco had endured. All the beatings he took. The endless days and sleepless nights filled with constant fear and humiliation. It was bound to leave scars that nobody else could see, the kind of pain that Marco would live with for the rest of his life. So who was Greg to deny his friend a little revenge?

He handed the gun over.

"Need me to come with you?"

"Thought you'd never ask."

Marco led the way to the cabin. The polished wooden staircase was narrow so they had to go single-file. That meant Magnus could end this quick if he was sitting down there ready to pick them off. But there was no other easy way down, and Marco wasn't leaving until he had some closure.

The music got louder as they descended. Some ridiculous seventies prog rock that neither of them could identify. The smell of marijuana smoke filled the air and made the tight space even more claustrophobic. They were almost at the bottom when Marco turned around.

"Thanks for coming to get me."

He took the last two steps at once and tumbled into the space below. Greg was right behind him with the knife in his hand. They both jumped to their feet to search for cover, but the bullets never came.

The room was small, but luxurious. Heavy brass lamps flanked a leather sofa behind them. Soft light reflected off the wooden walls to create an orange glow, like fire dancing in a cave. Lush oil paintings of grizzly bears hung on either side of a closed door. A carved bar and two stools took up the far corner. Magnus was seated behind a small table in the opposite corner, eating dinner. He set his fork down on the plate and leaned back with a glass of red wine.

"Welcome aboard, Greg. Happy holidays."

"Where's your other man?"

"Around here somewhere. Keeping you honest."

Marco moved toward Magnus, gun first. Greg went over to pat him down. Magnus had Greg's Glock under the cloth napkin in his lap.

"I was wondering what happened to this."

Greg took a few steps back. Magnus brought his wine up to drink. Tiny beads of red liquid clung to the stubble that grew around his sneering lips. He nodded to Greg.

"Why don't you take a seat?"

"Your business is with him."

They both looked at Marco. His face was an unreadable mask. Greg brought his gun up and walked over to the closed door. Locked from the other side.

"Where's the key?"

"Must've misplaced it."

Marco leapt at Magnus, bringing the gun down across the side of his head. Two streams of blood ran from either end of the narrow gash over his ear. Magnus grunted and sat back up. He sounded slightly less confident when he spoke again.

"I bet that felt good. Huh, Marco?"

Marco leveled his gun, the barrel trained on Magnus. Greg's eyes darted between the two doors and the narrow windows high up the walls. If anybody was coming to save Magnus, they were taking their time. Magnus brought the napkin up and held it against his wound.

"I know it did, because I've felt that kind of rage myself. Let it build up inside of me until I exploded."

Greg was getting antsier with each passing second. He could sense the phantom bodyguard circling, waiting for the signal to pounce. With everything else that had happened, he had no patience for another lecture from Magnus.

"Let's just go. Officer Bob can take care of him."

"No way. He's a dead man."

Greg was still staring at Marco when Magnus spoke up.

"It's more true than you know. Got diagnosed with brain cancer last year. Terminal. A bullet would honestly be a relief."

Greg's face flushed with rage.

"Is that what this has all been about? A last hoorah?"

"No man wants to go to the grave without leaving his mark."

"Come on, Marco. He doesn't need any help from us with his pathetic little legacy."

"You've already helped plenty."

Now Greg's gun was pointed at Magnus too. He knew that he could end all of this with one shot. Shut him up for good with a bullet right between the eyes. He could save Marco the trouble, and the crippling regret that would surely follow. But Greg couldn't stop himself from asking some of the questions buzzing around his mind.

"What the hell's that supposed to mean? Grizzly Bear was a lie from the start."

"People don't buy products any more, they buy the myth. I'm a marketing guy, not some 'mad scientist'. You said it yourself.

It didn't matter if Grizzly Bear was real, it mattered that people *thought* it was real—thought that they had to try it. I just needed somebody interesting to help me spread the word."

"How exactly did I fit into that equation?"

"Don't you get it? You were the perfect spokesman. A hero cop with a front man's ego who was already being chased by the media. I could have just hired somebody if I was selling jeans or watches, but this was a special circumstance—and there you were. It was a dream come true for an opportunist like me."

"I thought your plan was to sell your creation to the Mexicans and retire."

"You're giving me too much credit. I've been on the wrong side of that business relationship, and I'm not itching to go back. Trying to sell them something that doesn't exist is a great way to get yourself killed. You were the better option by a long shot."

"And Marco was your leverage."

"I was running out of time until you two came along. Honestly don't know what I would have done without you."

It was getting hard for Greg to contain his anger. Pieces of the puzzle were swirling around his head now, coming together to form a picture he couldn't stand to look at.

"But there's no way you could have known that Grizzly Flats would get raided."

"Please, Greg. Who do you think called them in? I manufactured the whole scene. It was a gigantic PR stunt designed to get media attention. And it worked. They fell for it, you all fell for it."

Greg felt used up and spit out. He'd fallen right into Magnus's trap and got swept up. He'd let himself be fooled into thinking he could play the hero again.

"You got everything you wanted out of me—out of us. So why come after Kristen?"

"My life won't only be judged by my career. All of this was for her. The kind of existence, the kind of *money,* that I never gave her as a child. I wanted to have her by my side when they end comes, to make up for all the years we missed. She's the only other person I ever truly loved."

"You threatened to kill her, and her best friend. That isn't love, it's manipulation. You're nothing more than a twisted control freak."

"Call it what you want, but everything was going according to plan—*my plan.* The only thing that I couldn't predict was that she'd fall in love with a failure like you. "

Greg took the words in. Let them roll around his mind until they disappeared. The shock, the anger, and the temptation to shoot Magnus—all of it was gone. Washed from his body with the realization that none of it mattered. He brought his gun down and turned to face Marco.

"I'll be up on deck. Do whatever you have to do, then let's go home."

The crisp night air felt like a slap to the face. Greg was struggling with the lifeboat levers when a shot rang out from inside the cabin. The noise echoed off the water for miles in every direction. Greg knew that sound would never stop ringing in Marco's ears.

CHAPTER TWENTY-THREE

E ddie grunted and groaned as he struggled across the sand. The wetsuit he'd borrowed was bunched up around his arms and legs, but taut across his gut. It was only nine in the morning and beads of sweat already dotted his forehead. He never would have made it to the shoreline if Marco wasn't prodding him along. Greg was waiting for them when they arrived.

A wave peaked and crashed not far from where they stood. Eddie jogged backwards from the whitewash that rushed at his feet. Greg couldn't stop from laughing.

"Don't tell me a tough guy like you is afraid of a little cold water."

"This is a bad idea, Greg. I haven't even been in the ocean for twenty-something years. You really expect me to maneuver this thing?"

He motioned to the paddleboard on the sand at his feet. Greg picked up a paddle and handed it to Marco.

"You'll be sharing a board with him."

Eddie started protesting even more.

"The water's freezing. No way, I'm not going to—"

"Take it easy, Eddie. You'll lay flat and Marco will do all the work. We aren't going far."

Eddie looked out to where Greg was pointing. Silhouettes glided along in front of the horizon a couple hundred yards out. Marco gave his passenger a slap on the shoulder.

"You ready, old man?"

It was the closest thing to a joke that Greg had heard from Marco in almost two weeks. He'd barely even seen him smile since that night on the yacht. And they still hadn't spoken to each other about what really happened out there. Probably never would. Which was fine by Greg, since Marco was still alive.

Eddie followed Greg out into the shallow water and Marco brought the board up alongside him. It took a little coaxing to get Eddie to lie down, but he finally relented. Marco stepped on at the back of the board and shifted his weight. The balance was as good as it was going to get. Greg climbed onto his board next to them and led the way across the waves.

Eddie's wiry grey hair was soaking wet when they reached the SUP Sober meeting. Pete watched the trio float up and swung his board around to greet them.

"Greg and Marco, together. I must be having a flashback. Who's your friend?"

He nodded to Eddie who was gripping the rails for dear life, cursing under his breath. Greg stepped in to make the introduction.

"That's Eddie. I'm sure you two have crossed paths."

"Most definitely. You threw me out of your bar more than a few times, back in the day."

Eddie perked up a little at the violent trip down memory lane, as if he briefly forgot that he was in the middle of the ocean waiting for his first twelve-step meeting to begin.

"I'm sure you had it coming."

"No doubt about it, but that was a long time ago. Stoked you're here today. I hope you stick around."

They joined the others and got their boards into a jagged circle. Greg watched Eddie's face as Pete brought the meeting to order, saw the dawning realization of what it actually meant to be out there with the people he once served drinks to. Admitting he was one of them now.

It was a start.

꿈

CHRIS WAS SITTING ON the sand with his surfboard. Greg walked up the beach and dropped down next to him.

The boy reached over to strap his leash on.

"Any good out there today?"

"Not bad. Little mushy for a pro like you."

Chris gave Greg an awkward punch to the arm.

"Whatever, dude. You take grandpa out to that meeting of yours?"

"Yep. Went better than I thought it would."

"Cool."

Chris looked out at the waves to watch his grandpa and Marco paddle in. Greg studied the boy's face. He could see a light brush of acne on his cheek, above a jawline emerging from under baby fat. Greg guessed that Chris would be shaving in a year or two. He searched his own memories for what came after that, but didn't like what he remembered.

"How are your meetings going?"

"Okay, I guess."

"Just okay?"

Greg noticed a confidence in the boy's gaze that hadn't been there before. Chris rolled his eyes.

"Want me to pretend that therapy's cool?"

"Beats the alternative."

Chris stood up and grabbed his board. Greg reached down, flipping a handful of sand at him.

"Did you learn that song I taught you?"

"Bet I can play it better than you can now."

"That might be true, but I'm the one who wrote it. Show a little respect."

"Whatever, *Fred Despair.* See you later tonight."

"Wouldn't miss it."

⤳

GREG TRIED TO BE quiet when he came through the back gate later that morning. He leaned his paddleboard gently against the garage and took his wetsuit off in silence. J.J. had worked the closing shift at Eddie's the night before and would be sleeping until well past noon.

Things between them weren't perfect, but he still liked having his old bass player around. Even if J.J. had been inadvertently spying for Magnus ever since he moved in. Greg knew that J.J. was really only guilty of trying to relive his glory years. And who could blame him? Getting old was exactly as terrible as they imagined it would be when they were still kids. Besides, it was nice to have somebody else in his life that could remember his brother Tim— the way he was before the drugs took over.

Greg turned on the garden hose and rinsed his feet off. Kristen hated it when he tracked sand into the house these days. She'd become a real neat freak ever since the baby was born. When she wasn't nursing or napping, she followed him around with a dustpan and broom. Meanwhile, the refrigerator was full of eggnog that neither of them would ever drink.

He opened the door and found her in the rocking chair. It always made Greg think of the cabin when he saw her sitting there, but he kept that memory to himself. She smiled at him while bringing a finger up to her lips. He walked over and gave her a kiss on the forehead, careful not to make a sound. Between J.J. and the baby, a life that was once full of loud music and gunshots had become relatively silent.

Their son was swaddled tight and sleeping in her lap. Greg still couldn't look down at his chubby little face without expecting to see Magnus. He wondered how much of his grandfather they would detect in the boy as he grew up. And if there was anything he or Kristen could ever do to stop that part of him from completely taking over. *There are so many things in our lives that are so far out of our control.*

Kristen stood up carefully and handed the baby to Greg.

"I haven't taken a shower all week."

"Take a bath. I've got him."

"Thanks. What time's your meeting?"

"Couple hours. Go relax."

She stumbled off to the bathroom in a sleep-deprived daze. Greg took her place in the rocking chair, holding baby Tim in his arms. The boy twitched and threatened to open his eyes, but drifted back to sleep in no time. A smile crept across Greg's lips as he stared down at his son, thinking of the future.

❧

TOMMY WAS ALREADY SEATED when Greg walked in later that afternoon. There was a laptop computer open on the table in front of him, and a couple of notebooks beside it. Greg looked around the empty South Bay café as he sat down.

"You sure this is a good place to do this?"

"It's fine. I work here all the time."

Tommy smiled and waved to the barista behind the counter. He held up two fingers and she got to work making a couple of lattes. It was hard for Greg to take Tommy seriously without his motorcycle leathers.

"Those reading glasses are a nice touch. How have you been?"

"Really busy trying to get this piece done. My editor thinks that I have a book here."

"She the tall woman with red hair?"

"That's the one. You really shook her up when you stopped by the office that day."

"She's a good actress."

Tommy stopped typing and looked up.

"I'll tell her you said so. Now, let's get this interview over with."

"You only have a few minutes to spare for your star source?"

"You read my column, so you know I already wrote your quotes. This interview is a formality."

They hadn't been face-to-face since that night on the mountain, but they'd traded plenty of texts and spoken on the phone several times. That's how Greg got the news that 'Tommy' was the nickname of newspaper columnist Leslie Thompson. It was a total shock, but a relief to know for sure that his new friend didn't work for Magnus. It also explained how so much of Greg's personal information kept getting printed. And why the news helicopter arrived before the police that day on the mountain.

Tommy whipped out a digital recorder, hit the red button and set it down between them. Greg felt instantly uncomfortable.

"No foreplay?"

"I thought you'd be used to getting recorded by now."

Tommy had been writing an investigative piece about illegal marijuana crops in the Angeles National Forest when Greg literally burst onto the scene. It was the kind of story that made careers, the kind that was worth putting your life on the line for. And now it was paying off.

Tommy flashed that familiar smile, diving right into the first question

"What happened out on that yacht?"

Greg's heart started pounding as he recounted the scene that night. Marco was standing just inside the cabin door when Greg rushed back in. The smoking gun was still in his friend's trembling hand, but his wide eyes were on the limp body at his feet.

Tommy nodded as Greg went on.

"I bent down to check his pulse, but he was already dead."

"Did Marco say anything?"

"No. He was in shock. Marco's done a lot of bad things, but that was the first time he'd shot anybody. I can tell you from personal experience that it takes a pretty big toll."

"The kid in Virgil Heights was your first one, right?"

"The only one so far."

The barista brought the drinks over and set them down. Greg sat back and sipped at his. Tommy flipped through one of his notebooks before asking his next question.

"Then what happened?"

"I mostly remember the laughter…"

It sounded like something from a horror movie. Endless screeching and squealing that seemed to suck the air from the room. Greg was overwhelmed with the need to make it stop. He grabbed the gun from Marco's hand and stepped over the guard's warm corpse. It felt good to bring the cold metal against the side of Magnus's head.

"That shut him up?"

"Long enough to radio the police. They were there in less than an hour, but that was one hell of a long night."

"And it was supposed to be a long trial…"

Tommy hesitated before finishing his thought. Greg already knew where he was heading, but let him go on.

"The D.A.'s saying that Magnus is too sick to go before the judge. They don't think he'll last through the end of the month."

"That's the word on the street."

"Do you feel cheated, considering everything he put you through?"

Greg took the question in, reflecting on everything that had happened. Not just in the last year, but the events that led up to it too. He knew that he was supposed to forgive and forget, but he wasn't there yet. Too many people he loved had suffered at the hands of Magnus Ursus. Part of him regretted not shooting the evil son of a bitch himself. He wanted to be as honest as possible when he gave his answer.

"Not if he suffers."

Tommy reached down and hit "Stop". Greg finished his drink, setting the empty pint glass down. It wasn't a beer, but it still made a satisfying sound.

"We through?"

"I got what I needed. Did you?"

"That's a loaded question."

"I guess it is. Thanks for taking the time to do this."

Tommy put his things in his bag. Greg pushed himself up and got ready to leave.

"Least I could do for the guy who saved my life."

"Come on, now. I was only doing my job as an undercover reporter. I didn't even fire a single shot."

"You keep saying that and maybe one of these days it'll be true. But, don't worry—your secret's safe with me."

"Wish I could say the same. You ready for another fifteen minutes of fame?"

CHAPTER TWENTY-FOUR

The white van pulled up outside of the rehearsal studio. Greg and Chris were standing there next to the El Camino when Marco jumped out of the passenger door. The scars on his face were already starting to fade now that he was regularly eating and sleeping again. He still wasn't speaking much, but at least he was out in public.

It took J.J. a minute to get the van into park before he jumped out too. He walked straight over to Greg with a huge grin on his face.

"What do you think?"

Greg recognized it from that night with Mary in the Valley, but he decided to sit on that piece of information.

"Where'd you get it?"

"I bought it off those girls I told you about."

Greg folded his arms and shook his head. Magnus was in custody, but most of the other people in his organization had gotten away. It would have upset him more if one of them wasn't the mother of his child.

All four of them took a stroll around the vehicle, stopping to admire the sticker-covered back doors. Chris spotted a sunbaked BCC sticker near the bumper. Marco crouched down and wiped off a layer of grime. The sticker didn't look like new, but it looked a little better.

"Haven't seen one of those things in years. First tour, right, Greg?"

"Looks like it."

A loud power chord roared from inside the rehearsal space. All three of them stood up to find Chris standing in front of his amp with the Les Paul Custom strapped on. He was doing windmills with his arm, letting the feedback ring out into the North Bay night. Marco was the first to speak up.

"Little dude's pretty good."

"He's got an awesome teacher."

They walked over and each took their positions. Greg brought the rolling door down from the inside while Marco counted off the first BCC song of the night. It ended as fast as it began. So they played another one. And a couple more right after that.

It wasn't long before long they'd played them all twice.

CHAPTER TWENTY-FIVE

The steel door slammed shut behind Greg. The guard escorted him through a metal detector and down a long hallway. He was trying to make small talk as they walked, but Greg was too deep in his own thoughts to do more than nod. Try as he might to distance himself from being a cop, he always ended up among them. *At least I'm still on this side of the bars.*

They reached the visiting room and Greg stepped inside. Sunlight poked through a small window high up on a cinder block wall. Everything in the room was painted battleship grey. He sat down on a cold aluminum picnic bench, shifting nervously from side to side.

Two guards walked in through a thick door in the opposite wall a few minutes later. A skinny kid was between them, his eyes fixed on Greg's. He had a shaved head and a freshly tattooed neck. Greg couldn't quite make out the design, and didn't want to get caught staring. The guards sat him down across from Greg and cuffed his hands in front of him.

"We'll be right outside."

Greg and the kid both stayed silent until the guards were gone. The kid smiled and shook his head the minute they were alone. Greg noticed the acne on his chin. He couldn't help thinking of Chris and wondering if this is where he would end up too. Or some place worse, if there was such a thing.

"You're the pig who shot me?"

The kid seemed skeptical. Maybe even disappointed. Greg could think of a million ways to respond, but only one seemed appropriate. It was short and sweet, just like his old Police Chief had told him to keep it. The old man even offered to come along for support, but Greg declined. He had learned that there were some things in life that you needed to do alone.

"Yes."

"Damn. You were a lot bigger and scarier in my head. Younger too."

Greg thought the kid looked like his older brother Manny when he laughed. Manny was an adult when the VHPD took his gang down, so he was doing a three-year sentence at a prison in Northern California. His kid brother was underage and ended up at this youth correctional facility in Oxnard. He wouldn't be eligible for release until his eighteenth birthday, a little less than a year away. Greg could only imagine what kind of animal he would be by then.

"Why did you want to see me?"

"Serious? You shoot my ass and *that's* the first thing wanna ask me?"

"I was doing my job. I hope you weren't expecting an apology."

"Shit. You ain't even a pig any more."

"Glad you did your homework. But I was when we met. That's all that matters."

"Whatever, man. I only made you come here to deliver a message for my brother."

Greg squeezed his hands into fists under the table. He wasn't sure what he was expecting from this meeting, but that wasn't it. His teeth were clamped when he responded.

"Still doing his dirty work? He could have just called me."

The kid leaned forward across the table.

"Manny wanted me to look you in the eyes when I told you."

"Tell me what?"

"This ain't over, pig."

ACKNOWL-EDGMENTS

Publishing this book was definitely a team effort. First I'd like to thank my supportive wife, Heather, and our two amazing kids. It should come as no surprise that I'm not much fun to be around when I'm writing; even less so when I'm editing. Heather has also become a valuable member of my inner circle of readers, which includes merciless feedback from the likes of Scott Ross and Paul Covington. I'd also like to thank my insightful editor, Elaine Ash, and talented lawyer, Kim Thigpen. And, of course, high fives all around to Tyson Cornell, Julia Callahan, Alice Marsh-Elmer, Winona Leon, and Navid Saedi at Rare Bird Books.

If you like this book, you can join the team, too. Please tell your friends, recommend it for a book club, request it at your local library or give it an honest review on your favorite online platform. Every little bit of support is greatly appreciated.